P9-BYO-735

DAY OF DAYS

ALSO BY JOHN SMOLENS

Angel's Head

Cold

Fire Point

My One and Only Bomb Shelter

Out

Quarantine

The Anarchist

The Invisible World

The Schoolmaster's Daughter

Winter by Degrees

Wolf's Mouth

a novel by JOHN SMOLENS

DAY OF DAYS

MICHIGAN STATE UNIVERSITY PRESS | *East Lansing*

♾ The paper used in this publication meets the minimum requirements
of ANSI/NISO Z39.48-1992 (R 1997) (Permanence of Paper).

Michigan State University Press
East Lansing, Michigan 48823-5245

LIBRARY OF CONGRESS CATALOGING-IN-PUBLICATION DATA
Names: Smolens, John, author.
Title: Day of days : a novel / by John Smolens.
Description: First. | East Lansing, Michigan : Michigan State University Press, [2021]
Identifiers: LCCN 2020003171 | ISBN 978-1-61186-381-9 (cloth)
| ISBN 978-1-60917-656-3 (pdf) | ISBN 978-1-62895-416-6 (e-book)
| ISBN 978-1-62896-417-2 (kindle)
Subjects: GSAFD: Historical fiction.
Classification: LCC PS3569.M646 D39 2021 | DDC 813/.54—dc23
LC record available at https://lccn.loc.gov/2020003171

Book design by Charlie Sharp, Sharp Des!gns, Lansing, Michigan
Cover design by David Drummond, Salamander Design, www.salamanderhill.com.
Photograph of cupola from Bath Consolidated School, which survived the bombing
in Bath, Michigan, May 18, 1927, taken by James Daggy, Michigan State University.

Michigan State University Press is a member of the Green Press Initiative and is committed to developing and encouraging ecologically responsible publishing practices. For more information about the Green Press Initiative and the use of recycled paper in book publishing, please visit *www.greenpressinitiative.org*.

Visit Michigan State University Press at *www.msupress.org*

▪

For Ellen Longsworth,
daughter of the Midwest,
who loves the lay of the land,
and to
Bath, Michigan,
past, present, and future.

▪

Acknowledgments

For so many reasons, I'm indebted to so many people.
The short list:

Julie Loehr & Dick Johnson

Kris & Bud Kipka

Meg & Peter Goodrich

Nancy Wynn & Bob Dennis

Marianne Brush & Don Crane

Susan Spellman & Jay McGovern

Kim & David Raymond

Linda & Peter Smolens

Elizabeth Smolens & Aron Hellingas

Berta Sutro-Harris & Michael Smolens

■

Io fui gia quel che voi siete e quel ch'io sono voi anco sarete.
I once was what now you are, and what I am, you shall yet be.

—Inscription, *Holy Trinity,* fresco, Santa Maria Novella, Florence, Italy
by Tommaso di Ser Giovanni di Simone, known as Masaccio (1406–28)

■

The past does not exist. There are only infinite renderings of it.

—Ryszard Kapuściński, *Travels with Herodotus*

■

I. Michigan Soil

1.

It's not what you know; it's what you believe. We like to think we can find the truth. There is a place between truth and untruth, a place where we dwell, driven by hunger and thirst, fear and desire. A place where the season's always disagreeable. Too much rain, not enough rain. A harvest so poor that there is scarce enough to get through a winter that locks the earth and will not release it until late April, only to be parched, caked, and cracked beneath a brutal July sun. A fall day when the air is so clear, so clean with the foliage downing through the trees, to bury the land for another year. A place where men and women look to the sky in awe, in hope. Where what is said is as important as what is left unsaid. Where a grudge can run through generations and elders speak in decades. Where mothers give birth until their hearts break and their bodies give out. Where conception, birth, and death share the same bed.

And now I have lain in this bed so long, I know every crack in the ceiling better than I know my own face. A part of me died a long time ago. The rest is preparing to go. Finally. I barely sleep. I rarely eat. Nurses and aides tend to me, wash me, see to my needs, some talking as though I were a newborn child, some treating me as though I were a useless piece of furniture.

I'm not a woman named Beatrice Marie Turcott; I'm the bed in #137.

I was usually just Bea.

The staff here seldom call me Bea. Dear or Honey, perhaps. But rarely Bea.

I only ask that when they leave my room they close the door to minimize the sound of the televisions that reverberate in the hallway—breaking news, game shows, commercials, and the weather reports that never effect the stale air in my room—the American symphony accompanied by a chorus of canned laughter. Shut it all out.

I used to welcome the occasional visits from my daughter, my granddaughter, and her small children. But there is now such a look of desperation in their eyes, and the little ones turning restless and bored—their visits a quiet ordeal we all must endure in our own way. We have all reached the same conclusion: *it is time.* We have known this for so long and we're tired just from the knowing of it.

Listen.

There is no fear of death, and little of dying. It is, in its own way, reassuring. I will go and it will all continue. But while I lie here, staring at the ceiling cracks, the lines suggest faces and figures that shift and fade and reshape themselves in the pale light that seeps through closed window blinds. And staring up at these lines I live it again. I see it, smell it, hear it: the days, the seasons, the lay of the land, the blessed scent of the sun's heat coming off the coat of an old mare named Daisy.

▪ ▪ ▪

In 1927, there was a new beast upon the land. Cars, trucks, tractors. We often called them machines. Not everyone had one. A machine couldn't be trusted like a cow. In '27, it was still common to see plows dragged by harnessed animal, but increasingly we witnessed this: a man driving a tractor. There was something proud, even dignified in the posture of a farmer as he sat in the steel bucket seat, hands on the wheel. It was not unlike riding a horse. You watched a tractor working a field and you could determine much about the man astride his machine. Bib overalls or dungarees. A broad-brimmed hat. Boots caked with honest dirt. Michigan soil.

But Andrew P. Kehoe, he was different. He worked eighty acres wearing a suit, white shirt, and necktie. Looked more like an attorney or a doctor, often without a hat on his head. A suit and tie spoke of a propriety that superseded the common sense of denim. There was something shrewd and yet faintly humorous about Kehoe, his sense of irony left us feeling uncertain, not always sure if he was being serious or was joshing. His wife Agnes Price, however, she came from a prominent family in Bath, with connections in Lansing, ten miles southwest. Everyone called her Nellie. She was the niece of Lawrence Price, who had been instrumental in establishing the new industry of automobile manufacture in the state capital, and who had sought election to the US Congress. Though he didn't win, he never lost favor in Lansing. Nellie Price and Andrew Kehoe, they married late, in 1912, both in their forties. Seven years later they moved from Tecumseh into the Price farmhouse on Clark Road, where she had been raised.

I remember the day I first considered the man. Andrew Kehoe came striding out of the barber shop, his wavy hair newly shorn and oiled, glistening in the sun. It was a Friday, after school had let out, and we were on the sidewalk near Crumm's Pharmacy: Warren and Jed, my sister Alma and me. The way Mr. Kehoe walked toward us, his suitcoat flapping in the April breeze, you would have thought him some big shot up from Lansing.

How old you were was so important. You wore your age like a badge. Warren would claim that he was almost seventeen, because he always looked to the future. He was like an older brother to Alma and me. Or so I wanted to believe. Alma was fifteen, not quite twelve months older than I was—and even though I was taller I was hard pressed to accept that I would always be the younger Turcott sister. Jed was twelve, and the way Warren clutched his shoulder I could see that it hurt, but Jed refused to let on. He wanted to be included in whatever we did, which required enduring small hazings and embarrassments, cruel payment for being allowed to tag along.

Warren leaned down and whispered, "Look at that suit, Jed. Check his coat pockets."

Alma smiled, knowing something, the secret she and Warren often seemed to share. Like she knew him better than anyone, better than he knew himself. Like she owned him.

"Go on," Warren urged, his fingers digging into Jed's shoulder.

It now seems so innocent. An early spring afternoon, the smell of the fields on the air. Jed had to show nerve. When he looked up at me, I wanted my eyes to say *Warren's really a scaredy-cat. He's using you, asking you to do something he's afraid to do.*

Even at twelve years of age, there was something fearless and belligerent about Jed. He ignored my tacit warning. As Mr. Kehoe approached, he shrugged off Warren's grip and stepped forward. The man came on, billowing smoke like a train. Jed stood in his way, and when he saw this boy wasn't going to step aside, Mr. Andrew Kehoe stopped walking. He placed his hands on his suspenders, his mouth a grimace around the stub of his cigar.

"Well, now, aren't you—" and seemed to be trying to remember.

"Jed Browne."

"Ah, yes. Alice and Jerome's boy."

He nodded.

"Is this a stick up? Or do you perforce require that I pay a toll?"

Perforce. People in Bath, most of them, didn't talk like that.

When a man like Andrew Kehoe talks around a fat stogie, it's difficult to tell when he's joking and when he's serious. At that age I tended to take things—particularly what adults said and did—in a literal sense. "Seeing as you don't appear to be armed," Mr. Kehoe said, "I will assume this is not a stick up."

Jed merely stood there, looking up at the man.

"So it's a toll you require?"

Jed ventured to glance over his shoulder. Warren and Alma and I couldn't help him. He was on his own. I looked down at my feet, contemplating the dust on my high lace-up shoes, Alma's hand-me-downs. This wasn't going to end well. Somehow I suspected that it was Mr. Kehoe who wanted something from Jed.

Mr. Kehoe's eyes were steady, unwavering, as though he were sizing up Jed for slaughter. He shoved his right hand deep in the pocket of his suitcoat, while his other hand removed the cigar from his mouth. "I don't have much money," he said. "And what I do have mostly goes to taxes, 'cept what Mrs. Kehoe takes off me when she travels down to see those doctors of hers in Lansing." He pulled his hand from the coat pocket, holding something in his closed fist. "You wouldn't be the tax collector, would you?" What an incredible idea. Jed shook his head. "Well. Tell me this, Jed Browne. Do you believe in getting something for nothing?"

I couldn't believe he asked this. Adults didn't ask such questions. Not of children. If anything, they usually told us what to do, what to think, what to believe. He had sought Jed's opinion.

"No, sir, I don't."

"Excellent. Neither do I. No advantage to it. Yet that's often exactly what taxes amount to: nothing for something. Catch my drift?"

Tentatively, Jed nodded.

"So, here's what we'll do," Mr. Kehoe said as he opened his hand. In his palm lay a flat shiny object. "I will give you this dime, but on one condition." He paused, seeing that Jed was distressed. "I will give you this ten-cent piece as a down payment. Toward services to be rendered."

Perforce. Rendered.

"You look like a strong young lad. If you accept this down payment, you will agree to come out to our place tomorrow morning. Eight o'clock sharp. And you will assist me in my chores about the farm." He must have seen Jed's uncertainty, but kept his hand extended. When Jed reached out and took the dime from his palm, he said, "Excellent."

The way he placed his cigar in his mouth signaled that their negotiations had concluded. Time to move on. Jed stepped aside and Mr. Kehoe continued down the sidewalk. Warren, Alma, and I lowered our heads, as though it would render us invisible, until the man turned the corner of the building and his footsteps faded away.

As Jed approached us, Warren seemed resentful. "A *dime?*"

Jed kept his fist closed. I thought Warren might hit him, a slug in the arm or a slap on the head. Jed thrust his hand and the coin in the front pocket of his overalls, infuriating Warren. Alma was indignant. The impertinence. It was not supposed to be this way. She and Warren were older. But it was Jed, our little tagalong who—at Warren's insistence—had stepped up before the man and stopped him on the sidewalk.

Jed gave us that boy's grin of his, dimpled cheeks, slightly crooked front tooth: "I have a job."

▪ ▪ ▪

Next morning, Jed and I rode Daisy out to the Kehoe farm, west of town. I was to drop Jed at the Kehoe's and then take the horse farther down the road and look in on Aunt Ginny. She was sickly and I was often sent out to help with household chores. I wore my leggings under my blue dress, figuring I'd be on my knees scrubbing her floors until they smelled like pine trees.

Daisy was a mare too old for fieldwork, so Pa let me use her to get around. It was a few miles and she walked a slow pace, so we set out while there was still dew on the spring grass. We rode bareback. I sat behind Jed, my arms about him. He was all ribs and backbone then. But something suggested that in no time he'd begin to fill out. His wide shoulders would thicken with muscle and sinew. Riding behind him, my nose was often pressed into his hair, and I detected the faintest scent of Round Pond or Looking Glass River, where I knew he and Warren and the other boys had been swimming since it had begun to warm up.

Jed didn't say much, which was not unusual. Though sometimes he would of a sudden blurt out a jumble of thoughts and feelings, so you'd know he was alive in there. I knew he loved me and had since we were small. I figured one day, when we were older, he'd get up the nerve to tell me. I didn't know what I'd say to that. At fourteen, I worried about how my life would turn out. Now I know. There's little relief in it. Instead of looking forward, you look back, and rather than wondering what might happen you consider what might have been.

"Mr. Kehoe didn't tell you how much this job paid, did he?"

Jed seemed perturbed that I'd even spoken.

"Just making conversation."

"No, he didn't," he allowed. "Just the ten cents as a down payment."

"Well, that's a good start!" Brightly, but he didn't pick up on my enthusiasm. "Think of what you can spend it on."

"Like what?"

"Candy."

He shook his head. Strange boy. Didn't care much for candy.

"Licorice."

He tilted his head. "Licorice, maybe."

"You just like the way it makes your teeth black. I see you boys smiling when you're eating it, thinking you're being so funny."

"Do not."

"Do to." I cinched in on his ribs, driving the breath out of him.

"Stop it."

I knew he liked it. I might have tickled him or tugged on his hair with my teeth, but we were on horseback. I'd taken a few falls from Daisy and it's no place to be messing with a boy. "Well then, you could save the dime."

"I suppose."

"Save it, and add your wages to it."

"Wages." Like he'd never heard the word.

"Open a bank account. Collect interest."

"Interest."

"I swear, Jed, sometimes I believe you were born last night."

We could see the Kehoe house up ahead. Impressive. Three stories. Steep-pitched roof with a large dormer overlooking Clark Road. Two front porches, first and second floor. I'd never been inside but had heard that it was as fine a house as there was in Bath. Mr. Kehoe had installed a gasoline-powered generator, so there were electric lights. And indoor plumbing on all three floors.

"If you save your dimes, Jed, one day you could have a place like that, with no outhouse."

He considered this awhile. Daisy's hoofs were like seconds ticking in the hard-packed dirt road.

When Jed pulled up the reins and we stopped in front of the house, he said, "That would take a real lot of dimes."

"You are a strange boy, Jedidiah Browne. You can make the obvious seem profound."

He considered this, too. "I hate it when you talk like that."

"Like what?"

"Like that."

▪ ▪ ▪

Jed had never had a job before, never had a boss. Mr. Kehoe came out of the screen door and stood on his front porch, suitcoat flared back while his hands rested on his hips.

"Tell me," Bea whispered in Jed's ear. "What kind of a man farms in his Sunday suit?"

It was the same suit Mr. Kehoe had worn into town the day before. The shirt might have been different. Hard to tell as it was also white, and the tie, it was the same gray with a vertical black stripe.

Behind him Mrs. Kehoe appeared inside the screen door. "Go on, ask her," she said quietly.

"What'd you bring her along for?" Mr. Kehoe asked.

Before Jed could respond, Bea said, "I will head on down the road to my Aunt Ginny's. Ma sends me out there to lend a hand."

Mr. Kehoe turned and gazed at his wife as if to say *See?*

She said something to him Jed couldn't hear.

When Mr. Kehoe turned back he was clearly displeased. "When you finish down there, Bea, you come on back here. We have Edith Witt helping with house chores, but she can't make it today. We're not relations, so you'll be compensated." He seemed to find this funny. "Now, Jed, let's get started."

"Yes, sir."

Mr. Kehoe came down the steps and began walking around the side of the house toward the outbuildings. His wife no longer stood at the screen door.

Jed swung his leg over Daisy's neck and slid down to the ground. Bea worked her way forward on the horse's back and took up the reins. "It appears I have a job, too," she said. "I'm going to save my wages. Collect interest."

"You'll be buying candy at Crumm's Pharmacy this afternoon."

"Will not." She gave Daisy a nudge with her heels and they started down the road.

Jed followed Mr. Kehoe around the side of the house. There were several outbuildings, and they entered the largest one, the barn. They walked down the length of the building toward the wide double doors open at the back, which gave a view out onto the pasture—empty except for two grazing horses. Jed had never seen a barn like it. Neat and tidy, more so than a lot of homes. There was a rake leaning against the back wall. From the way it stood crooked, tines up, Jed suspected it had fallen from its pegs. Mr. Kehoe picked it up and hung it on the wall with an assortment of hoes and shovels. Without looking at Jed, he said, "Implements have their place. Understand?"

"Yes, sir."

"This must have fallen during the night. The horses, they kick in their stalls and sometimes one of these gets shaken loose."

The way he said it reminded Jed of the school superintendent, Mr. Huyck, who spoke with the same directness that made it clear that something wasn't right. Was not *acceptable,* would not be *tolerated*—those were his words. In school, Jed supposed this was necessary, but here Mr. Kehoe was talking about a rake. Like it had misbehaved and deserved punishment.

They went out the back of the barn to a dirt yard, the chicken coop to one side and a large shed across the way. A tractor was parked in front of the shed, the engine covered with a tarp. Jed helped remove the tarp, happy to be doing something. Mr. Kehoe had been working on the engine, and there were parts neatly lined up along a board on the ground next to the front tire. He removed his suitcoat and took it into the shed, where he carefully draped it from a hook next to a workbench. Like the barn, the workbench was neat and tidy, all of the tools hung on the wall and some from the rafters. He came outside, rolling up his shirt sleeves and tucking his tie behind a button, which gave the impression that the tie had been cut off at an angle.

A lot of farmers still worked the land with equipment drawn by animals. Tractors moved so much faster, and there was the engine noise. Jed didn't know anything about them. Like everything else, the tractor was clean—except the large rear wheels. They were taller than Jed and there was dried mud caked in the metal spokes and tire treads. Mr. Kehoe had both hands in the engine compartment, and there was the clank of metal on metal as he turned something with a wrench. Jed watched for a minute, growing worried that Mr. Kehoe would not like him simply standing around. He decided to go into the shed and found a pile of folded rags on a shelf under the workbench. He took several rags and went out to the tractor, where he began knocking clods of dirt off the wheel rim.

When the rim was clean, the red paint shining, he straightened up. Mr. Kehoe considered him with a hard, assessing eye. "Excellent," he said. "You show initiative." He held an engine part in his palm. Jed was surprised that he allowed grease to get on his hands. "Now what might this be?"

"I don't know, sir."

"Haven't been around motors much. And electricity. Don't know about it either?"

"No, sir. We have kerosene lanterns at the house."

He nodded. "Mine's one of the few houses in Bath that has electric lights. When the power company finishes installing the lines this spring, everybody will have electricity."

"Everybody?"

"You'll wonder how you ever lived without it."

He must have seen something in Jed's expression. Disbelief, most likely. He nodded as though he'd made a decision, and held out his hand. "So you don't know what this is."

"No, sir."

"Spark plug."

"I've heard of them."

"Have you now? And what do they do?"

"Don't rightly know, sir."

"I see. You hold this while I remove the next one."

"How many are there?"

"Intelligence starts with the right question." He smiled as he handed Jed the spark plug. "Depends on the engine. This Ford engine's a four-holer. Now you take that plug and place it in that pan on the workbench. We'll soak them, and I'll explain what spark plugs do."

The plug in Jed's hand had a concentrated weight, which he liked. But its shape, he had no idea why it looked that way, with the metal threads and the ceramic end.

Mr. Kehoe clearly wasn't pleased that he was still standing there. "I said go on. Should I have to tell you to do a thing twice?" It was a question, but it sounded like a threat. "Well?"

"No, sir."

▪ ▪ ▪

I called her Aunt Ginny though that wasn't exactly accurate. Virginia Wheeler had been married to one of my grandmother's cousins, Ed Wheeler. Everyone called him Captain, or sometimes The Captain, as though he were the only one. He fought in the Civil War. He died before I was born. His wife Ginny was younger, his second or third wife, I'm not sure, but in 1927 she was in her sixties, and had been alone since he died. She'd been close to our family as long as I could remember. Came by for dinner on Sundays and holidays. Ma worried about her living out this way on her own, and had suggested she move closer to the village, or maybe have someone move in with her, but Ginny would have none of it. Because she was relations (as Mr. Kehoe called it), I was not to expect or accept any form of payment for work I'd done at the house: laundry, cleaning, sweeping, washing windows. But Ginny always made me a fine lunch, often using her good china. A real occasion, she called it while pouring our tea. We had cold chicken, mashed potatoes, carrots, followed by her blueberry pie—made with the last batch she had put up the previous summer.

"So, after you're finished here, you're going over to help out Nellie Kehoe," Ginny said slipping the cozy over the teapot. "Ever meet her?"

"No, I haven't." I picked up my teaspoon and began stirring, the sugar cubes rattling in the cup until they dissolved. The bell tone of that china teacup sounded like refinement. My fingers were white and shriveled as a result of the vinegar and water solution I had used to wash the windows. A kerosene film from her lamps covered most everything in the house, the wavy glass panes, the woodwork, the wallpaper, which was badly faded and pulled away at many seams. I sipped my tea.

"Fine family, the Prices. Nellie Kehoe, you'll like her."

"I expect so."

Her blue eyes came up and she stared at me. "Perhaps she won't have you doing windows."

"I don't mind. I know you like the way the world looks through a clean window. I do too." Aunt Ginny's head and hands had a slight tremor. Finally, I said, "Mr. Kehoe has strung the place with electric lights."

"He's a man of strong opinions." As though she had not heard me. "Nothing wrong with that."

"I suppose not."

"That a fact?"

With adults I was reluctant to express any opinion, for fear of seeming contrary, but with Aunt Ginny she often solicited my thoughts. "I don't really know the man," I said. "Only what I see of him in town." Small reward: the sugar was stronger now that I was halfway down the teacup.

"They are Catholics," she said with finality. "I don't hold that against them, though I suppose some people do. Irish, and all that. She has family down in Lansing, younger sisters, I believe. Her mother died when Nellie was in her teens, and Nellie, God bless her, raised them pretty much on her own. Tied her up until she was in her thirties. Guess that's why she married so late. They took the family farm over maybe eight years back. Seems right that Nellie has the place now."

"It's well kept," I said.

Aunt Ginny used both hands on her teacup so she could set it back in the saucer without a lot of clatter. Just fitting it in the center took concentration. "I guess I should use the past tense. They *were* Catholics. But then once a Catholic always a Catholic, so I don't know if the past tense is appropriate. They are Catholics. Not many of them around here. They just don't attend church any longer."

"They don't?"

Now Aunt Ginny turned regretful. "Dear me, I may have begun something I oughten to have."

I doubted that *oughten* was proper English but I wasn't about to the raise the point.

"It must be strange to live without your religion," she said.

I had never thought of this. In fact, one of the reasons my visits to Aunt Ginny's were of consequence was because we often discussed things that had never occurred to me before—certainly had never been talked about at our dinner table.

"I hope you don't think me too liberal-minded," she said, "but I don't reckon it matters much what church one attends. Or a synagogue, if you will. But to a*ban*don your religion. It must seem, I don't know, empty. We need the Lord. Without Him, there would be just . . . just chaos. Chaos worse than darkness. There would be little sense to anything."

This was one reason why I didn't mind helping out at Aunt Ginny's house. My mother would never talk this way. No, she would discourage it. It was not our place to question things. Ma believed what is *is,* and there lay virtue in acceptance. *It be God's will*—she would say things like that about most anything that had no clear and apparent reason. God's will was all the reason one needed. I realized that there was something brave about Aunt Ginny, the way she probed and questioned things. So I said what was on my mind, which, if my mother were there, would have been discouraged. "Why?" I asked.

"Why?"

"Yes, why have the Kehoes stopped going to church? I mean, how do you know?"

Those pale rheumy eyes settled on me. I think she knew I was stepping beyond my bounds and she was quite fond of such boldness. "Because Nellie told me so," she said. "Occasionally I stop in on the way back from town. She welcomes the company. Women's company. She's different when he's not in the house. So one visit—it wasn't long after they moved up here from Tecumseh, which is down by Ann Arbor, almost to the Ohio line—she told me, and I think it's because the previous Sunday I was being driven home from church in Josh Lealand's buggy and I saw the two of them, Nellie and Andrew, sitting out on the front porch and it just seemed like they'd been sitting there all morning. I think she felt she owed me an explanation, though I did not request one." Aunt Ginny picked up her tea. It took some time, her two hands bringing the china cup to her mouth. When she'd settled the cup in its saucer, she said, "It happened down there, in Tecumseh, before they moved up here. It was quite disturbing for Nellie, though she tried not to let on. She's a very lonely woman. It's different from my circumstances. I'm alone. She's lonely."

Then Aunt Ginny seemed to freeze. This would happen sometimes. She'd be in conversation and all of a sudden she'd not be there. She'd stop speaking and not look at anything in particular, and I would have no idea where she would go. But she herself was very much alone in the room. I know all about this now. I know I drift in and out, as they say. Old people, they can't help it. Where do

I go? Back. I go back, and I don't seem to mind. I now know that's where Aunt Ginny would go at such times. *Back.*

I offered to pour more tea, which brought her out of it.

She declined.

"So," I said. "The Kehoes have never gone to church since moving to Bath."

And I decided to leave it there, as though there was nothing more to say on the matter. But with Aunt Ginny there was always more to say, there were layers of circumstances that could be pared away like peeling an onion, until you get to the core of the thing, the reason why it was the way it was—she was, even then, in her sixties, in constant pursuit of that core. Some people, some in my family, thought Aunt Ginny was just a terrible gossip (though it never caused them to get up from the table when she got started). She believed it was the truth.

"It had to do with the church, down there in Tecumseh," she said. "They had torn down the old Catholic church and built a new one. Every family in the parish was expected to contribute its share to defray the cost of construction. They received a bill for about four hundred dollars. Nellie said it went back to Andrew's father, who had very strong views regarding taxes and such—hated to pay them, and only would do so if he believed that the money was spent in a way that would directly benefit him. Andrew just ignored the bill. When the priest came to the house to inquire about the four hundred dollars, Andrew told him to get out of his house, and if he didn't, he, Andrew, would remove him. To a *priest,* a man of the *cloth.* Afterward Andrew forbade his wife from ever going to church again."

Aunt Ginny saw that my cup was empty. "More?"

"No, thank you."

"Well, you should get on back to the Kehoe's. She could use a hand. She has that girl Edith come and help, but it's a big house. Big for just the two of them. They never had any children."

I wanted to ask why but *that* seemed too intimate a question, even for Aunt Ginny.

Her blue eyes turned toward the window light. "I believe they married too late for that," she said, as though she'd heard my question. "And, well, her health isn't that robust. She spends a lot of time in Lansing. Her sisters are down there. She's like a mother to them. And there are doctors' appointments. No, no children."

■ ■ ■

They monkeyed with the tractor until past noontime. Mr. Kehoe removed various parts, handed them to Jed, who took them into the shed, where he placed them in pans and buckets filled with a solution that would clean the parts after soaking overnight. He could smell cooking coming from the open window at the back of the house. Finally, Mr. Kehoe said they would stop for lunch and they walked up to the back of the house, and when he opened the screen door, he said, "You can sit out here on the stoop. The missus will bring you something."

When she came out of the kitchen, Jed got up from the wood step. She wore a print dress, green with some kind of white flowers on it that reminded him of trumpets. She gave him a plate with a sandwich and a glass of milk.

"It's cool here in the shade," she said. "I do hope you'll be comfortable."

"I'm fine, Ma'am."

Turning to open the screen door, she paused and gazed at the field beyond the outbuildings. Her concentration was such that she seemed to have forgotten he was there on the step below her. She might have been counting something. Her graying hair was pulled up and worked into a loose bun at the back of her head. There was something, a faint scent, that reminded Jed of one of the teachers at school, an older woman who had worked as librarian until she became ill. This was several years ago. Jed recalled that he thought she smelled like books, old books with yellowed pages. It was not unlike the smell of old wallpaper that is curling away from the plaster wall because the glue has gone dry. He wondered if it was something Mrs. Kehoe put in the bath or some cologne, or if it was just a smell that women acquire when they reach a certain age.

"Isn't that just beautiful?" The way she said it Jed wasn't sure if she was talking to him or to herself. He looked out across the pasture toward the trees at the back of their property. "The leaves, so green against that sky," she added.

It was one of those spring days when the heat rises off the land and clouds develop as afternoon comes on. Though there was sunlight on the trees, far to the north a thunderhead had built up into an enormous gray anvil. The brilliant green leaves backed by the dark cloud, that was what Mrs. Kehoe thought was beautiful.

Jed felt he owed her some response. "Maybe we'll get showers later."

"Yes. Perhaps." She sounded vague, and glancing up at her, he saw that she was now staring at something else, something to do with the pasture. "So much rain this year. So much rain."

She turned and stepped into the kitchen, and pulling the screen door behind her, she said, "Andrew, that one-eyed horse and the mare. You sell them off, that pasture will just go to waste."

Jed didn't hear her husband's response because she closed the kitchen door.

He sat on the stoop and picked up the sandwich: chicken, with what looked like a whitish mustard, on thick slices of bread. Then he realized that there was something else on the plate. Three jelly beans, red, green, and yellow. It was what his mother would call a thoughtful gesture, though she would never put jelly beans on his lunch plate.

After biting into the sandwich—the mustard was horse radish, he knew because his father slathered it on almost anything he ate—he chewed as he stared out at the fields. The soil had not been turned, and there were the two horses, their heads lowered to the business of grazing, with an occasional flick of the tail.

Strange farm. No chickens, cows, or goats. Just two horses.

He took the jelly beans from the plate and stuck them in the pocket of his overalls.

2.

Aunt Ginny was right about Mrs. Kehoe. She was pleasant but seemed to suffer some ailment that prohibited her from moving with any assurance, as though she constantly questioned her balance. She explained that her "regular girl" Edith Witt couldn't work because she had come down with a cold.

Mrs. Kehoe set me to oiling the woodwork in the parlor and dining room. Solid oak, which had a handsome sheen after I wiped and buffed it with a cloth. While I moved about the floor on my hands and knees, she sat in a stuffed chair at an oak table, turning the pages of a magazine. The skin around her eyes was dark and her face had a grayish pallor. She leaned over the magazine on the table, but often she would lean back in her chair, remove her glasses, appearing to be exhausted from the effort of merely sitting upright. Both she and Mr. Kehoe dressed as though they expected company. I liked the violets on her dress. The material was fine, pressed linen.

There would be silence, minutes where the only sound would be of my cloth wiping oak woodwork, punctuated by the sound of a magazine page being turned. But then Mrs. Kehoe would say something that seemed to come from nowhere. As though she were in a conversation with herself, or perhaps someone in the room who was invisible to me. But I wasn't sure, and if Mrs. Kehoe were addressing me, it would be impolite not to reply.

I didn't want to interrupt her, but when she said something about "taking a rifle to stop the barking," I sat back on my haunches and looked up at her.

"The Harte's little terrier across the street," she said. "He shot it."

"Because it barked?" I asked. "When?"

"Oh, this was some time ago." Her eyes were closed and she was leaning back in her chair, her face tilted toward the ceiling. She might have been trying to conjure spirits. I liked to read about the séances high society people in places like New York held, and imagined that this might be what Mrs. Kehoe was doing, speaking with a spirit, communing with the past. "He never admitted it," she said, without opening her eyes. "But it was obvious. I was in Lansing at the time. It was his rifle. I could smell that it had been fired. The Hartes didn't get home until after dark. They didn't find the dog until the next morning."

Mrs. Kehoe almost seemed in a trance, or asleep. I looked at her throat, the loose flesh there, and wondered if the woman was in pain. She seemed to be in a state of endurance.

I resumed wiping down the baseboard. When I reached the corner of the room, I stood up and began work on the back of the swinging door that led to the kitchen. I had grown several inches within the last year and I could now just reach the top of a door and run the oiled cloth along the uppermost panel—the top rail. The oak grain in the door reminded me of a tiger, the finish giving a deep, rich tone to the wood.

"The little thing barked often." It had been minutes since Mrs. Kehoe had last spoken. "But it never left the yard, never crossed the road. Just barked when it saw you coming or going, or if you were in our front yard. It would come to the edge of its yard and let you know it was there. Didn't bother anyone. Just barked like a dog doing its job, protecting the property." She opened her eyes, moved her head and stared at me as though she were surprised to see a girl standing there in her parlor. "It annoyed him, so he shot the dog."

She sat forward and turned a page of her magazine. I worked the cloth into the corners of each panel. I loved the feel of the ridges and grooves in the wood, and it made me appreciate the times I had spent in my father's workshop watching him use his miter saw and various block planes. Sometimes he'd let me help with the final sanding, saying to go very easy with the fine grit sandpaper over all the curls and edges; change nothing, he'd say, just make the wood fine to the touch.

"And now there's Kit, our one-eyed horse."

"He shot it, too?"

I kept working at the door, afraid I would be reprimanded for being so familiar, so inquisitive. There was silence from the other end of the room, and then a long slow sigh. I turned around. Mrs. Kehoe removed her glasses and laid them on the table next to her magazine. She wasn't looking at me, but there seemed to be no doubt that she knew I was in the room, no question that when she spoke she was responding to my inquiry.

"He gave Kit to our neighbor McMullen. He'd already sold off all the chickens, and Monty Ellsworth bought the hogs and an old shack that was out in the pasture. I asked, What did you get for that horse? He said, Nothing. He didn't sell it; he gave it away. With all our concerns, he gives the horse away. But he gave McMullen a bill of sale." She was looking toward me now—not necessarily at me, but toward me, as though she were trying to distinguish me from the door I was oiling. "McMullen returned the horse."

I didn't dare ask why.

▪ ▪ ▪

Work on the tractor continued through the afternoon. As they filled several pans with engine parts, Mr. Kehoe named each one and explained its purpose. There were valves and screws and bolts and springs and arms, metal parts so precise in their dimensions and purpose that it seemed they were not made but given. They were *manufactured.* That was Mr. Kehoe's word. They were *carburetor* and *intake* and *exhaust;* they were *spark* and *compression.* The engine, all of its stationary and moving parts, was designed to contain and utilize *combustion.* Somewhere—somewhere nearby, in Detroit and Lansing and Flint—parts were manufactured. Out of steel. *And what is steel?* It's iron ore that comes out of the ground up north, up in that land above the Mackinac Straits, that other peninsula where there were said to be wild animals and an abundance of fish in the rivers and lakes, but miners extracted iron ore in the Menominee, Gogebic, and Marquette ranges. *Taconite,* Mr. Kehoe said, which after being *processed* looked like rifle shot, round balls that big (forming a hole with his forefinger and thumb), and it was loaded in train cars and hauled down to harbors on the Lake Superior shore. Locomotive engines pulling dozens of cars out along enormous ore docks, some running over a thousand feet out into the lake, and the container on each car was on *hinges* so they could be *articulated* and the contents tipped so that the taconite *pellets* would pour through massive chutes that angled down from the side of the ore dock and into the holds of ships called *ore boats.* And as tons of taconite filled the ore boats—enormous ships of steel that could be seven- or eight-hundred feet, bow to stern—the sound was of a waterfall that could be heard miles away. And how was it possible that, when the ship full of taconite left the ore docks, it didn't simply sink, go straight to the bottom of Lake Superior, a body of water so deep, so big, that all the water from the other Great Lakes, Michigan and Huron and Erie and Ontario, all that water could be poured into Superior time and time again and never could fill the vast canyons created by the glacier that once cut its way down through the midsection of the continent? The ships did not sink because of what mariners called *displacement;* no, they floated and set a course due east, some under steam, some still plying under sail, heading for the only place where a vessel could leave Lake Superior, cruising hundreds of miles, often through fierce weather—famous storms that have wrecked countless ships, thousands of tons of cargo and hundreds of lives lost—until those ships that held course entered Whitefish Bay and found refuge in the *locks* at Sault Ste. Marie. There, the lock water was drained—miraculously, it took only a few minutes, tons of water rushing and creating a sound much like the sound of taconite filling the ship's hold—until the downriver gate was opened and the vessel could continue on the St. Mary's River, which was twenty-one feet below Lake Superior. At Detour Island the ship would head west, through the straits, and then down Lake Michigan to Chicago or Gary, or it would continue south on Lake Huron to Detroit, or even farther south to Toledo or Cleveland on Lake Erie, there to be unloaded and heaped in great piles—gray pyramids—next to *foundries.* Steel plants dotted the shores of the lower lakes, smokestacks on the horizon serving as landmarks for the coming ships, and there these pellets dug out of the northern mines were heated to incredible temperatures until they turned to liquid and a color of fire that was too strong for the naked eye. And then they were *manufactured.* Tool and die, Mr. Kehoe said, forms and presses. *Die?* Jed thought, but didn't ask. The molten steel miraculously shaped, cooled, and hardened. Each piece manufactured according to specific *dimensions* and *tolerances,* and this is what you see here in these pans. This carburetor screw, this bolt, all manufactured, and then sent to the Ford plants. Most of them in Michigan, Mr. Kehoe said. In Lansing, the General Motors Plant downtown and over on the west side the Durant Plant.

In Detroit, the Highland Park Plant and to the south the new plant being built on River Rouge. This is Michigan, where once there were fields and forest, now there are foundries and plants, all rising up off the land—and workers, thousands of workers, on the assembly lines. All for the purpose of making this Ford tractor. And when Mr. Kehoe said the word *tractor,* he might have been a preacher speaking the Word from the pulpit during Sunday service. *Tractor.* This machine, made from iron ore, could till the soil, scratch the land, open the earth so seeds could be planted. Many farmers still walked behind a beast pulling a plow. They were wary of the machines. Cars and trucks and tractors moving along the roads like an invasion of some alien species. They feared it because they didn't understand it—and that was Mr. Kehoe's point: *you've got to understand it.* And they didn't understand a man like Mr. Kehoe who wore a suit and tie as he rode up on the seat of his Ford tractor, as though he himself might be a god. A god of the earth. Lord of the land. Eighty acres. Cultivate the crops. Raise livestock. So we can eat. So we can live.

▪ ▪ ▪

Sometimes I lie here, staring at my ceiling cracks, and come to the thought that it was an act of mercy. I wonder if this might have been what was in the man's mind. The same hard empathy one feels when putting an animal down. An injured, wounded, ailing cow. An old horse. Or a dog. The rabid dog, turned vicious, we put it down with one shot to the skull. We are saving it from further pain, further hurt. There is no point to the suffering. Put a stop to it, put an end to it. Finish it. And we are protecting ourselves from the dog's teeth, from the vile rabies that might infect our blood, the blood of others. We kill to make the world safe.

But this, this is not a rabid animal, a sickly mare. There is no threat. Yet there is the belief—no, the conviction—that there is mercy here. It must be conviction. Conviction that comes after acceptance. Acceptance of suffering, of the fact that the innocent will suffer. They are destined to, if not today, then tomorrow. All hope, all promise ultimately gives way to the other. The loss. The ache. The grief and sorrow. The very anticipation of these. It all leads to the same place. The suffering. To accept that is to find a way out, a way of defeating the necessity of it. Relentless suffering. Inexorable suffering. Suffering that dwells within, waiting for that moment when it can break through, much as the crops push up through good dirt into sunlight. You cannot avoid it, cannot ignore it, cannot negotiate with it; you cannot defeat it. You can only kill that which will suffer, eventually, inevitably, you can only put it out of its misery. Maybe this was his reasoning, if that be reasoning—killing is the only true act of mercy.

▪ ▪ ▪

"Guess what I have in my pocket," Jed said.

It was a game we played. Guess what's in my hand, in my pocket, behind my back.

I tightened my arms about his ribs. "Okay. Is it from their farm?"

"Yes."

"Does it have a smell?"

"Ha. I suppose. But not too much."

"Does it come from one of the animals?"

"No."

"What color is it?"

Jed hesitated.

"You don't know what color it is?"

"It's two colors. Red and green."

"Does it grow, like on a stem or a stalk?"

"No. But you wish it would. Here's a hint."

"Thank you, a hint."

"Jack."

"That's it? Jack. Your hints, they always make it harder."

As though in agreement, Daisy nodded her head as she plodded along the road.

"That's all you get. One hint: Jack."

I looked out across the Kehoe fields. "What did you do all day?"

"Worked on his tractor."

"The land—he's not planting?"

"Guess not. He didn't harvest last fall either. Strange, isn't it? Two years in a row. And for all his talk about the need to raise animals, there's nothing but a couple of horses grazing."

"I know. Strange." I wanted to get back to the guessing game. "Does it make a sound when you shake it?"

"No. Wait. There are two of them, so if you shook them, they'd make a sound."

My strategy was to ask questions about physical attributes, but I said, "Did you steal it?"

"*What?* No, no I didn't steal it."

"So it was given to you. By Mr. Kehoe?"

"No." Jed was emphatic and quite proud of that.

I rested my forehead against the nape of his neck.

"Falling asleep?"

"I'm thinking."

"She's thinking. *Help!*"

"Then Mrs. Kehoe gave it to you."

A pause, and then a defeated, "Yes."

I pulled my head away. "You were in the house—when she gave it to you?"

"No."

"She came outside?"

"Yes."

"I know," I said. "Is it edible?"

"Yes." Disappointed.

"So she gave you something to eat?"

"Yes."

"But you didn't eat it, and it's in your pocket. So it's not, um, ice cream."

He laughed. "No, it's not ice cream."

"How many questions do I have left?"

"Two."

"Liar."

"Two."

"This is where you always cheat."

"Do not."

"Okay. Is it a . . . a fruit? Or a vegetable?"

"That's two questions."

"Right. Is it fruit?"

"No."

"And it's not from an animal, so—"

"One more."

"It's, oh wait. It's. It's gemstones. Colored gemstones."

"No. But that's a good guess, if you eat stones. Close your eyes and open your mouth."

"If it's something fuzzy or dirty, I'm going to kill you."

"It's not fuzzy. Or dirty. Closed?"

"Yup."

I could feel him leaning to his left and reaching into the pocket of his overalls. "You get one at time."

There was a moment. Anticipation infused with fear. But I trusted him.

Didn't I?

His fingers touched my lower lip, and then something was inserted into my mouth. It was smooth and round against my tongue. No, not round. Oval, like a miniature egg. But hard, clicking against my front teeth, like a pebble. Like a stone, but not a stone. And then a sweetness began to coat the inside of my mouth. Tentatively, I clamped the pebble between my teeth and bit down, it's brittle shell cracking and giving way to a softer sweetness that filled my mouth.

"Jelly bean!"

"Yes."

"Jack. And the beanstalk. Really? That's no clue."

He shrugged his shoulders. "Can you guess which color?"

"There are two?"

"Yes, red and green. I ate the yellow one."

I began to chew and the bean broke up, its contents dissolving, coating my tongue with a sugary paste. "I don't know. I can't tell."

"Guess."

"It's the red one. Red."

"No."

"Give me the other, and maybe it'll taste different and I can tell the color."

He hesitated. "What would your mother say?"

"Come on, Jed!"

"She would say, Too many sweets and you'll ruin your teeth."

I pounded my fist against his back. "You ate the yellow one."

Physical beatings never worked. He liked it, and it only strengthened his resolve. "We'll think of another game," he said, "and see if you can have the other one."

"You're cruel." I hit him one more time, for good measure.

"Why isn't he planting?" His mind was already elsewhere.

"Leaving the land fallow is good for the soil."

"But the entire farm, eighty acres. Two years. Without crops, how's he going to make it?"

"I don't know."

"And not even a chicken in the yard."

I was tired, suddenly very tired. Ma would say it's what happens after putting too much sugar in your tea, but it was also the work at both houses, much of it on my hands and knees. I rested my cheek against the back of Jed's shoulder. As the slow predictable rhythm of Daisy's gait massaged my brain, I closed my eyes, thinking only of the warmth of the sun on my hair.

I fell asleep.

It happened more than once, falling asleep on horseback, my arms around Jed.

So long ago now, but I can still feel it all, Jed's ribs, the heat rising off Daisy's coat, the sense of abandon as I drifted down into that dark refuge. *Sleep.* There was no sense of time, only acceptance and trust. It's what this old woman hopes for now, entry into the benign shelter of sleep that will carry me beyond this world at a sauntering pace along a country road on a warm spring afternoon.

And then I was awake. Startled, alert. Something in Jed's posture had stiffened as Daisy pulled up and stopped walking. I became aware of a sound approaching from the woods a quarter mile ahead, and then we saw it, the locomotive emerging from the trees, its wheels squealing as it slowly rounded the curve in the tracks. We watched the white plume of smoke chuffing into the clear spring sky, and then the endless cars, boxcar after boxcar, and the occasional flatcar, loaded with stacks of lumber. The train continued to issue from the trees, as though it were eternity itself, a perpetual parade of clattering wheels and rattling steel.

Two men stood in the open door of a boxcar. They tossed their sacks off the train, and then, after a moment of hesitance, they dropped down, their bodies rolling to the bottom of the grassy embankment. They got to their feet; one retrieved a hat. With their sacks thrown over a shoulder they walked away from the passing train, looking about like feral animals. They gazed in our direction but seeing only two children on horseback never broke stride through the tall grass as they disappeared into a woods. Finally, the caboose appeared from the trees and then the sound, that sweet, jarring racket that is a train, began to diminish as the line of cars continued on down the rails to Lansing.

"Hobos." Jed nudged Daisy with his heels and she continued down the road.

"Aunt Ginny hires them sometimes," I said. "Cutting and stacking wood, yard work. She gives them food and a little money."

"Mom once put a pie up on the windowsill to cool, and it disappeared. She was convinced it was hobos."

I laughed. "It wasn't you? You and Warren?"

"Naah. She'da known it was us and I'd be dead now." Daisy's hooves beat on the packed dirt with the slow persistence of a clock. Jed was thinking something through, I could tell. "I read about hobos in a magazine. Some can be dangerous. They can be drunkards and such. But many of them live by an honor system, and they leave messages for each other in hobo's code."

"Riding the rails," I said, "and all you do is end up here in Bath. Think you'll ever leave Bath?"

He laughed then. "If I'd'a stolen Mom's pie, guess I'd have to."

"Aunt Ginny likes to say, 'For most of us there's but one way out of Bath.'"

Weary, I laid my head on Jed's shoulder and closed my eyes again.

3.

The word that comes to mind is trauma. Afterward, when it was all over, when it had been done and everything that we knew was different from everything we had known, after that we picked up on conversations among the adults—often overhearing them because their talk, what they thought, what they suspected, what they believed wasn't meant for our ears. They were trying to piece it together, understand how it was done, why it happened. I used to think that's what made adults different from children, but now this old woman knows different. We are all the same. Age has nothing to do with getting closer to it, nearer to understanding, comprehending, imagining how any of it was remotely possible. Even the youngest child had to come to this: *it just is.*

But we thought the adults knew something we didn't know. We would hide because that was how we gained access, hide on staircases, in the next room, behind furniture and doors. Tight places where children could fit without being seen or heard. And then we would share what we had heard: a kind of cross-referencing. If my pa said this and your uncle said that, then there must be some truth to it. But there was so much uncertainty. So many details that may or may not be accurate. Or are just inexplicable. It left Bath in a state of suspension. A moratorium: we couldn't go back, we couldn't go forward. Yet, slowly, the days returned to something that appeared to be normal. We ate meals, did chores, worked, went to school, attended church, but it wasn't real somehow, it didn't have the same meaning. We weren't exactly living. Sometimes whatever we were doing seemed downright pointless. But we didn't know what else to do. Other times it would get to be too much.

Sometimes Ma would begin to cry. Once while making pie crust. I was standing by the table taking the small cuttings of dough, as I often did, rolling them in the flour on the board with my fingers, and eating them. There was no texture like those balls of pie dough. When Ma stopped thumbing the edge of the crust in the plate and began to daub at her eyes with the corner of her apron, I thought she was upset with me. I said I wouldn't eat any more, but she shook her head, really sobbing now, and she took me in her arms. I could smell the heat from her soft heaving chest and my cheeks were dusted with flour as her hands stroked my face and hair. I knew. I knew then what was the matter, and as she hugged me, I chewed the last ball of dough, feeling guilty.

There was that, too. It might not surface until years later. At graduation ceremonies, weddings, baptisms, wakes, and funerals, something would be said—usually a vague reference, for no one needed to mention it directly—and we would understand that they were addressing the guilt of surviving. Years later, I read about this after World War II. People who had survived those camps in Europe, how they felt guilty, as though they had no right to live. It often became worse as they got older; as the business of life, work, and family faded away; as all that receded into the past, they said they were left, old and infirm, with this guilt at having had those things, careers and children and grandchildren. It made no sense; it wasn't our fault, but we felt that, too. Survivors' guilt.

One night, sitting on the landing, my forehead pressed against the newel post, staring down through the balusters, listening to their voices rise up on the heat from the kitchen. I could tell that Pa and my uncle had been out to the barn for a sip from the jug that he kept on the shelf behind the cans of paint, linseed oil, and turpentine. Often Ma would chastise him, knowing what they'd been up to—and it was funny, Ma talking to him like he was one of us, a child who had engaged in some foolishness—but this was not more than a couple of months after it happened, late summer, with the cicadas sawing in the trees, and the four of them, Ma and Pa, and Uncle Clarence and Aunt Millie, sitting in the kitchen, trying to sort it out.

"It's the politics of this town," Pa said.

"No, the finances," Uncle Clarence said. His voice was accompanied by a clicking sound that his pipe made against his teeth. "He stood to lose his farm. We know now how far behind on taxes he was. And the mortgage."

There was silence—there often were these long silences. Until Ma said, "It was both. Money and politics. Kehoe was an ambitious man."

Aunt Millie, her voice always shrill, broken by the periodic cough which eventually turned into the thing in her lungs that killed her, "They made Kehoe treasurer of the school board, even though some members of the board were wary."

"*Wary!*" Uncle Clarence exploded.

"Listen," Millie said patiently, as though speaking to an excited child, "whatever you think of Kehoe, there was no question he was an intelligent man."

"That be your problem right there," Uncle Clarence said. "*Too* smart, if you ask me."

"When it came to figures," Millie continued, "when it came to toting them up, he was exact, right down to the penny. Everybody knew that."

"Which is probably why he was so much bother at school board meetings," Pa said.

"That may be so," Millie said. "But the numbers always added up."

"He was obsessed with money, with taxes," Ma said. "If things didn't go his way with the school board, he'd move to have the meeting ended."

Pa chipped in. "And as treasurer, it was his job to distribute the paychecks at school. I heard how he'd walk through the building, distributing checks to teachers and staff. More than once he'd 'forget' to give Huyck his check. The school superintendent!" Pa slapped the kitchen table as he laughed. "He wanted to make the fella come and beg for his money."

"Emory Huyck," Uncle Clarence said. "There was another smart fella. Two smart men and look, just look what happens."

There followed the silence of agreement.

▪ ▪ ▪

The second time Jed went out to help the Kehoes, he rode in Mr. Kehoe's Ford truck down the two-track that ran along the edge of his fields to the woods at the back of the property. Mr. Kehoe explained that for some time now he'd been cutting the woods back, adding to his pasture and cropland. Jed stared out across the untilled land under lowering spring clouds. It looked like rain. Black birds worked the field, which had not been planted the previous season.

"Crows?" Mr. Kehoe asked.

"I think so."

"Or are they ravens?"

Jed didn't answer. This was like in school, where teachers often asked him a question that just made him freeze up.

"They're both in the corvid family," said Mr. Kehoe. "Know the difference?"

"Afraid not, sir," Jed said. He expected a lecture on the difference between crows and ravens.

But one was not forthcoming. Mr. Kehoe kept both hands on the steering wheel, concentrating on keeping the tires on the tracks, though they weren't going faster than a horse's saunter. Grass ticked along the underside of the truck. "Don't they teach you anything in that school?" When Jed didn't respond, Mr. Kehoe snorted with satisfaction. "Nothing useful, apparently."

They arrived at the edge of the woods and climbed down from the truck. Mr. Kehoe walked into the woods, saying over his shoulder. "I've already set things up. But I thought you'd like to see how it's done."

"Yes, sir."

Mr. Kehoe stopped and took a handkerchief from the pocket of his suitcoat and unfolded it. There was a wooden box on the ground with a wire running from it off deeper into the woods. He spread the handkerchief on the ground close to the box. Then with effort, for he was not an agile man, he lowered himself to one knee, careful that the handkerchief protected his trousers from touching the ground. He leaned over the box, which had a metal, T-shaped bar protruding from the top. Placing his hands on the bar, he said, "Now, cover your ears and you keep your eyes on yonder tree stump."

Jed placed his hands over his ears and looked into the woods. The stump, sawn at an angle, was a fair distance away. Mr. Kehoe pushed down on the metal bar, causing metal gears to click inside the box, and then an explosion sent wood and dirt and smoke into the air. The force of the blast pummeled Jed's rib cage.

A cloud of screeching birds rose up into the air above the trees. Mr. Kehoe got to his feet and, folding his handkerchief, gazed skyward. Jed thought he said, "Crows, mostly." But he wasn't sure because his ears were muffled from the explosion. He could feel his blood beating inside his temples. As the smoke cleared, Jed looked at the hole in the ground where the stump had been.

He wanted to ask Mr. Kehoe if they could do it again.

■ ■ ■

When I heard the explosion, I thought this is it, the End of Time. The Resurrection.

As a girl, I was much taken with religion. Every Sunday we were assured that Jesus would return and my first thought was that the moment had arrived. The sound wasn't just noise, it moved the earth causing the house to heave and rattle so that I thought it would all come down on our heads. Judgement Day had come while I was lifting one end of the oak table in the parlor. Edith Witt dropped her end and let out a cry as she buckled over in pain. Miraculously, the house remained standing.

I went around the table and helped Edith to the nearest chair. She removed her shoe and inspected her foot, the big toe red and swelling up. I was beginning to have doubts about the nature of Judgement Day. Could this be Edith's adjudication? What form of sin warranted a swollen toe? I expected at any moment to experience some ill physical sensation, some hurt, some agony that would reflect the nature and scope of my offenses. At fourteen I believed it was my sacred duty to bear my sins honestly—I had to admit it, I was guilty. Envy. Greed. Pride. Those were the first to come to mind, but there were others, what I considered my most secret sins, which I harbored deep down where I hoped no one would discern them, though of course the Lord would, for He knew all and would know their number, the severity of each, and now that the day had arrived, it was too late for me to offer atonement. I felt shame, which only seemed to compound my fear. I wanted to climb back inside my mother's womb and be given a chance to live my life once again, pure and innocent and free of the slightest transgression against His will.

Edith, I was convinced, understood that we were both in this inescapable predicament. She could only hiss and take in deep breaths of air. Tears sprung from her eyes. Her hands shook. She was, I guessed, ten or twelve years older, though she looked so withered and pared down she might have been thirty-five, even forty years of age. She wasn't paid, I had come to understand, which was odd because I knew they weren't related. It wasn't the same as my helping out Aunt Ginny. It was not unusual, though, not then in Bath. Her family was fond of Nellie Kehoe, née Price, so it followed that they would send Edith to help out around the house. Edith was missing several teeth, which made her difficult to understand, particularly when she pronounced words with an *s*.

For some reason I had not yet been stricken by God's hand, and I began to sense that what seemed the end of the world was actually some detonation out behind the house. Acting purely on instinct, I went into the kitchen, where there was a teapot heating on the stove. I knew from the first time I had worked at the house that Mrs. Kehoe kept a jar of Epsom salt in the kitchen closet. I filled a porcelain pan with hot water from the teapot, added a fistful of Epsom salt, and returned to the parlor, careful not to spill it. "Soak your foot in this," I said, placing the pan on the floor, and glad to let go of the rim that was turning hot from the water.

"*Grathiouth me,*" Edith said, as she eased her foot into the pan.

I went to the window and looked across the fields toward the woods. Birds wheeled in confusion through the column of smoke that rose above the trees. In the field, the two horses were trotting away from the woods. "What was that?" I said. "I can see the truck—but I can't see Jed and Mr. Kehoe. Are they all right?"

"Another of his tree stumps." Stumps sounded like *thumpth.* "Never gives fair warning when he's going to blow one to smithereens. The Mrs. says he's like a boy toying with fireworks, the way he plays with his dynamite."

As if on cue, there came a thumping on the parlor ceiling. Edith nearly rose out of her chair in fear, but then settled back and exhaled. "I promised her tea. You best take it up to her." She inspected her foot in the pan. "Thank you for thinking of the salts. I don't believe anything's broken, but Lordy it smarts. Spend a few minutes with her, and when you come down, we'll get this rug outside for a beating." Edith glanced at the ceiling, and then at me, wide-eyed, as though she were about to divulge the darkest of secrets. "She is so fine a lady. This was her family's house—the Prices. They was always good to us." She leaned forward in the chair, whispering, "But *he* . . . he ain't paid no property taxes in a good while and there's a threat of foreclosure."

"You mean, they might lose the farm?"

"Right. I hear them talking and arguing over it." Edith leaned back in the chair, making a shooing motion with her hand. "Go, go on up."

I went into the kitchen and began to prepare the tea, occasionally looking out the window. The smoke was clearing, and I could now see Jed, gathering wood and loading it in the truck bed. It was difficult to tell what Mr. Kehoe was doing—smoking one of his cigars, and coiling up some kind of rope?

"There's cookies in the tin by the stove," Edith said. "Give her two. And insist that she eat them. She's fading away to nothing. Can't get her to eat not a morsel."

From upstairs I could hear Mrs. Kehoe cough, a wet, hacking sound.

I poured boiling water into the teapot. "What's wrong with her?"

"Lord if anyone really knows," Edith said, barely a whisper. "Goes into Lansing all the time for doctor's appointments. Maybe some allergies? Or some kind of asthma? But she's in a poorly way that give her these terrible headaches."

When I had the tea, cup and saucer, and plate of cookies on the tray, I came through the parlor. There were three cookies on the plate. I broke one in half and handed it to Edith. She took it reluctantly, looking as though she would be struck dead, but then she put the whole thing in her mouth and grinned at me.

I climbed the stairs with the tray, and when I reached the landing and was out of Edith's sight, I whispered under my breath, "*Cookieth, thmithereenth, grathiouth me,*" half expecting that I might be struck dead myself for committing yet another of the seven deadly sins. Or perhaps the eighth: mockery. But I wasn't felled by the Lord. In some odd way I felt saved. I continued upstairs, where the polished hardwood reflected God's light as it poured through the window at the end of the hall.

▪ ▪ ▪

Kehoe loved dynamite.

He loved the way it made the air smell volatile and dangerous.

While coiling up what was left of the wire to the detonator box, he regarded the hole in the ground with great satisfaction. He had instructed Jed to gather wood and load it in the truck bed. The tree trunk had been shattered and blown to pieces, some as long as the boy was tall, some not much more than splinters that would make good kindling.

Kehoe removed a cigar from the inside pocket of his suitcoat, cut a wedge from the tip with his jackknife, and patted his trousers for matches. "Jed, you ever see anything like that before?"

The boy paused, a bundle of wood in his arms. "No, sir."

Kehoe settled on the front fender of the truck and slowly inhaled as he moved the match flame about the end of his cigar. "Ever smoke one of these stogies?"

Jed took the wood to the back of the truck. "Me? No, sir."

"Not even once?" Kehoe smiled around his cigar. "How old are you?"

"I'm twelve."

"That a fact? And not yet smoked a cigar, or a cigarette. I'd had my first by the time I was ten." He considered the smoldering end of his cigar. "Not good for you, I suppose, but once you get used to them, it becomes a habit. And we are by nature habitual creatures, wouldn't you say?"

The boy bent over and picked up a stick. Of course he'd smoked a cigar. All boys did, wanting to be like men.

"This here is the future, Jed." Kehoe rapped his knuckles on the metal fender of his truck, and then pointed toward the ground where the tree stump had been. "That hole, it's the past. But this Ford machine, this is the future. Combustion engines and electricity." He drew on his cigar in contemplation. "Dynamite. And pyrotol. Left over from the war. Reprocessed from military surplus. It's cheap. But to detonate it you need electricity. To turn the lights on in that expensive new school of yours, you need electricity. Go into Lansing, you see power lines above the street. And it's coming here to Bath. You see the crews erecting the poles and stringing the wires along the roads. It's coming, Jed. Every house: electricity. You know who's responsible for it?"

The boy shook his head. His mouth was slightly open. He wasn't slow, but he needed time for a thing to register. Kehoe had seen that when he explained how a spark plug functioned inside the tractor engine.

"The future is something people don't give enough thought to," he said. "They simply expect it to happen like the rising sun. Just like those horses out there in the field. Electricity is the new sun. But it's different—and you know why? It's manmade."

Jed nodded, because he was expected to, but he glanced out at the grazing horses as though expecting them to share in his uncertainty.

"And who do you think made it possible?" Kehoe removed the cigar from his mouth. "Mr. Thomas Edison. He's changed the future in the way few other men have. More than the president, more than any general. Thomas Edison and George Westinghouse. And Henry Ford, who has set up the manufacture of these here trucks—by the thousands! These men, they're responsible for the future. If I were you I'd study the combustion engine, I'd learn about alternate currents and the alkaline battery. That's if you want to have a future. That's if you want a future that doesn't mean you're wedded to a bit of acreage that your creditors can reclaim when they damn well please. Land is the past. Machines, they're the future."

Jed added more wood to the pile in the truck bed.

"You give much thought to the future, Jed?"

"I guess not so much."

"You think you have one? A future?"

The boy's shirt and overalls were covered with bark and wood chips. "I reckon."

"You reckon." Kehoe stared at his feet and smiled. He was tired. Weary. The truth of it was he'd been weary for a long time. "What if you knew what your future was, Jed? What if you knew that you would lose everything, everything you ever worked for, everything you wanted in life? Your wife. Your family. Your house. Your farm, with all the land and animals. Every cent you ever earned. Everything you ever owned, everything you held dear. If that's your future, to lose it all, what would you do?"

The boy folded his hands on top of the tailgate, as though he were praying. He pulled his lower lip in behind his small front teeth, a sign that he was thinking. "Work," he said, helpless, knowing it wasn't the answer Kehoe wanted. "I'd work harder?"

"Why? Why work if you know it's going to come to no avail."

Jed removed his hands from the tailgate. Clearly, he was thrown by the word avail. He resumed collecting wood that was strewn about the ground.

"See, there's a flaw in that kind of thinking, Jed. You believe in reward. That's what they teach you in that fancy new school we all pay for. In church, too. They tell you if you work hard you earn your reward. You pray and avoid sin, then you die and earn your reward. It's a lie. It's *all* a lie. There is no reward, son. Once you appreciate that, you'll see things clear."

The boy continued to pick up wood. "Yes, sir."

"You'll come to your senses." Kehoe got to his feet and tapped the ash from the end of his cigar. For some reason he'd always found satisfaction when the ash dropped away clean, as though it had been cut by a knife. It said something about the quality of the tobacco, how it was aged and wrapped, the way it burned slow and even. "If you're lucky, you'll come to your senses before it's too late. It happened to me—happened most recently in these here woods." He chuckled. "People now call 'em Kehoe's Woods."

Jed had his hand on a stick, but straightened up. Turning to Kehoe, he said, "Here?"

"A tree did it. I was out here, shooing a cow back to the field—this is back before I sold the herd. They'd wander into these woods and get caught in the brambles and bawl till you come and walk them out." He pointed at the place, deeper in the woods. "Back there."

"A tree, sir? What happened?"

"Branch fell on me. I heard this crack above me and it came down on my head. Knocked me clean out, I tell you. Lucky I wasn't killed. I lay there unconscious I don't know how long. When I opened my eyes the cow was standing next to me, dumb as spit."

"Were you hurt?"

"Cracked me good on the back of the skull. Had a lump like you wouldn't believe." Kehoe laughed, causing Jed to look wary. Almost as a means of self-defense he made himself busy collecting more wood. "I wasn't right for some time. Wasn't myself. I just wandered around here in the woods, the cow walking with me, and then I made my way back across the fields to the house. There was a woman there. Strangest thing. Know who she was?"

Jed shook his head. He looked afraid to hear any more.

"Old woman. Sickly. Looked to be wasting away. I hadn't a clue who she was, and when I asked her she looked at me all funny and said 'I'm your wife. Nellie. Why Andrew, I'm your wife.'" Kehoe puffed on his cigar. "Nellie was my wife. And my name was Andrew. It was news to me." He studied his cigar, wedged between his fingers. "And that's not the first time."

"First time for what, sir?"

"First time I took a good lump on the head. There was another time, years ago, when I was working out west. This is before I married that woman over there in that house. I was working for an electric company, doing what these crews are doing here in Bath, stringing the poles with wires that bring electricity to the countryside. Did it in St. Louis, and then up in Minnesota. It was decent work, and I was good at it. I was young, of course, and could climb those poles all day long. But I took a fall one day and got a knock on the head. Funny thing is I wasn't myself that time neither. But in a way, it was the first time I began to see things clear."

■ ■ ■

I don't know about time, that's for the philosophers, ministers, and mathematicians. But I suspect that it's an enormous wheel that goes round and round, causing us to relive the moments in the past. We are so obsessed with what *was*. It just won't let go. Moments come at us so bright and distinct we can't often see the present.

When I was a girl climbing those stairs to the second floor of the Kehoe farmhouse, carrying a tray of tea and cookies, I had this notion, this sense about the future. I couldn't see it, but at such moments I could feel something coming our way. I had no idea what it was, but I was convinced it loomed before us—something that would cleave time, an irreparable fissure, a black abyss. That explosion out in Kehoe Woods set something off in me, in my head, in my heart, something as real and inevitable as the light, God's light, glancing off the floorboards in the Kehoe's house.

Upon entering Mrs. Kehoe's bedroom I had a fleeting glimpse of the future. There lay a woman, frail, old (so very old, I thought then, though now it doesn't seem so—she was only in her fifties). Her color was not good. Her face, her hair, everything about her pale. Not even gray. Not even a color.

When she opened her eyes they possessed a recognition, an understanding of my understanding, if that makes sense. She saw what I saw, or so I believed. She saw herself as I saw her and she knew how horrifying it was—but then she smiled, weakly and with a sense of irony, because she knew that I knew I was staring at myself someday. I was seeing myself as I am now (though I'm well beyond my fifties). It was a secret we shared from that moment on: I was the girl she had been; she was the woman I would become. One day it would be my turn, as it was hers at that moment.

And then she said, "Place the tray on the nightstand, dear, and help me sit up, would you?"

Kind as can be. It was effortless, gentle, and I knew that it was a sign of strength, the only strength left in that frail body. She was saying we must play our roles, we should not acknowledge what we both just recognized; it's better to pretend. I helped her sit up and arranged the pillows and counterpane (no one uses that word anymore, but she did) about her.

When I placed the tray across her lap and turned to go, she said, "Won't you stay a moment and sit with me?"

"But Edith," I said. "I'm helping her move furniture so we can take the rug outside."

"Edith will be fine," she said. "There, pull the bench over from my vanity, won't you? Edith will appreciate a few minutes rest, don't you think?" I was reluctant to answer, to let on that she was at that moment downstairs, soaking her swollen toe. "She works so hard," Mrs. Kehoe said. "Let's let her be, just for a spell."

You'd think Edith was the lady of the house. I went to the vanity and brought the bench closer to the bed. It had a cushion upholstered with a green, black, and gold fabric that was so fine. Once I sat down, I kept running my fingers over the material. It might have been a satin evening dress, a gown.

Mrs. Kehoe poured her own tea and added one teaspoon of sugar, no milk. She looked at the plate, and then I saw them: the crumbs, the evidence that there had been another cookie on the plate. I felt the heat come to my face as it always did when I was embarrassed or felt caught in a predicament—not a lie, but also not the plain truth. At fourteen you sense that you are culpable most of the time, and you're just waiting to be found out. There was a long moment when nothing moved but the steam rising off the teacup.

"I couldn't possibly eat both of these." She held the plate out to me. "Won't you help me?"

Reluctantly, I took the smaller of the two cookies.

"I know Edith is always trying to get me to eat and she brings something, some sweet, most every time she comes to the house. So you'll tell her I ate both cookies, won't you? Don't want to hurt her feelings." I shook my head. "It'll be our little secret."

I nodded and bit into the cookie. Oatmeal with raisins, soft in the middle, like the first one I had shared with Edith.

"You can keep a secret, can't you, Bea?"

I stopped chewing.

"For some reason, dear, I know you can."

I nodded my head.

"I thought so. I may have a secret or two to share with you. Sometime."

I waited, but as the silence lengthened I realized that no secret was forthcoming immediately. I resumed chewing my cookie, studying the pattern of the patches on the counterpane. There were pineapples in some squares, and other fruit in others—oranges, strawberries, pears, apples, watermelon. I wondered if watermelon was a fruit or a vegetable.

In the silence, Mrs. Kehoe sipped her tea, which seemed to revive her somewhat. Finally, she said, "Of course, you heard it?"

I finished chewing and swallowed. "I didn't know what it was at first. I thought—" and I hesitated. "I thought it was Judgement Day. Really, I've never heard something so loud. Except maybe the time, when I was quite small, the lightning bolt struck our chicken coop and started a fire that my father and other men worked through the night to put out. It was Mr. Kehoe's doings in the woods across the fields?"

"They're all such boys. He loves to tinker with the engines. And experiment with his electricity. Did you know that our chicken coop is heated? Of course, we don't have any chickens now. He sold them off. He has wires running all over this place. It's quite ingenious." She put her cup in the saucer, creating the distinct click of fine china that reminded me of Aunt Ginny's tea set (in our kitchen there was only the hefty clatter of clay mugs). "But the tree stumps, they're his favorite. In less than a second, he'll say, it's blown to bits out of the ground, work that might have taken him all day. I ask him to warn me before he sets one off, but he doesn't. Boys do so enjoy the element of surprise."

She drank her tea and we ate the cookies. I don't remember everything we said. It's not important. But the way the light from the window struck her from the side, the way she often stared out that window, these images have stayed with me all these years, until it was my turn to be the old woman in bed. Her world had been reduced to the weight of the counterpane, the warmth of a cup of tea, the sweetness of oatmeal and raisins, all surrounded by worry. Her eyes, gazing out at the fields beyond the barn and outbuildings, were desolate. It was as though she knew what was coming, she knew the horrors that would descend upon her, upon all of us—and she understood the source of these things to come. She was merely waiting. And in the waiting she maintained such poise, which is what I remember most about that afternoon, the first of several when I would sit with her. Now, here, now in the telling of this, in the recollection of it, it's her poise that has stayed with me.

Poise that is a form of grace. Poise that is a virtue.

I don't know how long I remained in the bedroom. When I picked up the tray, she placed a hand on my wrist. Lightly.

"He lost last year." Her voice was no more than a whisper. "And he will lose again this time. He knows it but won't believe it. He lacks the ability to accept things as they are. It is rare that one does. It all becomes . . . a test of wills."

The sincerity in her gaze made me feel, I don't know, revealed. Perhaps this was the secret she wanted to tell me? I wasn't sure, but I wanted to put the tray down, I wanted to tell her things that I feared and desired, things that I kept to myself. I believed she—and only she—could understand them. I was afraid to expose myself, which seems unfortunate now. When she removed her hand from my wrist, I thanked her and went to the door. I was baffled. I didn't understand what he had lost and what he stood to lose again. I didn't doubt her, and later, when I came to understand what she meant, it only confirmed what I had first felt from Mrs. Kehoe.

4.

Jed remembered when Bath Consolidated School was being built five years earlier. In 1922, he was seven and he loved to watch the construction crews and equipment that were transforming the hill overlooking the village. Prior to that, his parents explained one night at supper, Bath's public education had been a series of small schoolhouses. "Your father and I learned the three Rs in a one-room schoolhouse, but you won't." They wanted him to understand that the new school was the future, and he was going to be a part of it. Jed's father said, "It's expensive, but it will make all of you better citizens." It had never before occurred to Jed that he was expected to become a citizen, to assume responsibilities associated with citizenship.

When construction was completed, it seemed impossible to imagine the town without the Bath Consolidated School. The school had a life of its own, a sense of uniformity and routine that had daily, seasonal, and annual cycles, overseen by the superintendent, Mr. Huyck, and the principal, Mr. Huggett. Most of the teachers were single women, many of them living in the DeLamarter Hotel down in the village.

Once Jed was asked to run an errand during class. His teacher gave him a large envelope to deliver to the superintendent. When he entered the main office, Mr.

Huyck's secretary glanced up from her desk and commanded, "Knock first." She resumed pounding on one of those contraptions, a typewriter.

Jed looked up at the office door, black letters, edged with gold leaf, printed on the frosted glass:

Emory F. Huyck
Superintendent
Bath Consolidated School

Mr. Huyck was everywhere, patrolling the halls, making unannounced visits to classrooms. You could see that these incursions made even the teachers nervous. Everyone knew how the home economics teacher, Mrs. Babcock, lost her job because her education philosophy somehow differed from Huyck's. He was a force both raw and sophisticated, always talking about changes and improvements that would make Bath Consolidated a better school. He was respected more than he was liked, and it was clear that there were rules that must be observed. Mr. Huyck believed in consequences.

Jed knocked and opened the door. Behind him, the secretary's typewriter keys snapped rapid-fire machine gun bullets. He entered the office, with its intimidating cabinets stocked with sets of books so large and uniform that they reminded him of soldiers marching in formation. The knowledge of the world, all there in rows flanking Mr. Huyck's oak desk. The superintendent wore a maroon bow tie that day, and it appeared that he'd recently had his hair cut—the sides of his head were shaved clean a good two inches above his ears. He wore thick-framed tortoiseshell glasses, perfectly round, making his eyes seem inordinately large. His beaked nose contributed to the notion that he resembled an owl.

He was preoccupied, leaning over papers on his ink blotter. "Yes," he said, reaching across the desk, "I've been expecting these."

Jed handed him the large manila envelope and then turned to leave, but stopped when the superintendent cleared his throat. Jed had not been formally dismissed, so turning back to the desk he expected a reprimand.

Mr. Huyck placed the envelope on top of the neat stack on the side of his desk, and then there was a moment where he appeared uncertain. The eyes behind those glasses did not possess their usual authority, and then he did the strangest thing. Mr. Huyck was accustomed to speaking to students in groups, to classes, to assemblies, to addressing students in the plural, but having a one-to-one conversation seemed to pose a very different situation. He attempted a smile. “It’s Jed, correct?”

“Yes, sir.”

“As in Jedidiah . . .”

A worm of fear drifted down Jed’s spine. The superintendent was trying to remember something, some infraction, some breach of the rules.

“Browne.” Mr. Huyck looked oddly pleased with himself.

“Yes, sir.”

“Browne, Browne,” as though he were trying to recall some important fact. And then his face lit up in a way Jed had never witnessed before—the man’s eyes were bright and curious. “I remember now, I remember noting your name once while reviewing class rosters. Your name—your full name—it has true historical significance, so to speak.”

One of those phrases Jed never understood. *So to speak.* But he wasn’t about to question Mr. Huyck at that point. All he could manage was, “My full name, sir?”

Mr. Huyck sat back in his chair—a swivel chair that allowed him to lean back—and crossed his legs, folding his hands on the knees of his striped suit trousers. He was now fully engaged. “Yes, tell me your full name.”

“Jedidiah Solomon Browne.”

“This is interesting.”

“What is, sir?”

Mr. Huyck adjusted his glasses on his nose. “Jedidiah Solomon Brown—except Brown is spelled without the *e*. Do you know who that was?”

This must be a trap. “No, sir.”

“Well. You’ve heard of ‘the shot heard round the world’?”

It was a trap, a quiz. “Yes, sir. 1775, in Concord, Massachusetts. Colonials first fought with the British soldiers.”

“Lexington.”

“Oh. Yes, sir. Lexington.”

“Early in the morning of April 19. They first gathered on Lexington Green and engaged British soldiers that had marched out from Boston during the night, and then the fight moved a few miles away to the village of Concord. But very good. Your teachers, they’ve said you are one of our prize pupils. Though I believe it was suggested that your best subject is mathematics.”

Why was he being complimented if he’d been wrong? “Thank you, sir.”

"But the name, Jedidiah Solomon Brown, without the *e*—it has no significance to you?"

Jed didn't know what to say. He shook his head.

"Well. Some historians believe that Jedidiah Solomon Brown was the one who fired the first shot, 'the shot heard round the world.' He was only in his teens, seventeen or eighteen, I believe. Of course, historians differ on this. But you should be proud that your namesake has—or may have—such a prominent place in our history."

"Yes, sir."

The superintendent sat forward, placing his arms on the ink blotter, and said as he gazed at the papers before him, "Well, then. We mustn't keep you from your studies any longer."

"No, sir. Thank you, sir."

Jed left the office, fearing he might stumble over his own feet.

▪ ▪ ▪

The wheel turns, bringing them all back to me: Frank Smith, the bees, Miss Weatherby, Ali Baba.

Frank Smith was the janitor at Bath Consolidated School. Mr. Smith, to us students. His day started early, well before anyone else arrived—he and his wife, Leone, lived right across the street from the school. During the long Michigan winters he began work while it was still dark, to see to the furnace and be sure that the walkways and stairs to the building were clear of snow and ice. He would greet us in the morning, while doing his chores. He was as much a part of the school as the brick and mortar, our desks, our teachers. If a child threw up, which was not uncommon, Mr. Smith would arrive, seemingly without notification, to clean up the mess and sprinkle sawdust on the floor, which would help eliminate the smell. We all knew that smell.

But there was a limit to what he could do. A couple of years earlier there had been the incident with the bees. For some reason, a nest of yellowjackets became active during the winter, probably due to heat from the furnace. Bees swarmed the halls. Doors to classrooms had to be kept closed. No one could explain why it happened, and Mr. Smith could not figure out how to eliminate the problem.

We didn't concern ourselves about the school's operation. The supervisor. The principal. The teachers. The school board. Bath Consolidated School just *was*—it was the place we went to Monday through Friday. We were aware of a certain pride regarding the school. It was new, having been built just five years earlier. Prior to that, Bath's public education was what it had been for much of the nineteenth century, a series of small (often one-room) schoolhouses. Bath Consolidated School was the future. It was going to bring changes to the town, to its inhabitants in ways we, the students, didn't fully appreciate or comprehend. I recall Aunt Ginny saying—this was during a dinnertime discussion about property taxes and how they'd be affected by the new school (a subject of little interest to children who were only concerned with the food on their plates)—she said, "It's expensive, yes, but it will give them a greater appreciation of life." Them being us. This irked me, though of course I didn't question or contradict Aunt Ginny. I was who I was; I didn't really think that what I learned in school would make me any more appreciative of life. I could read; I could write; I could think for myself. As a child, I didn't connect who I was, how I developed, slowly, painfully at times, into an adult, with what I experienced at school.

Now, of course, I know different. We all do. We look back differently on the school, that new brick building with the cupola and, high above the front doors framed by stately columns, the triangular pediment above the entrance, which we were told was intended to connect the school and, indeed, the town of Bath, with the ancient civilization in Greece. (Both Greek and Latin were on the curriculum.) We learned about Athens, and its rival city-state Sparta. It was impressed upon us that Bath was more like Athens, a place where people could live in harmony, with each other, with the land about them. Fragments of Greek remain still, such as *demos,* which means "the people," and is the root of the word democracy. That's what that triangular pediment and the cupola, perched atop the roof peak, represented—not just a place, but the ideals that are associated with the place. Such architectural details go beyond functionality; they are expressions of our dreams, of all we hold dear in life. At fourteen, I felt that when I looked up at my school, but its value, its true significance didn't fully manifest itself in my heart and mind until later. Much later.

But then there were also the bees.

No one, not even Mr. Smith, could get rid of them.

The school board (we learned later) was an extremely contentious entity. The adults who were elected to the board held great responsibility. They argued among themselves, bitterly at times, apparently to the point where long-held resentments developed that influenced decisions made by the board. The politics of Bath were concentrated in that school board.

I was not afraid of bees. Some of my friends in school kidded me that it was because my name was Beatrice. I wasn't afraid of bees because our neighbors, Harvey and Mirna Lubeck, kept bees. Their hives were in a series of boxes with drawers, and I often stood (at some distance) and watched the Lubecks collect honey. They wore special broad-brimmed hats with mesh to protect their faces, and heavy gloves. Bees filled the air, but they weren't in a state of alarm. The Lubecks moved slowly and methodically, and when they were finished, the bees would return to their hives, seemingly content that nothing invasive had occurred, nothing had been disturbed. At such times, I would sometimes walk up to the boxes. Bees would come and go from the hive, in warm weather in search of flowers, I assumed. Sometimes they'd hover about me, right in front of my face, and sometimes they would land on me, my cheek or a bare forearm. I learned not to panic, not to swat at them. I learned to trust the bees.

But in the school they presented a problem. They were seen as a dangerous invasion, a health concern, a threat to the children of Bath. No, more than that, they were, for some, the embodiment of evil. Some parents wanted to keep their children home until the bees were eliminated. Some people directed their anger toward certain members of the school board, as though they were personally responsible for allowing the bees into the school. Eventually, the board asked Andrew Kehoe if there was anything he might do. Everyone knew that he was good with machines and electricity—he'd studied electrical engineering at Michigan State College down in East Lansing. (Another thing that made him a curious figure in Bath: he'd attended college, yet he farmed. Somehow the college education justified the fact that he wore suits all the time.) He said he'd inspect the building and see what he could do.

He got rid of the bees. No one seemed to know how exactly. All that mattered was that they were no longer a nuisance in the building. Subsequently, the school board requested that Mr. Kehoe oversee the school building's maintenance program. He obliged, and for several years came and went from the school day and night. He scheduled routine cleaning projects and inspected the gasoline generator and plumbing system; he arranged for tradesmen to make necessary repairs. Like Mr. Smith, the janitor, Mr. Kehoe was a familiar figure around the school.

I recall one afternoon—it was after classes were finished because I had stayed behind to help Miss Weatherby, the new third and fourth grade teacher. My cousin Wilma was in her class, and I had gone to get her, as I often did, so we could walk home together, but Miss Weatherby said she had already left with some of her classmates. Miss Weatherby was new at Bath Consolidated. She was twenty years old. She had a beautiful smile, and girls often talked about her marcelled hair. Miss Weatherby was cleaning the classroom, and while she did so, she talked to me in a way that made me feel I'd known her for a long time. I helped her wipe down the chalkboards and together we lined up the desks in neat rows, which was part of her routine at the end of the day.

As I was leaving school, Mr. Kehoe was coming up the front walk. I turned to open the door that had just closed behind me, but it had locked, and I apologized to Mr. Kehoe for not holding the door open for him.

He smiled as he dug into the pocket of his suitcoat, and said, "Not to worry."

It occurred to me that he didn't realize that I was the girl who sometimes came to his house and helped out with the chores and cleaning. I was just a girl, and there was something about the way he looked at me that gave me the sense that he had something else on his mind, which was not uncommon among adults: children are often invisible to them. For decades, I came to miss that invisibility, until I reached an age where I was no longer an "adult" but "old," and rendered once again invisible.

But then Mr. Kehoe looked at me—at *me*—and whispered, "I have the secret."

From his pocket he produced a ring of keys. There must have been at least a dozen. He whispered, "I can get in any door in this building," as though this was a secret that gave him a rare and even mystical power. "But the problem is—" and he began sorting through the keys, "finding the *right* key. Ah, here we are, let's try this one."

He inserted a key into the front door lock and turned the knob, saying, "Open sesame." As though he had performed a magic trick. "Call me Ali Baba."

I stared up at him, having only the vaguest notion of *One Thousand and One Nights.*

"You must be one of the forty thieves," he said as he pulled the door open. "And this I gather is your mountain cave."

▪ ▪ ▪

For years I considered making a list that goes beyond the Seven Deadly Sins: *The Other Vices, as Perceived by Beatrice Marie Turcott.* After I died I planned to present the Lord with my list and say, "With all due respect, you missed some."

The list will include the sin of Speculation.

Also overheard from the stairs: speculation about why Andrew and Nellie Kehoe had no children. (As though being childless were itself a sin, so unspeakable it had no name.)

"Making babies," according to Cora Minor, Cousin Wilma's mother and Ma's best friend, "is as easy as blowing a chicken feather off your knee. And usually takes half the time."

Which made my mother slap the kitchen table and laugh, though I didn't yet understand why.

Cora, who needed no encouragement, went on, "Goodness me, when you look at some families in Bath you'd think raising children was the only thing they can do—a might better than raising crops or livestock. If some of the men around here spent more time tending to the fields than hanging their trousers on the bedpost, instead of another mouth to feed they might bring a profit at harvest time. Some of these folks must be closet papists. Nobody produces like Catholics. The Kehoes, they don't go to church, but everyone knows once a Catholic always a Catholic."

Cora was someone whose conversation frequently needed to be tamped down like the tobacco in Pa's corncob pipe. Ma said, "Oh, Cora. They're too old for making babies. Married late, you know. I'm sure both he and Nellie were the far side of forty."

But Cora was having none it. "My mother had nine children and lost at least two more that I know of. I was born when she was over forty, and I wasn't her last." Then in one of her stage whispers, she said, "She said she married him because of his longevity."

There followed one of those silences. Ma and Cora loved to disagree—on anything, from a recipe to local gossip—neither one ever conceding the point. Sometimes they just fell into this silence that said there wasn't anything more to say about that. *Oh, dear Ma!* How she wept after Cora passed following a lengthy spell of rheumatoid arthritis, which eventually left her curled up and bedridden, unable to even feed herself. After that it was like Ma had nothing left to say to the world. Except this: "There comes a point when life is over and there's nothing left but the dying." When she'd say it she would sound hopeful, for she was committed to the notion that she'd see Cora—and Pa—again.

▪ ▪ ▪

In 1927 we lived by what we called Bath time.

Though it had been nearly a decade since the federal government had standardized time zones across the United States, some towns continued to keep time according to local proclivities. Bath remained on central time, while much of the rest of Michigan had shifted to the eastern time zone. It gave our six-square-mile township a sense of singularity; some would say insularity. When visitors asked the time, we would say "You're on Bath time now."

Nineteen twenty-seven was the year we began to notice the rest of the world. That place beyond the fields of Bath. Beyond Lansing, a handful of miles down the Michigan Central Railroad line. That place beyond Detroit, and even Chicago.

Evidence of the rest of the world began to show up on the wall above Jed's bed: photographs from magazines and newspapers, cartoons, sketches. There was George Herman Ruth. Since the Red Sox sold The Babe to the Yankees in 1920, he kept breaking his own home run records. His record stood at fifty-nine in one season, set back in 1921. Warren, Jed, all the boys talked about this as if it was beyond human capability. Jed loved to play ball and he had a head for stats. He could tell you the Tigers' record against any other team; he could compare pitchers' ERAs; more than once he noted that by the end of the season in 1926, Ruth had hit a total of 307 homers in seven years for the Yankees. But no one, Warren argued, could hit sixty home runs in one season. Jed believed if anyone could, it would be The Babe.

And there was the Great Atlantic Air Derby. I remember the first time we saw an airplane above Bath, a biplane that must have been not more than fifty feet above the treetops.

"How's it stay up there?" Alma asked. "Shouldn't it just drop out of the sky?"

"The engine," Warren announced. "It pulls it through the air." But he was unable to elaborate.

Jed added, "The wings are shaped like a bird's, allowing them to lift the plane up on the wind."

We looked at him. I knew that pinned to his wall were photographs of pilots, a French World War I ace named René Fonck, and the American explorer, Richard Byrd. They stood before their flying machines, wearing leather helmets and jackets, goggles, and jodhpurs. The Derby, as it was sometimes called, was sponsored by a Frenchman, Raymond Orteig, who'd made a fortune investing in New York hotels. Orteig offered a prize of $25,000 to the first pilot to fly between New York and Paris without stopping. There were many disastrous attempts. Planes fell out of the sky, or they simply disappeared somewhere over the Atlantic. During a trial run, Fonck's plane failed to get off the ground and exploded (Jed explained that it was loaded with 2,850 gallons of gasoline), but Fonck managed to escape while the other members of the crew were incinerated in their seats.

Hitting baseballs out of Yankee Stadium, flying a plane across the Atlantic, these exploits spoke to Jed in a way that I didn't fathom. There was also the occasional mention of that fool, a former sailor called "Shipwreck" Kelly, who sat on flagpoles for days and days, while his redheaded wife down on the ground collected money from onlookers. I thought such news from the rest of the world only appealed to boys of a certain age, daring feats that drew us up and out of the fields of Bath.

But it was the flood that exposed Jed's true self. Through the winter of 1926–27, America had never seen such rain, and in the spring there was the snowmelt from the north. The major rivers in the country overflowed their banks. From Illinois down to Louisiana, the Mississippi turned the middle of the country into a lake. Along with photographs of baseball players and pilots, Jed's wall was covered with newspaper articles about the Great Flood. There were photos of houses and barns and swollen animal carcasses and debris being swept along in the floodwaters; of men, women, and children stranded on levees and dikes and rooftops.

Jed's Wall: spectacular achievements, horrific disasters.

▪ ▪ ▪

Jed had never seen anything like it. Farms were not supposed to be like this. Mud, dirt, dust, animal hair, manure. Mr. Kehoe wanted none of it. Everything had to be clean. If he didn't have Jed digging in the dirt—more tree stumps, more explosives—he had him cleaning something. The barn. The sheds. Each tool in the workshop—soaked until the rust could be removed. If not wiped, then sanded with steel wool. If not sanded, then put to the grindstone. He wanted metal to shine, paint to maintain its gloss. When he walked into one of the outbuildings he looked about him as though something—a harness, a hoe, a greasy engine part—was waiting to leap at him and soil the fabric of his suit. In the course of one afternoon Jed saw him go into the house and return wearing a fresh white shirt three times.

Clean.

The Kehoe farm was clean.

It was unnatural.

But it was a job and Mr. Kehoe paid with change in his pocket, doling out nickels, dimes, and quarters as though he had no need for them.

Jed liked blowing up tree stumps. He'd dig the holes around the stumps, at Mr. Kehoe's direction, getting in under the roots. He would then stuff the sticks of dynamite and pyrotol in the ground, while Mr. Kehoe connected the wires to the blasting caps and walked them back to the detonator box. Jed was careful, following instructions exactly. He liked handling what Mr. Kehoe called ordnance. When the plunger was shoved down into the detonator box, he liked the sound of the whirring gears that preceded the blast. But Jed didn't understand why tree stumps, and sometimes boulders, were being removed, yet nothing was done with the land. Mr. Kehoe had Jed collect the wood and load it into the pickup truck, but the holes weren't filled in, and the newly cleared soil wasn't prepared for planting. It was spring. Planting season was beginning, but not on the Kehoe farm.

Certain places Jed wasn't allowed to enter, particularly the henhouse. Mr. Kehoe said he had sold his poultry stock, though he didn't say why. The door was always locked. It was, Jed knew, where the dynamite was kept. Mr. Kehoe would give Jed a job to do—clean something—and then he'd drive the Ford truck around to the henhouse. He'd unlock the door and load the truck with dynamite and equipment necessary for the next tree stump.

One afternoon as Jed walked back from the outhouse beyond the corncrib, he noticed that the henhouse door was open, swinging in the wind. He went to close it, but stopped when he could see inside the coop. Though there were no birds, it still smelled of chickens. The shed was stacked with wood crates. Stamped on the boxes were names: *Hercules Powder, The Giant Powder Co., Dupont Explosives.* Several boxes were stamped:

1¼ × 8
50 lbs.
PYROTOL

Allotted by the
Bureau of Public Roads
U.S. Dept. of Agriculture

Mr. Kehoe came around the back corner of the barn, smoke from his cigar drifting up in the breeze. Jed stepped back, feeling guilty, expecting a reprimand.

Mr. Kehoe stopped outside the open door and removed the cigar from his mouth. "Must have forgotten to lock it."

"This is all for the forest?"

"I have a lot of trees out there."

"You plan on taking it all down?"

"These long Michigan winters, we need a lot of wood to heat the house." When Mr. Kehoe smoked a stogie, it often made his lips wet, and they turned a color that reminded Jed of a plum. His smile revealed one slightly discolored front tooth. He looked out across his land. "You think these fields just happened? We did this. We came out here and it was all forest. Takes generations to make good farmland." Nodding toward Kehoe's Woods, he said, "Might say I'm carrying on a tradition."

The crates must have contained hundreds of pounds of explosives. Jed looked at the stack of crates marked *Bureau of Public Roads.* "Where do you get all of it?"

"Different places. Lansing. Sometimes I go down to Jackson. The dynamite comes in sticks. And the pyrotol is those ropey brown cords we wad up in the holes. It's made with nitroglycerin, petrolatum, and something called guncotton. You might have noticed it doesn't smoke like dynamite."

Jed nodded.

"Combustion." Mr. Kehoe chuckled and spit tobacco juice. "Combustion, without the engine. No pistons, no rings, no cam shaft. Just the boom." He worked his cigar around his mouth, staring at the ground. "Keep this between us, son. You don't want to go telling anyone I'm letting you handle this stuff."

"No, of course not."

"You're good with it. You're careful. But some folks might get the wrong idea."

5.

There was an election that spring. Another election. In a town like Bath local elections take on a life of their own. Factions. Rumors. Hints. Allegations. Adults spoke in a form of code, which they believed we could not understand.

Promises: another vice to be added to my list of Deadly Sins.

Running up to the day of the election, promises are made. *If I am elected, I will do this, that, and the other thing. I will make what has been wrong right. I will change the way it's been so that it will be better.*

Promises are the work of the devil. They are Eve's apple.

This election was to select Clinton County's justice of the peace.

Justice of the peace. It was a phrase that confused me in 1927. The two words, justice and peace, there was a connection between them—one would hope that exercising justice would lead to peace—but *the* justice of the peace was a person? An elected official? I came to understand the duties of the office, primarily involving minor legal disputes and small claims. But primarily civil matrimony, a notion that appealed to a girl in her early teens. All the stories of daring elopements, of couples knocking on the door of the justice of the peace in the middle of the night, requesting that they be married immediately. True love that couldn't wait till morning, that had to be consummated tonight. True love desperate for legitimacy. True love that could not find its way down the aisle of a church. What did justice or peace have to do with holy matrimony? I can imagine what Cora Minor would have to say about *that.*

The election took place during a town meeting. Children who had accompanied their parents to the town hall remained outside. There was a game of hide and seek. Some kids climbed a beech tree. It was dusk on a warm night. There had been a great deal of rain, but the day had been clear and the sun seemed to have broken open the earth's winter crust, unlocking the smell of soil and vegetation and the planting season that was beginning. Peepers and frogs could be heard from the wetlands back in the woods.

Alma had stayed home with the croup. I didn't know where Jed was, so I walked with Warren down to the railroad tracks. I can't explain the allure of the tracks, but it was strong; when there was nothing else to do, nowhere else to go, we usually found ourselves wandering along the Michigan Central rails. We walked each rail tightrope-style. The day's heat filled the air with the smell of creosote rising up from the railroad ties. Occasionally, I lost my balance and stepped down on a gravel bed until I could get both feet back on the rail. Warren, always the show-off, never lost his balance, and continued to walk with his arms spread as though he were on the high wire under a circus tent.

"For my birthday in August," he said, "my dad says he'll take me on the train to Detroit to see a Tigers game. Grandstand seats, third base side. I've never been to Navin Field."

Warren was going to be eighteen. I was fourteen and eighteen seemed so far off. You weren't an adult but you were no longer a child. Warren liked to say that at eighteen you couldn't do everything legally, but you could do what you could get away with. Sometimes I was mistaken for seventeen because I had a growth spurt, three and a half inches since the previous summer. Ma told me to let my hems down twice. At school many boys were now shorter and regarded me warily, as though I were some alien being. They looked up at my breasts, which occupied the space between them and my face, and then away, embarrassed. Otherwise, I was still skinny. Coltish, Ma said.

Warren dropped down off his rail and walked beside me as I continued my balancing act. Up ahead there was the small house where railroad section gangs, responsible for maintaining the railbeds, kept tools and supplies. On a short spur off the main line was a caboose, which had been stored there so long it was surrounded by tall weeds. All of the windows had been smashed and the door at the back hung on one hinge. Strange things happened in the caboose. Hobos were seen to come and go from there. There were stories of escapees from the Jackson prison hiding out there, and about runaways and lovers' trysts.

We walked the spur as far as the handcar, where I lost my balance and Warren caught me as I stepped down onto the railroad ties. My shirt was untucked and his forearms were warm, slightly moist with sweat where they clutched my lower back—it was a humid night for so early in the spring. I thought of Alma, back home lying in bed, reeking of petroleum jelly. Ma believed in the Lord Our Father, Hellman's Blue Ribbon Mayonnaise, and Vicks VapoRub. At the time, I believe all mothers did. I was letting Warren hold me a moment too long. Pulling myself free of his arms, I continued around the handcar to the caboose.

"Think there are any hobos around?" I asked.

"Doubt it. You usually see or smell the fires they build to keep warm and maybe cook a can of beans or something. I'll check."

He pushed through the weeds and climbed up the steel steps to the small portico on the back of the caboose, and then shoved the angled door and disappeared inside. Then there was silence. I could feel my heart behind my ribs.

It was nearly dark now. I could barely make out the treetops against the night sky. Other than the peepers in the woods, there was no sound. The caboose was silent. I waited. And waited.

"Warren," I said finally. "I know what you're doing."

There was no sound from the caboose.

"You're not fooling me."

Nothing.

"Fine." I sat down on the rail and folded my arms. "Fine," I repeated.

I waited, and eventually said, "You are not scaring me, you know."

There was no sound from inside the caboose.

I don't know how long I sat there. A few minutes felt like a silent eternity. When I got to my feet, I said, "All right," trying to sound slightly fed up with this silliness. "I know what you're thinking." Still nothing.

I climbed up on the back of the caboose. It was pitch dark now, except when I looked back down the railroad tracks the lights from the town hall glinted off the parallel steel lines. I stepped through the door and into the cooler darkness of the caboose. The air was musty, smelling of mold and, I thought, straw, which I suspected had been brought in to sleep on.

"Come on, it's too dark now," I said.

No response. My eyes began to adjust so I could see the few window openings on each side of the caboose, and there was also a dim glow from an opening in the raised portion of the roof. Though I told myself to hold my ground, I walked forward, taking small steps and keeping my arms outstretched. There was something in the center of the car, something dark that seemed to rise up to the roof. When I was close enough to touch it I realized it was the stove, and I placed one hand on the cool iron as I worked my way around it.

At the front end of the caboose, I stopped and turned around, just to be sure he hadn't somehow hidden so that I'd go past him. There was no movement, no sound, nothing.

"Warren," I said. Not fed up now. Angry. No nonsense. "Cut it out."

Again, I waited for what may have only been a minute but felt like a long time. Standing in the dark of an abandoned caboose, waiting for a boy approaching the age of eighteen to do something, leap out or scream or whatever, so that he can have the satisfaction of scaring the Dickens out of a scaredy-cat girl. What is it about boys that need this? What is it about girls that want it? This was a game, a game on the verge of another thing all together, something dark and foreign and terrifying. I wanted to scream, I wanted to cry, but I was not going to let him win.

So in the vast silence I said, "I'm not going to play anymore."

There was a door in front of me but it was closed. He couldn't have gone out that way without making noise, could he? I walked back down the length of the caboose, now moving with confidence, knowing where the stove was, eager for the clean, sweet night air outside.

When I reached the switch where the spur joined the main rail line, I paused to listen. Still only the peepers and an occasional frog claimed these woods. As I continued down the tracks toward the town hall, I was like a moth drawn to the warm light that streamed through the trees. Part of me wanted the safety of that light, but I was also reluctant to leave this dark moist place. It's so long ago but I recall a girl's images—no, not images, but notions—of what might be, what it might be like. Notions of Warren's skin, the fine hair on his forearms, and the back of his neck. Of what happens during a lovers' tryst. The moment when his arms encircled me, when his bare skin touched the skin above my hips, this was where we weren't supposed to go. Not yet, at least. We were cautioned, instructed, we were forewarned: *you mustn't.* We were told that even to *think* about it was immoral. Your mind, left to its own devices, was capable of sin. But

I couldn't help myself. None of us could. I could see it in their eyes. The way Alma would look at Warren. The way Warren would look at Alma, and sometimes at me. The way most the boys looked at Annie Dunne, who was developing a reputation, and the nickname Annie Does. The place we weren't supposed to go, in the dark. A pure dark, where there was no knowing what lay up ahead. Whatever it was, once we got there—at fourteen, eighteen, twenty-one—there was no return. That was the true transgression. That was the sin. The track went on into the dark, and we could not turn around and go back.

Such notions ceased when I felt his hands on my shoulders.

I screamed.

Of course I did.

Warren laughed and he broke into a run, down the center of the tracks, silhouetted against the town hall light. For him, it was just a game. Hide and Seek. Tag. I was relieved, and I was angry.

But I rejoined the game and gave chase, my feet carrying me along the ties and the rock gravel, bound by the gleaming rails.

▪ ▪ ▪

Jed didn't finish his chores until it was nearly dark, and then he walked across the fields to the village. When he reached the town hall he could hear children outside the building playing games. Girls were singing a round, not quite in tune.

He stood in the road as the town hall doors opened and the adults spilled out into the night. In 1927, there were some three hundred residents in Bath, Michigan. Jed recognized everyone there. They gathered in front of the building in small groups. Husbands and wives. Relatives. Neighbors. Talking quietly. It reminded Jed of Sunday morning after service let out of church, but it was different. It was nighttime, but there was something else that he didn't recognize. He sensed that they didn't want to linger. The adults were eager to collect their young and get on home. Their muted haste was barely concealed. They were, he thought, embarrassed.

Amid the confusion, the mustering of kin, Jed saw Warren emerge from the woods between the town hall and the railroad tracks. He was running but slowed down to a walk, as though to prove he hadn't been up to something. He was winded, his chest heaving as he joined his parents, who were climbing into their truck.

Engines cranked over and headlights split the dark. As Jed turned to walk back home, he noticed someone else coming out of the woods. At first he thought it was a boy, a thin boy, but then he noted the hair, chopped at the shoulders, and the chest. Bea. He watched her walk toward the crowd, also out of breath—winded because she'd been chasing Warren. They'd been in the woods, probably over on the tracks.

Jed understood part of it. Warren was dangerous. He was older. Jed knew how Alma looked at him, but Bea? Jed had failed to see this about her—that she too would chase after Warren. Maybe it was because of Alma. Bea and her older sister competed for everything. Alma, being older, acted as though she deserved to win, to get what she wanted first. Bea would have to wait, which she would not settle for, not for second. Maybe she be chasing Warren simply because Alma wanted him.

Jed shoved his fists deep in the pockets of his overalls and started back toward home in the dark.

▪ ▪ ▪

I didn't think anyone outside the town hall took notice of me, or of Warren, when we returned to the fold, so to speak. I stopped running and walked into the crowd gathered before the building. Headlights washed villagers in a brilliant horizontal light which cast long shadows.

Then something peculiar happened: Andrew and Nellie Kehoe appeared in the doorway of the town hall. For the briefest moment they stood on the threshold. He was dressed in a suit, as always. She was on his arm, as we would say, and she wore a lilac dress with a white lace collar, which I thought quietly elegant. It was not something most of the wives in Bath would wear. Her hair was pinned up and her tiny silver earrings caught the light. Standing in the open doorway, they might have been newlyweds, presenting themselves to the world as man and wife. I would not have been surprised if the crowd had broken into applause and tossed rice into the air.

Instead, the adults seemed frozen by a collective response: guilt. I remembered that during the town hall meeting a vote was going to be taken to determine the new county justice of the peace. Andrew Kehoe did not win. He had lost his position on the school board earlier, and now he'd been defeated in the election for JP. I don't remember who was chosen but I heard later that Kehoe didn't just lose, he was soundly rejected.

I love the democratic ways in this country, despite its inconsistencies and flaws, particularly the idea of casting your vote by private ballot. But this was different. The legal voters of Bath, Michigan, had assembled in the town hall to cast their votes, which were then and there tallied, and the winner announced. Democracy had been served.

But when Andrew Kehoe, with his wife Nellie at his side, descended the steps, men toed the ground with a boot, or busied themselves with a cigarette or a pipe; women stood with arms folded. Andrew and Nellie Kehoe walked among them, both looking straight ahead. Mr. Kehoe had the faintest smile on his face, while his wife maintained a somber, dignified gaze. Anyone could see from the pallor of her skin that she was not in good health, but during that short walk to their machine, she was an erect, even statuesque, presence in the moment of her husband's defeat.

▪ ▪ ▪

"That poor woman," Aunt Ginny said. It was a warm afternoon for early May, and I had brought our tea on her pewter tray out to the porch. (She often mentioned how the tray had come down from her great-grandmother, and I can still see the fine scrollwork etched into its dull surface.) Despite the sunlight cutting through the budding leaves, Aunt Ginny kept her parlor quilt over her legs. "The embarrassment," she said. "And now I understand that she's back in St. Lawrence Hospital again."

"Mr. Kehoe drives down to Lansing to see her every day," I said. "He gives Jed chores to do, but I haven't been to the house to help Edith."

"He locks himself away in there, only venturing out when he's going to Lansing."

I poured our tea. "She has this awful cough. Can't control it at all. And headaches. She would lie in bed with a damp cloth over her eyes for hours."

Aunt Ginny surveyed me with care. I was a legitimate source because of my recent access to the Kehoe household. It made me feel important, valuable, but at the same time deceitful. I was a turncoat, a spy. Whatever I told her might be contributed to the local gossip mill.

She looked across the road at the fields, which in the coming months would be lined with green rows of sprouting corn. "I don't know what they're going to do when they lose it."

"Lose what?"

“The farm! They haven’t paid taxes on it for years.”

“They’ll really have to give it up?”

“That’s the way the world works, dear.”

“But . . .”

“He blames it on the school tax.”

“The school tax?”

“Says it’s well over three-hundred dollars for their eighty acres. You don’t think your education is free? We’re all paying for it; we’re all contributing. In my day, we went to one of the little country schools. But now, now it’s all different with the consolidated school.”

I was speechless. I felt guilty.

“That’s a might hard turn, to lose the place where you were raised,” Aunt Ginny said. “Who knows where they’d go.”

I drank my tea. I didn’t want to hear any more, didn’t want to be a part of this. I wasn’t sure what was true, what was conjecture, but it was all ugly and vile. For some reason I thought of the dress Mrs. Kehoe wore the night of the town meeting, the fine material and the lace collar. A woman in such a garment should not have to suffer the indignity of losing her home. “They have nice things,” I said. “Furniture, shelves of books, and a patterned rug in the parlor. The woodwork throughout the house is oak. I’ve polished it.”

Aunt Ginny didn’t seem to hear me. “He’s peculiar, I’ll tell you that, but then as often as he’s rubbed someone the wrong way, he’s also helped neighbors. He’s right handy. He fixes things most people don’t understand—boilers and machines and such.”

“I know,” I said. “He’s at the school so much that he has set up his own workbench in the basement. Nobody knows how he got rid of those bees.”

As if this confirmed her deepest suspicions, Aunt Ginny said, “All men are contradictions. He can’t stand this young superintendent, Mr. Huyck, but at one of the school board meetings he was in favor of giving Mrs. Huyck the job as music teacher. And you know teachers are not ordinarily married women.”

I nodded. This was common knowledge. I wanted to ask why.

I was about to do so when Aunt Ginny said, “Then there was that other business.”

“What other business?”

“About his animals.” She hesitated, but then realized she couldn’t restrain herself. “He beat a horse to death. This is sometime back. And then I heard recently that he gave another horse—it was blind in one eye, I understand—to McMullen. Just gave it to him. It was like, 'Take it because I can't care for the beast any longer. Just like I can't tend to my fields.' And a few days later, he goes to McMullen and presents him with a piece of paper. It was a bill! It said McMullen owed him $120 for the one-eyed horse. Of course, McMullen protested, declaring he'd never offered to *buy* the poor thing. *My!* You don't know if Kehoe is that desperate for money—I imagine he is, what with the unpaid taxes and the hospital bills—or if his's just a bit addled. *And—*" She raised the cup to her lips, steam drifting above her head. "I heard tell of an incident down in Tecumseh, where he grew up, on his father's farm. He'd bought six cows from a neighbor and put them out to pasture when the hay was terrible wet. Two cows got the bloat and died. So he goes back to his neighbor and demands his money back for the two cows. Like they were defective, when everyone knows you're responsible for feeding your own cattle." She put her cup down in its saucer. Click. "You wonder what goes through the mind sometimes. That poor woman."

6.

There were few secrets in Bath. Alma made her feelings known Saturday morning while we were both in the barn milking. I was on my stool, pulling, when she walked down the row of cows and, rather than depositing her milk in the jug, came over and stood behind me. When I turned to look up at her, she dumped the milk from her bucket over my head. If Pa had seen it he would have been furious that she was wasting milk. It was warm.

I was encroaching on my older sister's territory. Message delivered.

■ ■ ■

Those first days of May I felt restless—we all did. The classrooms were warmed by sun on the brick building. Some of us couldn't sit still; others had to be poked so they wouldn't nod off. School would be out in a few weeks.

At the end of classes on Friday, I went to Miss Weatherby's room on the pretense that I was going to walk my cousin Wilma home. But she had already left with some other girls, and, as usual, I was happy to help Miss Weatherby straighten up her classroom. After everything was neat and tidy, we left the building together. The Bath Consolidated School gave me a sense of pride. The concrete walkway from the front door to the street was lined with trees. They had been planted when the school had been built five years earlier, and each spring they budded, taller than the year before.

"Would you like a ride home?" Miss Weatherby asked.

"A ride?"

"Yes, he'll be by in his car any minute."

Then I understood the scent I couldn't place while we were in the classroom: she was wearing perfume. "All right."

When we reached the sidewalk, Miss Weatherby sat down in the new spring grass, her back against the nearest trunk, and smoothed her skirt over her knees. She patted the ground, indicating that I should sit beside her.

When I was settled, she said, "You know, Beatrice, you're one of our finest pupils."

I was seldom called Beatrice—usually when Ma was upset with me.

"What's your favorite subject?" She already knew. "English, right? You like to read." I nodded. "My colleagues and I, we've talked about you, you know. You're one of the few students who have read all of *Julius Caesar,* not because you know there will be a test on the play, but because you want to read it. You're fourteen?"

"Yes."

"You realize how close you and I are in age?" I'd never had a teacher speak to me this way. I could barely conceal my embarrassment at such flattery. Miss Weatherby said, "When I was your age, it was only about seven or eight years ago—I asked myself what I wanted to do when I grew up."

She wasn't looking at me, fortunately. I was staring at her now, expecting her to answer the question that had been haunting me for a long time, throughout that school year. What *was* I going to be when I grew up? This plagued me. I would lie awake at night often, completely at a loss. When you are fourteen, people speak to you about your future as though it's an object, something you already possessed, something you can hold in your hands, but the fact is the notion of the future—*my* future—caused me nothing but anxiety and fear. Though I loved Ma and Pa dearly, I didn't want to stay on the farm. But then sometimes I did, thinking it would be the best thing, because it was familiar, but more than that because it was all I should ever need—to want more, to have expectations led to doubt and even guilt.

"I do think about it," I said to Miss Weatherby, barely whispering. "I just don't know what it is that I want to do, that I should do."

Beneath her marcelled hair and the bangs that came down her forehead, she had a small face, with a dimpled chin, but her eyes were large so that she often had this expression of wonder. Sometimes the students would make fun of her (when she wasn't around, of course) simply by opening their eyes wide. But they were pretty eyes, compassionate and understanding. When she looked at you, when she spoke to you, she was really seeing *you,* not just any student. Now she stared at me with those eyes and said, "You like school." It was not a question. I nodded. "Have you ever considered becoming a teacher?" She seemed to understand that I didn't know what to say. "Well, there's time. You give it some thought." She got to her feet. "And we can talk again, if you'd like. But right now, our ride's here."

I stood up, too, and watched a car pull up to the curb. It was a Chevrolet, very smart, and sitting behind the wheel was a young man in a tweed suit, a starched collar, and a maroon tie. I got in the back seat and Miss Weatherby said, "Dan, this is Beatrice, one of our prize pupils. We're going to drop her off at home, all right?"

Dan looked over his shoulder. I could smell his aftershave. "Where to, young lady?" He had a wide smile, which formed dimples in his cheeks—and good teeth. (Cora Minor believed that you could determine much about a man and a horse by examining their teeth.)

Before I could answer, the car accelerated down the hill through the village. As we drove out to my parents' farm, they discussed what they would do with the evening. It seemed such an adult way of putting it: *do with the evening.* Dan suggested dinner, and then dancing at Lovings up on Round Lake. I couldn't take my eyes off of Miss Weatherby. She had her right elbow propped on the open window of the passenger door, and though her hand was pressed against the side of her head, her hair was being blown back by the wind. It made her head seem even smaller, her face that much younger.

As I stared at her, I had a frightening thought. Nearly all the teachers at Bath Consolidated School were young, single women (exceptions being the shop teacher and Mr. Huyck's wife, who taught music). Many of the women lived in the DeLamarter Hotel in the village. They were hired with the understanding that their comportment would have a direct influence upon the children in their care. Thus they were seldom seen venturing out on their own—if they were on the sidewalks in the village, they usually traveled in pairs or small groups. On weekends, some of them would together take the train into Lansing, where they would shop, have lunch in a restaurant, and perhaps go to a movie. Always, they would return to Bath by late afternoon, ensuring that they were safe in the hotel before dark. These young women were not expected to "fraternize," and their social activities were carefully monitored. (In Bath, what was said about someone in an unofficial capacity could lead to the most severe condemnation and, in the case of these teachers, expulsion.) To say that dating was frowned upon is an understatement. And Miss Weatherby was planning on going dancing with her beau. *Dancing!* This was not done; it was not allowed. But my horror, then, in 1927, wasn't that these restrictions upon women was frightfully absurd and unjust, but that it could only mean that Miss Weatherby planned on leaving Bath Consolidated School.

At that moment, riding in the back seat of Dan's Chevrolet, I feared that Miss Weatherby planned to marry this man from Lansing. He worked in an office at one of the automobile plants. Though I didn't know exactly what he did, the fact that he wore a suit and tie to work suggested that he would make a good husband. They would have children, three, perhaps four. What I couldn't determine, as we drove through the fields of Bath, was if Miss Weatherby understood that after she married she would no longer be allowed to teach. In my mind, my adolescent mind, I dreaded unexpected change. Miss Weatherby had only taught at our school one year—her leaving so suddenly seemed catastrophic. As Dan's car slowed down in front of my house, I wondered if that was why Miss Weatherby had suggested the possibility of my becoming a teacher, so that I might one day replace her in the classroom.

▪ ▪ ▪

Every day Nellie spent in the hospital, Kehoe drove into Lansing to visit her. Though she had been given something to ease the wet, crackling cough, which caused her ribs to ache, she was very weak. He sat in the straight-back chair and engaged in the kind of small talk that made hospital rooms mundane sanctuaries.

Periodically, he held the glass of water to her mouth so she could take a sip. His other hand cradled the back of her head, lifting it from the pillow. They rarely touched any more, not by intention, at least. It had been years. She used to be quietly disappointed. But what did she expect? They were both in their forties when they'd married. In the first years she'd endured it as a necessity, an undignified yet required act of nature. Twice, even three times a week, her nightgown raised, knees bent and accommodating. It was a means to an end.

There was no end. Each month she had her days. Sometimes while coupled she might sigh, sounding as though she were urging him on. *Finish it, finish it, finish it.* When he did, she said she could hardly breathe with him collapsed on top of her. He could feel her heart beating in her ribcage, there beneath the flattened breasts. And then he would find the strength to roll off on to his back and stare at the ceiling in the dark. Always in the dark. Once he asked if he could have the light on, and she said, No, you just do your business. And then it all ceased. She no longer had her days, and over the winter months her hair looked heavier, brittle as it turned to the color of iron. While she prepared for bed, he took to remaining in the parlor. He read—newspapers, farm journals, manuals about electrical circuitry—the floorboards overhead creaking as she changed into her nightgown, and only after an extended silence would he climb the stairs, put on his pajamas, and get in bed. He would lie on his back, usually, while she lay on her side. He could tell from her breathing whether she was really asleep. They rarely spoke, there in the dark, in bed.

What was there to say?

They both understood that it would end with them. So often, when neighbors and friends spoke of their children, of the fevers and colds, the cuts and scrapes, the things kids did even though they were told not to, times when they about drove their parents to distraction; when those conversations began she made herself busy, pouring the tea or coffee, cutting another piece of cake, anything to avoid participation in the discussion of what children should be learning in school, what chores they did around the house and farm, what they might become when they grew up. From all these worries and fears came hope. That their children would get good grades; that they would go on—to what they often couldn't say, but on into the world, bearing the family name. That they might take over the farm one day. That they might marry and have children of their own. The women in particular, over the tea and coffee and the cakes and cookies, looked toward the day when their children would have children of their own, as though that were the sole reason, the ultimate reward, for all that they were enduring now. And while they discussed the children (the word itself an assault: *children, children, children*), Nellie would migrate away from the moment and busy herself with the teapot.

Once, just once, he came in from the barn and found her seated at the kitchen table, weeping. Weeping as only a woman can: silent, cheeks glistening, handkerchief useless in her lap. Before her, a magazine on the table, open to an advertisement for baby clothes. Sketches of dresses and sailor suits, Sunday clothes that parents insist their children wear to church or holiday dinners so they look like miniature adults. She wept over these images and didn't bother to look up. He poured a glass of lemonade from the pitcher—her mother's pitcher—she kept in the icebox and drank it while staring out the screen door. It was late summer. The corn was high that year. This was not long after they'd moved to Bath, before the consolidated school was built. Before the taxes went up. He didn't even own a car or a truck yet, only a tractor for the fields. But he paid his taxes; he harvested his crops. He stood at the screen door, drinking lemonade, surveying all that they had, the barn and outbuildings, the chickens and livestock, and there was nothing to say to it. Her family, those sisters down in Lansing, they held the mortgage on the farm, $12,000. Too much for eighty acres in Bath. Nellie wanted to return to the place where she grew up, where she raised those sisters after their mother died. You pay dearly for such sentiment. It would have been better to buy a farm from strangers; it was as though he'd been penalized for marrying into the family.

He finished his lemonade, placed the empty glass on the counter, and went out the screen door; took a cigar from the breast pocket of his suitcoat and paused in the yard to light a match stick, and as he drew on the cigar, the tobacco rich and sweet filling his lungs, he stared out toward the woods at the far side of the field, and at that moment he realized what he should do. Those trees—cut them back. Fell the trees, remove the stumps, enlarge the field. Not all at once, maybe ten percent a year. In five years, he'd have removed fifty percent, and gained several acres of arable land. Put it to use for grazing or planting. The remaining trees would continue to serve as a windbreak. He would cut the wood, split the logs, and let them season before burning them in the stove. Cords of wood to get them through the Michigan winters. The stumps and the rocks (there were sizable rocks back in those woods, too), they would need to be removed, which would require the purchase of dynamite and pyrotol.

Plans. He couldn't explain, couldn't say to Nellie: weeping is pointless. She needed plans. Make a plan and stick to it. But now, years later, as he sat in the straight back chair in the St. Lawrence hospital room, making small talk while she struggled to breathe, he never mentioned his new plan.

And he couldn't tell her that it didn't have to be this way, that she only had herself to blame. It went back years to when they'd first met, both enrolled at Michigan State College. She referred to it as their courting days, even though it didn't lead to marriage—not until years later. They would meet after classes, have dinner, do what other young couples did. Nellie was not quite pretty, but handsome. Other boys mentioned how lucky he was to get his hands on a girl like that, their hands gesturing in the air, creating breasts and hips of mythic proportions. He could have taken it as an insult, but he didn't, instead going along with the ruse that he was getting a good thing. In the end, they all wanted the same thing. There was the fellow who left school and returned to Grand Ledge because he had to get married. There was the boy in his electrical engineering course who stopped attending class and word went around that he'd gotten a girl from Sarnia, Ontario, in trouble. Word was he moved to Port Huron, where he repaired cars, and they had twins. They got what they wanted, like it or not, and it gave them children, like it or not. That was their end. At the time, Kehoe thought they'd arrived at the end of their own lives. But they'd gotten what they wanted.

But not he, not Nellie. At the end of the night she'd let him kiss her, standing on the front porch of her uncle's house, with the light from the vestibule slanting through the yellow, pink, and purple stained glass in the front door—it was like being in a church. Mouth closed, arms folded protectively. The few times she put her arms around him, he could feel them tense up if his hands began to wander. That sort of thing wasn't for Nellie Price from Bath, Michigan. No. So he couldn't say now, as she lay in that hospital room, that she should have let him. Back then she should have let him do what the other boys did. We'd be like them, now. Our lives over, but for the children.

Instead, they drifted apart—that's how she referred to it, drifting apart, though after they married years later she acknowledged that she was sad when he simply stopped calling on her. He lost interest, in Nellie, in his classes, and he went west. West, because there was nothing stopping him. Spent several years in Missouri and Minnesota, always able to find work with a new electric company, repairing lines and transformers. He was good at things most people didn't understand.

After visiting the hospital, he'd drive along East Michigan Avenue, toward the high dome of the State Capital building. When the wind was right, you could smell cow manure in downtown Lansing. At hardware stores he would purchase more blasting caps and wire and dynamite and pyrotol. Before driving back up to Bath he might stop at Emil's. He liked that Italian food. Something you couldn't get in Bath, spaghetti and meatballs. Once he asked the waitress what he tasted that he couldn't recognize, the flavor that stayed with him on the drive home, and she said, "*Aglio.*" And then, "Garlic. Your wife *non cucina mai* with garlic?" She made a face, mean, brutish, but then she laughed. "*Aglio.* Make you, *l'uomo grande!*"

■ ■ ■

Sometimes I see Bath from the sky.

Sometimes I think of myself as a bird, a hawk wheeling above the fields in search of prey. Sometimes from a jet plane, thousands of feet up, where I can see the combed fields in their quilted patterns. And sometimes I can see Bath then, and see it now, decades later, as though a transparency were laid over the land, adding paved roads, houses, and buildings, eliminating woods, barns, and silos.

I'm an old woman with a girl's eyes, the clarity, the detail so sharp I can see corn husks peeling away from their stalks in the summer heat, the wood knots beneath sun-faded paint on a clapboard wall. The more I see, the less I understand. But I know. We all know. We have known for so long.

What is it that we know? That it couldn't have been avoided? It couldn't have been stopped? The children couldn't have been saved?

We know something, but we do not know that.

Do we?

From the height of decades, I can look down, I can look back, and I can see us riding bareback as Daisy plodded from the Kehoe farm east toward the village, her head bobbing with the effort of every step. I can feel the heat coming off of Jed's back and passing through my blouse, where it warmed my breasts. It was approaching suppertime, the second week of May. A warm afternoon, with the threat of rain in the piling clouds, the moist air pulling scents from the ground that suggested the coming months when the crops would work their way toward the sky.

"I saw another hobo today," Jed said. "Sign of spring."

"Where was he?"

"I came out of Kehoe's barn and looked across Clark Road. He was running across Harte's field toward the woods. Seemed to be carrying something delicate. I think he'd been in the chicken coop."

"Eggs."

"I think so."

"Not a chicken. He didn't steal a chicken?"

"No. I don't think so," Jed said. "But I wish he had."

I was surprised. "Why?"

"He must be hungry is why."

"But he was stealing."

"I know." We listened to the clop of Daisy's hooves, the rise of the night's first crickets from the culvert alongside the road. "Have you ever been hungry? Really starving?"

"No," I said.

"Neither have I. But I'll bet if we were we'd steal a chicken."

"Even though it's wrong, though it belongs to someone else?"

He didn't answer. "They must have been somebody once. They must have come from somewhere, had mothers, fathers, places to live. Then, somehow, they became hobos."

I had no answer to this.

"Something must happen to them," he continued, speaking slowly, as though he were figuring an arithmetic problem out as he went, pausing to make further calculations in his mind. "Something is done to them. Or maybe *not* done. And they run off. They run away from everything they've known. They run from who they are, and they become hobos who are hungry enough to steal from a chicken coop."

"It's sad, true. Ma tells me to keep my distance if I see one. And you know we're not supposed to go near the tracks, not alone, anyway."

He didn't seem to hear me. "You'd think they'd do something, anything to get off the rails to get back to where they'd come from so they'd have a bed and something to eat and people who know their names, but they don't."

"Well, they can't."

"But why?" he asked. "Why can't they go back?"

"It's a conundrum."

"What's that?" Jed asked.

"A word that was in our vocabulary exercise this week. It means a mystery, a puzzle, something that has no clear explanation."

"You and your vocabulary," he said.

"'Words, words, words.'"

"That's what I said."

"No, Hamlet did."

Neither of us spoke. My attempts at humor often brought silence. Daisy plodded on. Vaguely, I understood Jed was talking about time, not just place. Even at twelve there was a kind of courage to the way he went at a thing, a conundrum. He wanted to understand it, to figure it out. Too often we ignore that which we don't know, we take the easy route. What Jed didn't know he didn't ignore but tried to meet head on.

He said, "They're afraid."

"Hobos. You think so? I wonder what they think of us, of a place like Bath."

"Maybethey envy us," he said. "We have homes, families, food on the table."

"I don't know, maybe," I said. "I guess it's a real conundrum." But I didn't say it as a joke and Jed didn't laugh. "If they *could* go back to who they used to be, I think they would feel trapped. Caught."

"That's *it,*" he said.

"That's what?"

"Hobos, they're free."

Our farm was visible farther down the road. Daisy always picked up the pace some, knowing the barn and her stall and dinner were near. I can still feel the rhythm of her ribs, rolling under my thighs, the heat rising from her coat. How we loved that old horse.

"Mr. Kehoe said a strange thing today." Jed paused and I waited. Sometimes I thought he did it on purpose, hesitating like that, fueling my anticipation. But it wasn't that. He just thought through a thing at his own pace. Plodding, but steady. "He asked me 'What's a criminal?'"

"He saw the hobo, too?"

"No, this was before that. Besides he was in the house, changing his shirt the way he does, when I saw the hobo in the field. No, he was smoking one of his cigars, inspecting a tree stump we were going to dynamite. He studies them carefully, to figure where he wants me to dig around the roots, where he wants to place the stuff."

"Did he have an answer—what a criminal is?"

Jed shook his head. "Nope. He didn't say. We just blew that stump to kingdom come. He seemed quite pleased with the job. Sometimes everything doesn't go the way he likes. Big sections of tree will still be hard in the ground. But this one just made a big hole, and there was a lot of wood for me to collect while he sat on the fender smoking his stogie."

■ ■ ■

Mr. Kehoe asked Edith and me to be at their house the afternoon he brought his wife home from the hospital. As he helped her from the car, she looked like she'd never been in the sun. Her pale skin reminded me of the underside of our piglets. To climb the stairs to the front porch, she needed one hand on the bannister, and to pause a moment after each step, yet when she reached the porch, where I took her arm while Edith held the door open, she said, "So much rain this year, Bea. But isn't this the grandest day?" We got her into the house. Mr. Kehoe remained outside, doing what, I don't know. He just seemed relieved to pass her off into our custody.

The next hour or so was spent getting her upstairs, where she wanted a bath before putting on a clean nightgown. Once she was in bed, I thought she'd sleep, but she asked if I'd bring up a tray with tea and cookies. (Edith was somewhat resentful when Mrs. Kehoe asked me to perform such tasks, which left her to return to housecleaning and the endless laundering and ironing of Mr. Kehoe's white shirts.) When I brought the tray in, Mrs. Kehoe insisted that I have a cookie and sit with her a spell before she slept. I sat on the vanity bench next to the window that looked out back toward the barn, outbuildings, and fields.

"It's so good. To be home. In my own bed." Her voice was hoarse, and she had to take a breath after only a few words. "I don't know. How long. I'll be here."

I didn't understand, and she must have seen it. "I've spent so much time. In that hospital of late. This last time for a procedure." I took a small bite of my oatmeal cookie, thankful for the sweetness of one chewy raisin. *Procedure.* A word as haunting as it was vague. I conjured images of incisions, of sterilized instruments, of masked doctors and nurses hovering over exposed internal organs. "The thing. About getting old, Bea." I stopped chewing. "Is that you don't believe it. That it's happened to you. Inside." She pressed a bony finger against her sunken chest for emphasis. "In here. *You.* You think you are still. Still young. I'm the same girl. Who. Grew up in this house. But now I'm buried. In. This. This body." She offered me a smile. "Please, dear. Have the other cookie."

While I ate the other oatmeal cookie, she wanted to get caught up. Wanted to know how I was doing in school. If there was any news in Bath. When I shook my head, she laughed until she began that awful cough. It took minutes to subside. "It's the same as when. I grew up here. Nothing ever really seems. To happen. You don't appreciate it. Until you spend time. In a Lansing hospital room." She gazed at the ceiling a moment. "White. All I could see for days. The white ceiling. Your mind, it works differently. When you just have. That ceiling to stare up at. Day after day. And the nights. They're worse." She looked past me, out the window. "It's just beginning to green up this spring. Don't you love the colors? Of the soil after the rain? And the budding trees. That's all. I could do on the drive up. From Lansing. Look at the colors."

I knew what she was talking about, but I didn't think it was so extraordinary. It was spring. It happened every year. She spoke of it as though it were a miracle. As though she'd never seen it before.

She was right. The girl I was still resides in this ancient vessel, which now stares up at the white ceiling. I know that she was right. But it's almost as though I'm not alone in here. *We.* We inhabit this ancient vessel now. I would like to think that we are all here as a matter of solace, of comfort. For all the pain, all the sorrow, it's reassuring to know that, at the very least, we are not alone. Sometimes I have lost sight of that, and it has made me deeply remorseful, some would say now, depressed.

What gets me through it is just that.

We are not alone.

7.

It was Friday night. Warm and buggy. The parents were at one of their socials, so we took the opportunity to walk up to Round Lake. I can't recall, maybe eight of us. Some wanted to swim or at least wade in the lake, but what we really wanted to do was to hear the music and watch the dancing at Lovings.

It was like being a spy. We hunkered down as we came out of the woods and crossed the grass toward the club. Lovings had a generator and electric lights. There was a dance band. When we got close enough we could see in the windows. The band members all wore white dinner jackets. Couples seemed to glide and shimmer beneath the spinning light globe suspended from the ceiling.

And then I saw them, Miss Weatherby and Dan, her beau from Lansing. They were in each other's arms, dancing closer, it seemed, than the other couples. Closer and a bit slower. He was much taller, and she pressed her cheek against his shoulder, occasionally looking up at him when he spoke. Despite being on the crowded dance floor, they seemed alone, only seeing each other. When she raised her head, I liked the way her hair fell on the shoulders of her green dress. It was not what she'd worn to school that day. It was not a dress she'd ever wear to school. She had a lovely neck, and an ivory broach was centered between her collar bones. When she laid her head against his shoulder, she'd close her eyes as though she were going to sleep.

After a time, I realized that our group had split up. Some of the kids had wandered back into the woods. This was to be expected, especially the older ones who had walked hand in hand out from the village. I found myself crouched in the shadows not far from the dance hall, along with Jed and Kate Burrell, who wore a wedge in her shoe to compensate for her short leg.

When the dance band took a break, some of the couples stepped outside, and we retreated, crawling on our bellies to the nearest bushes. Voyeurism is a delicious sin, particularly when you're witnessing what are believed to be forbidden acts. We saw men and women light up cigarettes, and we could see that some couples got in their cars and began kissing. A group of men passed a flask. But not Dan and Miss Weatherby—they sat on the steps, where he removed his coat and put it around her shoulders. They were holding hands.

It was too much; I couldn't watch anymore. Such voyeurism only reveals your own unrequited yearnings. "We should go." I looked around. "Where's Alma?"

Jed shrugged. Kate just shook her head. She did so in a way that suggested she understood something that I didn't get.

"Where *is* she?" I said. "And Warren? We need to find them and head on home."

As we began walking back along the shore of Round Lake, I saw them emerge from the dark woods.

Alma and Warren.

They walked side by side, but they weren't holding hands or anything. It didn't matter, they looked guilty as sin. When we reached them, I could see Alma's face in the light streaming from the windows of Lovings. Her eyes were proud, victorious. Warren's hands were shoved in the pockets of his overalls, and he looked everywhere but at me.

"It's getting late," I said to Alma. "We're going back."

"Yes, we'd better," she said, and she glanced toward the woods. "The others already left."

As she turned I noticed something wrong with her blouse. It was one of the shirts Ma had sewn, pale blue and much faded from countless washings. She made most of our clothes, often combining fabrics salvaged from other garments. Because Alma was older she got most things first, and then they were passed down to me. I never questioned this. That's just the way it was. It made sense when we were younger, but during the past year I had grown a couple of inches taller than Alma, but still, I wore the hand-me-downs.

I said, "Your buttons."

Turning toward me, Alma said, "My what?"

"They're done up wrong."

Her glare: she could have killed me at that moment.

I said it again, "You're done up wrong."

And then I walked past her toward the woods. I could hear Kate and Jed's shoes in the grass behind me. Alma called my name and said something. She'd taken to swearing recently. It was like a privilege, something one acquired at a certain age. She used a word that, had she said it at home, would have gotten her mouth washed out with soap. Parents used to do that. Some of us called it the Bath bath.

I broke into a run, my thin legs taking me into the darkness of the woods. I loved to run, and felt I could go on forever, my feet barely touching the ground. I heard Jed and Kate trying to catch up to me, but their footsteps faded as they fell behind.

I was alone, running through the dark woods, my lungs filling with the night air.

▪ ▪ ▪

Kate gave up the chase once they reached the woods, but Jed kept running, weaving around tree trunks, his arms raised against unseen low branches. Bea was fast, faster than most boys. Her long legs carried her away in the darkness. When he couldn't hear her up ahead, he slowed down, and finally stopped, bending over to catch his breath in great heaves. He walked on, and just as he emerged from the trees into a field he heard her.

Not a scream. A cry, something released at the moment of sudden, unexpected pain.

The land sloped downhill, high uneven grass. He jogged carefully, trying to see her against the blackness of the next tree line. And then he heard Bea again. She sounded like she was struggling, speaking to something or someone. He saw movement, rising up out of the grass. Jed ran faster down the field, calling her name. Then he stopped.

A man, tall and hulking, stood at the edge of the field, facing Jed. Too dark to see any features other than a bulky coat and a fedora with a crumpled crown. He turned, and there was something familiar in the way he lumbered downhill into the woods, carrying Bea in his arms.

▪ ▪ ▪

When I was fourteen, I believed we shared a creed. We believed not in fate or fortune, at least not in any mystical sense. We believed in something larger. Something as real as it was inexplicable. We called it God, though now such notions too often need to be qualified. In Bath, the evidence was all around us. It was in the fields, in the crops we planted, the harvest's reliance upon an unpredictable Michigan climate. For us, the sky held the key to the land. Not our land, God's land. The joke was the farm belonged to the People's Bank of Bath, and to the Lord. We were tenants; it was a privilege to reside on that land. To work it, to cultivate it, to look skyward and think about rain. What the land needed. What we needed to survive. The pigs, cows, horses, chickens, goats, and sheep, they never looked to the heavens in wonder. They bent to their grazing, their pecking, their trough, taking whatever was given. When you watch a hog work through a pail of garbage you are closer to God, to all the mysteries of this earth, than when you sit through a Sunday sermon on salvation. Belief was like the air we breathed. You didn't need evidence; you didn't need to see it to know it was there. We believed, and we believed in a way that we did not need to put names to it. Our deeds; our daily rituals; our attending to the chores; the milking; the constant repairs to house, barn, fence, and machine were our most eloquent prayers. We all believed we were God's children and were thankful in the same way those hogs went through the slop. The way we are thankful when we eat the bacon from that carcass on a winter's morning. God works in mysterious ways, indeed, and just say grace at your table.

That's what I believed.

Then.

That night in May near broke me. Watching Miss Weatherby dance in the arms of her young man with the Chevrolet gave me hope, while my sister Alma's wrongly buttoned blouse sent me into despair. The kind of teenager's despair that seems abysmal, fathomless, and so unfair. Warren, for reasons I can't clearly recall, was my young man with a Chevrolet. Maybe it was his straight back, his delicate eyelashes, or his good teeth. Whatever it was, I knew when I saw those misaligned buttons on my sister's blouse that I would never have him. Love, I believed then, wrongly, was a matter of possession. I felt crushed, defeated. At that age my only response was to run, to run away as fast and as far as my legs would carry me.

Until it happened. Something in that field—a hole dug by some burrowing critter, a chipmunk, a squirrel, a vole, or maybe a skunk—caused my right foot to twist, and I heard the crack, felt the pain in my leg, knowing something was broken before I sprawled in the tangled grass. The pain drove everything out—all hope, all fear—and I writhed in agony, until I realized that I was not alone. And my pain was compounded by awe, the recognition of something I had always known yet had never witnessed.

A presence loomed in the darkness above me. I didn't understand it, but in my helpless, injured state, I trusted it.

He bent down and lifted me up in his arms.

As he entered the pitch-black woods, I lost consciousness.

▪ ▪ ▪

Jed understood that Bea was not like the rest of them. He could not place his finger on it exactly (if he'd say such a thing, she would silently chastise him by pressing a fingertip against his forehead), but she was different. Some suggested that she was peculiar or odd. No one ever really said why, they just knew that Bea was off by herself somewhere. Jed saw it in the way Bea looked at everything. As though she were attempting to crawl inside a squirrel on a tree limb, or a dog sleeping in the shade of a porch. She wanted to see everything, touch everything; she wanted to *be* everything. Bea. She read books looking for answers (that seldom seemed complete or satisfactory); she listened to sounds, voices, words as though they might deliver the truth.

Words.

Once, while riding bareback on Daisy, she began to say the word milk.

"Milk." Barely a whisper. "Milk. Milk. Milk."

"Milk?"

"Isn't it an incredible sound, Jed?"

"Really? Why?"

"I don't know. *Milk.* Say it out loud and it's so strange, but perfect. How did milk become *milk.* Who named milk milk? *Miiillk.* It's not just a word but a note in a song."

Jed tried: "*Miiilllk.*"

"See?"

"I suppose."

"Why didn't they call it *shoe* or *melon?*"

"You got me there."

"It seems so random."

"It is. Random."

And then she laughed. Laughed so that the pitch of her voice rose high enough that Daisy's ears twitched and she thought she was being told to stop. They sat on her swayback, and Jed waited for Bea's laugh to end.

"What?"

"Some words, they aren't random."

"Like?"

"Like udder."

"Udder?"

"Yes, an udder could only be an *udder.*"

"Udder. Ud-der." He shouted, "*Udder!*"

They both laughed.

Daisy took this as a signal to proceed, and she continued to plod along.

The music from Loving's faded into the night as the man had carried Bea into the woods, and Jed followed. Occasionally, he thought he heard something up ahead in the dark. A twig snap, the brush of a branch. But he didn't see the man or Bea. When he came to the other side of the woods, he entered the deserted village.

As he came around the corner of the town hall, Jed saw movement. He stood still, until he realized that the man was kneeling on the town hall steps, and that Bea was lying on the stoop. The man got to his feet and turned toward Jed. He had a beard, and though it was a warm night the collar of his tweed coat was turned up around his neck. He took a step toward Jed, who backed away.

"You friend's hurt, son." His voice was deep, scraped clean from sleeping in boxcars and outbuildings and forests. "Best you fetch some help."

He turned around and disappeared into the trees that ran alongside the railroad tracks. There was a slight hitch in his gait. Jed recognized that stride.

The egg thief.

■ ■ ■

I can't recall much of that night. Jed told me about how he ran to get my parents, who then sent him to get Dr. Taggart. Once I was home in my bed, the doctor gave me something for the pain. Before I slept he told my parents that it was a fracture in the fibula, that it would have been much worse if I'd broken my ankle. When I awoke in the morning my right leg was in a cast up to my knee. I could only get around on crutches. Inside the cast, my skin was hot and itched terribly. I missed several days of school, and once I returned it was difficult getting around. Pa drove me to and from school in the truck, and just getting up the walk and into the building was an effort. Jed often helped with my books.

And Alma. It was as though the business outside of Lovings hadn't happened. Or maybe it was because of Warren. I don't know. We'd always been contentious as only sisters can be. I spent a great deal of time—too much time—in bed, or in the evening, out on the glider that hung from the ceiling of the front porch. Alma brought me cookies and glasses of lemonade. And books. I read so much Ma said I'd go blind. I suspected that Alma's kindness was the result of our parents' admonishments, that they had made her feel responsible for my injury. At some point I realized that it was her own doing.

I was at first confused about what exactly had happened. I remembered running through the woods and the moment when I stumbled and broke my leg. But how I got to the town hall steps was a mystery, not only to me but to Ma and Pa, not to mention Dr. Taggart and our neighbors. They assumed that Jed carried me—he was smaller than me and they were in awe of his strength—but he denied it, saying that I had managed to walk from where I fell in the field to the town hall, that I merely leaned on him, using him like a crutch.

It wasn't until later, much later, that Jed told me about the egg thief.

▪ ▪ ▪

Jed walked the tracks out to the caboose. He went there for several days after Bea broke her leg but he never saw anyone. The hobo probably thought it best to move on, because the town might think he was responsible for the girl's injury. No one would believe that a vagrant had rescued her. Jed didn't intend to tell anyone about the egg thief.

A few days later he went out to the Kehoe farm. Mr. Kehoe let him in the kitchen door—Jed had never been inside the house, and it was so neat and fancy he felt intimidated. He was led into the parlor, where Mrs. Kehoe was lying on the couch beneath a blanket, despite the heat. Mr. Kehoe went upstairs, and she arranged the pillows behind her so she could sit up.

"I understand," she said slowly, "Bea had an accident."

"Yes, Ma'am."

The woman was having great difficulty breathing. "You tell her. I hope she heals up soon."

"I will."

"What grade are you in."

"Sixth grade, Ma'am."

"Oh." She sounded disappointed. "You won't be here. For the picnic."

Jed had no idea what she was talking about, which she realized immediately, and she seemed to have regretted bringing it up. "You see, one of the teachers called my husband." She paused to take a deep breath. "They asked. If they could bring some of the children. Out to our field. To have a picnic."

Jed nodded, unsure of what to say. Then he said, "I hope they have good weather."

"Yes, with all the rain we've had. Those poor people down on the Mississippi. For the children. It would be nice. A picnic to end their school year."

Mr. Kehoe came down the stairs, snugging his knotted tie up to the collar of his fresh white shirt. He went into the kitchen and out the back door. It was like his wife wasn't even there in the room.

When Jed turned to follow, Mrs. Kehoe said, "I hope Bea can visit me soon. You tell her I send. My regards."

"Yes, Ma'am."

Jed followed Mr. Kehoe out to the barn, where they put new tires on his Ford truck. While Jed was tightening the lug nuts on the last wheel, Mr. Kehoe settled himself on a barrel and lit one of his cigars. "Have you given any thought to my question?" He gazed out the open back doors of the barn. "When we had our last—" He paused a moment to draw on his cigar. "Our last discussion."

Jed stopped working and looked at Mr. Kehoe, who continued to stare out at his field. The afternoon light illuminated his eyes in a way that made Jed think of marbles. "What is a criminal?"

Kehoe nodded as his finger tapped ash that floated to the floor, light as snow.

"It's someone . . ." Jed hesitated. "Someone who does something he shouldn't."

"That so? And who decides what someone should or should not do?"

"God?"

"God." Mr. Kehoe shook his head, slow and deliberate. "People think that fellow's responsible for it all. But they got it backward, you see. God didn't create us. We created him. Now why would we do that?"

"I don't know."

"Because we're weak. We think he'll make us strong. Strong enough to know right from wrong. Strong enough to know when we shouldn't do a thing. For instance . . ." Mr. Kehoe paused to draw on his cigar. "Well no, why don't you give me a for instance."

"Somebody steals something. Like eggs."

"Stealing eggs." Kehoe repositioned himself on the barrel. Elbows on his knees, he might have been sitting in an outhouse. "That's a crime?"

"I guess so."

"Uh-huh. Ownership, I suppose that applies. Ownership of the chickens and their eggs."

"There's laws against it."

"Indeed. It's called private property."

It occurred to Jed that Mr. Kehoe might also have seen the egg thief crossing the Harte's field. He'd be the kind of man who would know if eggs were missing from his neighbors' coop. How exactly, Jed wasn't sure, but he believed if anyone could keep track of such things it would be Mr. Kehoe.

"It wasn't me," Jed said in haste. "I didn't do it."

"You didn't?" Mr. Kehoe considered him for the first time since he'd sat down on the barrel. "Do what?"

Now Jed felt caught. In a lie, though he didn't think he'd actually told one. But there was the sense that he was guilty in some way. He felt the heat in his cheeks. "Steal eggs," he mumbled.

"What? Speak up."

"I didn't steal any eggs from the Harte's coop."

Mr. Kehoe thumped his wide thigh. "That's a relief!" He rubbed the material of his suit pants for a moment. "You know somebody who did?"

Now Jed couldn't find any breath. Yes or no. Lie or truth. "No," he said. "I don't know who did it." This felt tight, as though he were squeezing through the eye of the needle.

"But you know eggs have been stolen."

Jed was clutching the long handle of the lug wrench. Rust had built up in the socket. His fear was tinged with an anger that he could not identify. The authority of adults was absolute, but somewhere in his mind he saw himself swing the tool like a baseball bat and hit this man squatting on a barrel while smoking a cigar. He could hear him gasp, see the blood spurt from his wounded head. He could drive this man to the ground, beat him until he ceased to struggle, and then there would be no need to answer questions about theft and eggs and private property. He would be a real criminal, a murderer.

"Yes," Jed said. "Yes, eggs have been taken."

Mr. Kehoe worked his cigar a long moment. Considering, as only an adult can. Jed expected an outburst, some accusation that he was an accomplice—that he was in cahoots with an egg thief. But Mr. Kehoe pursed his mouth as he leaned forward and dropped a heavy wad of spit on the packed dirt floor. As he straightened up, he said quietly, "I know that. Transients. Vagrants. Hobos. Whatever you want to call 'em, they steal from our farms. Last year they took a couple of my chickens."

Jed's sense of relief made him lightheaded. It felt like a stay of execution.

"Know *why* they do it? *Why* they steal from us?"

It was such a fundamental question. Such questions required some interpretation on his part. Some judgement. "Why?" he said. "Why do they steal?"

"That's what I asked, yes." Mr. Kehoe looked at him hard.

Jed had been through this with Bea, but he could speak his mind with her. "Well. They steal because they're hungry."

"Hungry?" Mr. Kehoe leaned toward Jed slightly, as though to see him more clearly in the dim light of the barn. "Of course! Why else would they steal?" Then he got to his feet and pulled up his trousers by the belt loops the way he often did. "But I'll tell you this. There are different kinds of thieves, different kinds of theft. Outside the law and inside the law. Some'll look you in the eye and tell you they're only doing what's right, only doing their duty. No, sir. No, they won't be stealing from me much longer. Not my farm." He gazed out the barn doors as though he could see hobos coming out of the woods and crossing his field. "*Why* is not the question in this matter," he announced. "It's how. *How* are criminals made? Are they born that way? Or does something happen to them that makes them criminals?"

Mr. Kehoe jammed the stub of his cigar in the hole of his mouth, his fatty lips about the soggy end a sickly purple. He strode out of the barn and into the sunlight, blue smoke trailing behind him.

■ ■ ■

After several days in a cast, and primarily being confined to bed, I said to Ma, "This must be what it's like to be old."

I was cranky. She ignored it, which was her usual response to childish whims. Tantrums were curtailed with a slap, or even a spanking. My view of the world seemed to have gone from vertical to horizontal. I had recently encountered the word *untenable* in something I'd read, and after dutifully looking it up in the dictionary, I deemed everything untenable. This Ma found harder to ignore. Though I know she knew what the word meant, she acted as though I were using foul language. I expected to be given a Bath bath.

Most of the time I scowled at the ceiling above my bed, though in the afternoons I would make a great production of moving myself and my books out to the living room sofa, or if the weather permitted out to the front porch glider. My anger was fueled by the fact that I had been reduced to being an observer, when I was born to be a participant. It wasn't fair, none of it. My sense of injustice was only exacerbated (a word I had not yet added to my linguistic arsenal) by how my sister treated me. Alma, to use Ma's words, was a perfect angel. Driven, I thought (or hoped), by guilt, Alma behaved as though she were my personal maidservant. She brought me things. She sat with me—even when I didn't invite her company. She gave me reports from the outside world. When she'd tell about the day's events at school, I would listen with arms folded, eyes averted, suppressing a scream. It would have been preferable had she provided me with the local news and gossip as a means of vengeance. But there was no gloating, no goading, no victor's hubris. Her sympathy toward me was pure and genuine. For the first time in her life, she was capable of a truly selfless act, and I hated her for it. The fact that she had Warren, that she would always have Warren (who I assumed was by then familiar with her absurdly plump breasts), that was beside the point. Perhaps. There were moments when I dragged my pathetic plaster-of-Paris leg down the wormhole of romantic jealousy. At fourteen the black abyss of sexual desire yawned beneath every moment of existence. The problem—or one of them, at least—was that I had witnessed how pigs, cows, and horses did it, but when it came to human sexual congress, I was utterly confused, mystified, and unschooled. Being primarily supine, with idle hands, was a torment I did not deserve.

But my restricted horizontal state taught me a few things. Despite my impatience, I observed my parents as I had never done before, and in retrospect I believe I came to know them better as a result of my convalescence. It seemed that I was able to see their daily routines from afar. Sometimes while staring at my ceiling I managed to reverse my perceptions, so that I felt I was viewing our house from above, as though it was a kind of doll's house which had removable walls and roof. I would chart by ear my mother's movements, hearing her in the kitchen preparing a meal, or in the parlor sweeping the floor, or in the yard beating the hooked rug. My father spent much of the day outside, of course, but I could monitor what he was doing from the sound of shed and barn doors squealing on rusted hinges, or by the clang and knock of tools in his workshop, or by the reaction of animals. Chickens scattered before him in the yard, pigs fought over slop buckets, and the mournful sound of the cows, which I had always loved, came from the barn during milking. One morning I lay in bed muttering the word *udder* over and over. When Ma came to take my breakfast tray away, and she noted that I had not eaten the hardboiled egg, I told her I was *udderly* stuffed. It was a joke, I thought, but her response was to place a wrist against my forehead to check for fever, and to suggest as she left my bedroom that Dr. Taggart might have to pay another visit.

It was clear that my parents' daily routines, which ostensibly were intended to keep house and farm in good working order, were actually designed so that the least direct contact between them could be maintained. Even at the kitchen table, they seemed to work in a parallel fashion, their comments seldom directed toward each other but often deflected off of Alma or me, or perhaps toward the food on their plates. Pa might say, "More potatoes" or "Salt"; Ma might offer an opinion about the chicken or pie crust. They lived, I concluded, a life of avoidance (a word I conflated with abstinence, after I found it in the dictionary). They had married, borne two children, lived under the same roof for nearly twenty years, and their one mutual desire appeared to be to not communicate with each other—at least not in any meaningful way. Nothing certainly beyond expressing the need to close a window or pass the butter. Why, then, did they marry? I had no idea. Was it simply to produce two offspring?

At night, I would lie in my bed, staring at the ceiling in the dark, listening. For years, Alma and I shared the bedroom and bed, but once we reached our teens, she was allowed to move into what had been Ma's sewing room. I could hear her turn in her sleep, and when she slept on her back there was often a nasal snap that occurred with every breath, steady as the ticking of a clock. At the back of the second floor, there was our parents' bedroom. Without fully realizing it, I was listening to them, listening for some sign of them being in the same bed in the middle of the night. I would hear an occasional box spring when one of them turned—I could tell if it was Pa because the effort would interrupt his snoring. I would hear Ma get out of bed and pad barefoot to the corner of the room, where she'd squat over the chamber pot.

What I didn't hear were words. They never spoke in bed. Not even a whisper, as far as I could tell (and I had, and have always had, very keen hearing). As with their daily routines, at night they went through practiced rituals of dressing and undressing, and then settled into their bed much the same as the cows often curl up in the pasture. They slept together, man and wife, because they would need their rest for tomorrow's chores. It was all about work. Silent, relentless labor performed day in and day out, whatever that means.

I was disappointed, and frightened. Disappointed because I had hoped to discover—to hear—some hint of affection pass between them. Some moment when the thing that brought them together in wedlock so many years ago still simmered, if only briefly in the dark of night. A sigh, a groan, the rhythmic protests of box springs—which I had heard when I was younger, before I had any idea what it meant. But there was nothing. And that's what frightened me. That it all came to nothing. They merely continued to exist together because that's what they were supposed to do, what they knew how to do. No different than the livestock in the field, the chickens in the yard.

It was a terrible realization for a teenage girl, particularly when she's laid low by a broken leg. And I didn't know that all of it, everything, was on the verge of breaking open. For me. For my parents. For Alma. Jed. Warren. Miss Weatherby. Aunt Ginny. The Kehoes. For Bath. For all of us.

I saw how the world works.

It all ends.

And then it begins again.

II. Day of Days

8.

It was the day of days, around which all other days pivot.

Wednesday, May 18, 1927, Bath time came to an end. Not literally, because the township continued to be on central time for several years to come. But after May 18, Bath was a different place. Time seemed different.

It's still impossible to say with certainty what happened on that spring day. There is no definitive record. Facts, yes. There are facts, but they are too often contradictory. For years I have lived with what I knew, what I saw, and, later, with what I read and heard—recollections, observations, perceptions, they all vary. I lie here, an old woman, staring at this ceiling, believing in only how little I know—how little any of us can know.

■ ■ ■

Monty Ellsworth's first thought that morning was of melons. It had rained overnight but by dawn the skies were clearing. The ground would be soft and damp, perfect for planting. Before 8:00 Bath time, he went to his garden and began digging in the soil. He could hear the chickens in his coop, many of which he had recently purchased from Andrew Kehoe—earlier in the spring he had abruptly sold all of his chickens to Monty.

Throughout the township, people were beginning their daily routines. Farm chores habitually started at first light—in winter, well before sunrise. Household tasks began early. Breakfast was made; children were urged to get ready for school. Wednesday, May 18, was a day like no other, of course, but in the first hours of daylight it promised a kind of familiarity. And in such familiarity lies possibility, particularly in the spring. For Monty Ellsworth planting melon seeds was a form of hope.

▪ ▪ ▪

Jed walked across the fields to the Turcott's farm. Though Bea had missed a number of days at school because of her broken leg, she was determined to take her final exam so there would be no question about her eligibility to go into ninth grade the following September. Since her leg had been put in the cast, Jed had left his house earlier than usual and walked to her house. Prior to her injury, they often walked to school together, but because of her broken leg, her father drove them into the village. When they climbed out of his truck in front of the school, Jed would carry her books while she worked her way up the front walk on crutches.

That morning the Ford pickup wouldn't start—no matter what her father did, the engine wouldn't turn over.

Jed saw it in Bea's face, the singularity of purpose that made her different from the other kids in Bath. Her cheeks flushed as she watched her father work on the truck.

"Eight thirty," she said. "School starts at eight thirty sharp, Bath time."

"Don't be so impatient," her father said as he leaned over the Ford's engine.

"You don't know how Mr. Huyck can be, Pa. There is no *tardy*. We're expected to be inside the building by eight thirty. I cannot miss my exam."

He closed the engine hood and tugged a rag from the back pocket of his overalls. "I will talk to Mr. Huyck, and everything—"

"Everything will *not* be all right." Seldom did she raise her voice with her parents.

Wiping his hands on the rag, her father said, "Don't take that tone with me."

Bea looked toward the barn. "*Daisy,*" she nearly shouted. "We'll take Daisy to school."

"With that leg?" Her father turned to Jed and shook his head as though they were in agreement. Jed wanted to disappear. Looking at his daughter, Mr. Turcott said, "And what are you going to do with Daisy, bring her into the classroom with you?"

"I'll tie her up to a tree."

"Honey, you can't keep the horse there waiting in the front of the school all day."

Now Bea stared at Jed. "You don't have an exam, do you?" He shook his head, feeling guilty. "Then you can bring Daisy back to the farm."

Bea turned herself on her crutches and began to hobble toward the barn.

Her father tucked the rag back into his pocket. "How you going to mount her?"

Bea keep swinging her body between the crutches until she reached the open barn door. Then, over her shoulder, she said, "Jed'll give me ten fingers."

■ ■ ■

He did.

Pa watched, his expression a combination of incredulity and exasperation. But Jed followed my instructions, lacing his fingers into a stirrup, and once I had my good left foot in it, he lifted me up so that I could throw my other leg over Daisy's sway back. "Now," I said, "hand me that satchel and get up here."

Jed handed up the satchel that contained our schoolbooks, and then he climbed up behind me. I looked at Pa, leaning against the gate. "The reins, if you please."

I was glad Ma wasn't there. She would never tolerate such insolence, but Pa would take it, up to a point. In a house full of females, he just wanted to keep the peace. "You're leg's all right?"

"The reins," I said.

I knew that I sounded much like Ma—wasn't about to take no for an answer. I detected the faintest smile as Pa untied Daisy from the gate and handed the reins up to me.

■ ■ ■

As Daisy plodded toward the village, Jed was reluctant to speak. His arms went around Bea's middle, clutching her ribs beneath her breasts. He could feel the tension in her back muscles, and her silence seemed to even have an effect on Daisy, who maintained an unusually steady pace. Finally, Jed said, "You could cross the field here, cut through the trees to the village."

Bea turned the horse off the road and began to walk around the perimeter of the field. They took the path under the trees, where the cool, shaded air smelled of lilac. Going through the woods, rather than continuing down the road to the corner of Main Street, saved a few minutes.

"Daisy's too old—she's just got the one speed," Bea said. "We may not make it in time. It's the last week of the year. Maybe Mr. Huyck'll let us in, even if we're late."

"I doubt it."

"I do too, despite . . ."

"Despite, what?"

As they entered the shade of the woods, she said, "He's not coming back to Bath Consolidated next year."

"What?"

"I heard Ma talking with Cora. Mr. Huyck told the school board he's moving on to another position. I don't know where."

"You think this will soften him up some so he'll let us in late?"

"It is the last week of school, but then there are exams." Bea hesitated, and then she laughed. "We'll find out." She did not sound all that confident.

"How's the leg feel?"

"It's fine."

"You are a lousy liar."

"Am not."

"Am too. Always have been."

When they came out of the woods, Jed looked down Main Street toward the village, and he had one of those moments when nothing seemed to make sense: there was a man who appeared to be climbing into the sky.

▪ ▪ ▪

Kehoe left the house not long after daybreak, carrying a sealed wooden crate to his truck. He drove into the village and parked in front of the post office, which hadn't yet opened. He took the crate from the back of his truck and walked down the street toward the railroad tracks. This was yet another source of aggravation: the insistence on operating on central time in Bath. Unlike most people in Bath, Kehoe set his watch to eastern time. But round here they didn't change. They didn't understand progress, true progress, things like electricity and the combustion engine. They'd be content to walk behind a horse-drawn plow for generations to come. By rights, the post office should be open now—it was a service of the United States government.

Instead of the post office, Kehoe entered the railway depot, which was open because the Michigan Central trains didn't run on Bath time. The railway agent, D. B. Huffman, came to the counter and studied the wooden crate. On the side was stenciled: *High Explosives. Dangerous.*

"Needs to be delivered to Lansing this morning," Kehoe said. "It's going to the law office of Clyde B. Smith." Huffman stared at the crate a moment, and Kehoe added, "Books. It's packed with books. What else would you send an attorney?"

Huffman took up his fountain pen and leaned over the order form on the counter. "Address?"

Kehoe gave him the street address, watching as he printed in careful block letters. When he was finished writing, he took a blotter and pressed it on the paper. "It'll go on the next train to Laingsburg, and then from there, it'll be transferred to the first train to Lansing." He toted up the charges.

"Ten miles," Kehoe said. "Be cheaper if I drove it down myself."

"Sure," Huffman said. "If you've got the time to drive down and back."

Was there a smile beneath that ragged mustache? Kehoe suspected there was—they all thought him to be a tight wad, a contrarian. Kehoe smiled, too. "What do they say about time and money?"

Huffman looked up from his form, a finger pushing his glasses up his nose. "Something about too much of one and not enough of the other? I could never keep that straight." Now he laughed, indicating he was going to tell a joke. "All I knows is I spend most of my time in this depot and ain't got but a dime to show for it."

Kehoe obliged with a chuckle as he placed some bills and change on the counter. "Take what you need."

Huffman seemed to think this was odd, the way he said it. As though a grand gesture. He took the bills and sorted out the necessary coins. "We'll have it on the first train to Lansing, and it'll be delivered to this address before noon."

"Good." He turned and started for the office door.

"Mr. Kehoe?"

He stopped. "Yeah?"

"Your change?"

He was tempted to just leave it. What would they say about that? But he returned to the counter, sweeping the coins off the counter and into the palm of his other hand. "Right."

"You'd be surprised at how often folks do that." Huffman picked up the crate, and as he took it through the door to the storeroom, he said, "Mind's elsewhere."

■ ■ ■

When Bert Detluff drove to his blacksmith's shop in the village, he saw Kehoe walking toward his truck, parked on Main Street. He pulled up behind the Ford and Kehoe came to his door. He looked distracted, but staring at the carton on the seat next to Detluff, he asked, "Whatcha got there?"

"Picked me up some duck eggs on the way into town."

"Duck eggs." It might have been a foreign phrase.

Detluff asked, "When's next school board meeting?"

Kehoe turned and looked down Main Street, which was lined with new poles taller than many of the trees that rose above the sidewalks. A Consumer Power crew was stringing thick black cables between the poles. "Not sure. It's either the nineteenth or twentieth."

"Maybe we should discuss the generator at the school."

"Why?"

"Got a call from Frank Smith this morning," Detluff said. "Generator's down again. No power in the building. Smith called Harrington, but didn't know when he'd get in to look at it. They can do without lights on a sunny day like this, but the water pump's not operating." He grinned, but Kehoe didn't.

"I suppose a fella like Harrington, with one arm, is busier than people with both." Detluff thought this was Kehoe's attempt at a joke, but he only kept staring down the street. "If we've got our hands full, must be tough for a fella with only one."

"He's a character," Detluff said. "Clamps a kid's head under that stump of his, and gives his scalp a playful rub with his knuckles. They love him."

"Where's your little girl?" Kehoe asked.

"She usually rides in on the bus."

Kehoe nodded. "Must be tough, widowed, raising a little girl."

Detluff raised a hand off the steering wheel and rubbed the back of his neck. He wanted to ask Kehoe what he meant, or how he meant it. The way Kehoe said it, he might be saying Detluff was fortunate to not have to deal with his wife, or he was burdened with having a child to care for—it was hard to tell. But that was Kehoe. Blunt, difficult to read, willing to say things that people didn't like to hear. No kids, a sickly wife, he had his own burdens. There was a time when Detluff would not have let such a comment pass without demanding clarification, but since Mabel had died, it was enough to just get through each day. Stick to the moment, which was the generator at school. "Why don't you come up and have a look?" he said.

"Now? Harrington will fix it."

"Just take a few minutes. We don't know when Harrington will get there."

Kehoe looked in the other direction, up the hill. "I suppose."

He got in his truck and followed Detluff up to the school. They both parked and started up the walk to the front doors.

"Eight twenty-five," Kehoe said, looking at his watch. "Almost time for classes to start."

"It's only seven twenty-five," Detluff said. "Plenty of time."

"Oh, right," Kehoe said. "Bath time."

The school was still quiet. The halls were empty, though they could hear the sound of teachers' shoes on the floorboards as they prepared their classrooms for the day. Detluff and Kehoe descended the stairs to the basement under the south wing, where they found Frank Smith in the small pump house. The janitor didn't know what the problem was, and, as had often been the case, he and Detluff looked to Kehoe to figure it out. For several years he'd been the one responsible for maintenance and repairs of the building. So much time spent there that he'd set up his own workshop in the basement. Kehoe looked over the water pump, and then inspected the generator. He didn't touch anything—being careful of his suit—he just examined wires and gauges, until he turned to the two men and said, "I'm in an awful hurry."

Before they could respond, he was rushing up the staircase to the first floor.

Detluff and Smith remained in the basement, looking at the equipment but concluded that they'd have to wait for Harrington, who was hired by the school board to make such repairs. Overhead they could hear children arriving for classes. They were generally quiet—Superintendent Huyck insisted on maintaining order—but the sound of their feet on the floorboards rumbled overhead. Finally, Detluff and Smith went upstairs, where a sea of children was now moving through the halls—there would be well over two hundred students in the building by eight thirty. Smith said he'd go to tell the principal, Mr. Huggett, that there would be no power until the generator was fixed. Detluff went out to his truck and drove down Main Street to his blacksmith's shop.

▪ ▪ ▪

Sometimes, when I imagine myself a bird—a crow, a raven, or a hawk—I am wheeling hundreds of feet above Bath, high enough that I can see the quilt pattern of the fields, the row of buildings along Main Street in the village, and the farmhouses and barns and sheds scattered across the countryside with a randomness that makes me think of rolled dice. If I were a bird, I suppose I wouldn't admire the landscape for its beauty, for that scent of lilac rising on the air—I'd be occupied with gliding and turning in the wind currents, constantly looking for activity on the ground, in the fields, along the roadside culverts, seeking the movement of a rodent or a hare. My only concern would be my hunger, the key to my survival. Things such as cars and trucks on the roads, tractors plying the fields, these wouldn't interest me; I'd have learned to avoid them. I'd know that prey were seldom found near such disturbances, with their noise and capricious movement. They were things not of this world, the natural world. If I were a hawk, I wouldn't wonder how the houses had come to be; I'd only connect them with the two-legged beings that dwelt within them. They were something unnatural and foreign that had come to inhabit this land. If I had been a bird in the sky above Bath that morning, I would see and hear sounds, threatening sounds. I'd keep my distance. All of us, all of the birds would stay clear, seeking safety from whatever it was that was going on down there.

9.

As Lulu Harte reached down into the straw, her fingers touching a warm egg, she heard it—like a gunshot, but different. A muffled thud, which caused a faint tremor to run through the packed earth beneath her feet. Lulu's days usually began with a trip to the henhouse. She loved its confined warmth, the fecund smell of chickens and straw. They had a variety of breeds: Buff Orpingtons, Black Australorps, Rhode Island Reds, and Araucanas, which laid blue-green eggs. She spoke to the chickens, gave them names. Her husband David had once suggested that she thought too much of her birds. "You shouldn't love something you eventually have to kill." When she asked how she was supposed to feel about them, he said, "Grateful." She understood that, but she still loved them. Sometimes she thought she understood her chickens better than she understood people. You raised layers for their eggs, for their bones that made good soup stock. She believed chickens felt deep sorrow—or perhaps it was resentment, evidenced by their awkward, desperate leaps into the air, accompanied by a frantic flapping of wings—that they would never really fly, never lift themselves up into the sky like the birds of prey that constantly soared above the fields.

The second thud was louder, closer—again, the earth jounced and the coop's wood joints groaned as the hens stirred fearfully.

She went outside, raising a hand to shield her eyes from the angled light of the morning sun. Across Clark Road, smoke rose from the Kehoe's corncrib. She ran toward her husband David, who had come out on the front porch. "They've got a fire over there," she said. "I saw Andrew drive off around seven."

David came down the porch steps, staring across the road. Turning, Lulu saw that it wasn't just the corncrib, but smoke was pouring from the barn. She thought of Nellie, alone in the house, only recently having come home from the hospital in Lansing.

When Lulu began moving toward the road, her husband caught her by the arm. "Don't go over there," he said. "He certainly set it himself."

She looked at her husband. He wasn't making any sense.

Andrew Kehoe would do this . . . on purpose?

David kept a firm hand on her arm.

They watched the smoke billow into the sky, thick, black, drifting on the faintest breeze. There was the sound of crackling wood, hay and dry timbers igniting quickly, feeding the fire. As if to confirm David's assertion, there was another explosion. Lulu couldn't tell exactly where it came from, and then it was followed by another explosion.

And another.

And another.

▪ ▪ ▪

Daisy got us to school with only a few minutes to spare. Our days at Bath Consolidated were usually predictable and uniform, structured with procedures and rules and expectations. That Wednesday felt different, because for many of us we were to take final exams, and for others it was the last day of school—graduation was the next day. So as I swung on my crutches along the walk toward the front doors, with Jed at my side, carrying my books in a satchel, I felt somehow freer and bolder than I might on any other Wednesday morning.

I was relieved—and I suspect Jed was as well—to see our principal, Mr. Huggett, standing outside the front doors as students raced into the building. Relieved, because Superintendent Huyck wasn't there. He was simply was not one to make exceptions. But Mr. Huggett was another story. He was only twenty-six, yet this was the fourth year he'd served as principal at Bath Consolidated. His lean face and dark wavy hair led some girls to think he was quite handsome.

We paused at the front step and said together, "Good morning, Mr. Huggett."

"Good morning." He seemed to be distracted, which was unlike him. "I'm glad to see you've made it to school, Bea. I hope that means your leg is better."

"In the cast, it seldom hurts," I said. "Though it itches something terrible."

"Terribly," he said.

"Yes, sir, terribly. Particularly at night." I was aware that I might be laying it on too thick. "It's fine, thank you, and I'm glad to be here to take my final exams." Once started, I couldn't stop myself. "But we have a problem." Mr. Huggett was looking out toward the street, and I suspected he already had an inkling where this was going. "Pa's truck wouldn't start this morning," I said, "so Jed and I rode Daisy in. And we can't leave her tied up to that tree all day."

Mr. Huggett nodded. "I suspect that would naturally lead to unfortunate results." This was another thing about our principal. There were moments when he appeared to express things in a subtly humorous fashion, something Mr. Huyck had never been known to do.

"Realizing that we can't leave Daisy tied up in the front yard of the school," I said, "we were wondering if Jed might be excused long enough to return her to our farm."

Mr. Huggett looked at Jed. "Do you have exams today?"

"No, sir," Jed said.

Mr. Huggett ran a hand down his clean-shaven cheek. "This is proving to be one of those days." Jed nor I knew what to make of that. We stood there, waiting while he seemed to check to see that he hadn't missed a whisker on his face. "It seems," he said, "that the generator is malfunctioning again, so we have no electricity. And . . . we have some water in the pipes, but the pump isn't operating, which inevitably will lead to problems, if we don't get power back soon."

Now he considered us with a seriousness of intent that was almost frightening. It meant we were in for one of his lectures. There was nothing to do but endure them, to nod and not shift from one leg to the other in a display of boredom or impatience. "These crews about town, from Consumer Power? It's none too soon. Bath is long overdue. We should have joined the twentieth century sooner. Other towns have already been wired for electricity—it's the future! We should have done this by now. The good news is that these crews are erecting their poles and stringing them with the necessary cables, so that soon everyone, every house, every building can be connected to the electric power grid." I glanced at Jed—I'm sure that neither of us had ever heard the phrase *power grid*—why would we?

"What this means," Mr. Huggett concluded, "is that when school opens next fall we will no longer be reliant upon the generator in the basement. Power will come up from the plant, miles away in Lansing. It will be a new day for Bath. But leaving a horse tied up in front of the school—and all that that *entails*—that might run counter to any sense of progress, don't you suppose?" We both nodded. "Yes, Jed you should return the horse and then hurry back here. When you return, come to the main office and we'll issue a note for your teacher." He drew back the sleeve of his suitcoat to consult his wrist watch. "It's nearly 8:30. Because we don't have power in the building, I will have to ring the opening bell manually." Something told me that he enjoyed the prospect of yanking on the heavy cord that hung from the bell in the hall outside the main office.

Jed handed my satchel of books to me, which I slung over my shoulder. As he walked quickly back toward Daisy, tied to a tree by the sidewalk, Mr. Huggett said, "And don't dawdle, young man."

"No, sir," Jed said as he untied the reins from the maple tree.

I followed Mr. Huggett inside the building, and continued down the hall, the rubber caps on the bottom of my crutches squeaking on the floorboards as I made my way to class. What was I feeling at that moment? Relief? Life's problems had solutions. I would take my exams, Daisy would be returned to her stall, and Jed would not be penalized for coming to class late. Other children walked past me, walked with a great sense of urgency—running was not allowed in school—desperate to get to their classrooms on time.

And then, behind me, from the far end of the hall came the sound of the bell. You didn't just hear it, you felt it. Mr. Huggett pulled the cord twice, and, if anything, the resonant chime seemed louder than on days when he merely set the hammer to metal by the press of a button. I remember thinking that, even after our school was connected to the *power grid* that would miraculously convey electricity to Bath, Mr. Huggett should continue to ring that bell by tugging on that cord. Progress wasn't everything. Something was bound to be lost. Some actions should be maintained until they become an established tradition.

Maybe those weren't my thoughts. I don't know. At the very least I know this: I loved that bell, which sounded more definitive, more authoritative when rung by hand.

In class, we often parsed sentences, drawing ornate diagrams on the blackboard: determine the parts of speech, the subjects, predicates, adjectives, adverbs, articles, and prepositions; and then carefully drawn horizontal and diagonal lines (using a ruler to make them straight); and write each word in its appropriate place, according to the rules of grammar, syntax, and punctuation. If successful, we could establish whether the sentence was correct. If not, its meaning and intent were not only compromised but inherently flawed. It was a game, a puzzle for some of us; for others it was a bloodless form of torture.

Though we have tried for years—for decades—we have not been able to parse the events of that morning in May. Despite the inquests and inquiries and investigations and examinations and interviews and studies, no one can say with absolute certainty what happened. We know the result, but we will never be certain of the how, let alone the why. In fact, the more I have learned over the years from reading (and rereading) about May 18, 1927, and from discussions with others who witnessed these events, the less certain I have become about all of it. Even recollection is clouded with doubt. Too often I've heard others question their memories—as have I—often concluding that they may not remember the sequence of events with anything that might approach objectivity or accuracy. We think we remember something, some moment, some feeling, some thought or impression. But then, we're not sure. We could be imagining it.

At times I've thought it peculiar that what we find to be most reliable are images. We all have images from that spring morning. We've carried them throughout our lives. They sustain us, even while they haunt us. They cannot be ignored or forgotten. They're a part of us, and we come to cherish them, for they're really all we have—suspended in our minds, lacking any corroboration or factual support, these images are everything.

Images tell the story.

Still, we try to parse it, break it down into its logical components and construct a diagram on the blackboard. But it's the images that bear a semblance to the truth.

▪ ▪ ▪

David Harte didn't know why, but the fire seemed to confirm something he'd known for a long time, at least since their dog had been shot. There were signs, so many signs that the man was tightly wound.

The explosions, they had to be Kehoe's doing.

The smoke and flames rising above the fields caused neighbors to rush to the Kehoes' farm, some on foot, while others arrived in a truck, car, tractor, or on horseback. It wasn't just the house or the corncrib or the barn. There was a rapid series of explosions—how many David wasn't sure—and everything on the property was ablaze. Smoke towered into the blue sky. He thought of the word engulfed—which likens fire to liquid. The house where Nellie Price was raised was entirely engulfed by flames, as was the barn, and all of the outbuildings except one. Burning wood creates a roar unlike anything else in nature. The fire generated such heat that it forced people to keep their distance, the air so hot—hot and windy, for the blaze seemed to have created its own miniature weather system—that they feared their clothes might burst into flames, that their hair might be instantaneously singed.

And then, incredibly, Kehoe was there. He arrived in his truck. Suit and tie, as always. He drove up past the burning house, his Ford disappearing in the smoke. No one could see what he was doing back there. But then he reappeared, emerging from the smoke and returning to his truck with a funnel in his hand. Why a funnel? No idea. Had he put anything in the truck? No idea. He had an almost a gleeful expression on his face. But what could this mean? At such moments people often react in an inexplicable manner. They laugh, they smile, with disaster and devastation all around them.

What was clear is that Kehoe showed no interest or surprise in the fact that his farm was burning up, nor that his wife was unaccounted for—that she might be trapped somewhere in the fire. He got in his truck, backed out to Clark Road, and drove east toward the village.

▪ ▪ ▪

As Jed rode Daisy along Main Street he watched the man in the sky. He wore a harness, a tool belt, and had large spikes strapped to the inside of his boots, which enabled him to climb to the top of one of the dozens of tall poles that had been erected along the roads in Bath by crews from Consumer Power. Jed loved to climb trees, loved to be high above the ground so he could see the lay of the land. The man's gear allowed him to do the impossible, climb a thick pole that went straight into the sky. No branches, no limbs. Defy gravity. Impossible: a current, an unseen power generated in a plant miles away, runs through wires, enabling you to turn on a light in your house.

Like Mr. Huggett, Jed's father had often said it was the best thing to happen in Bath during his lifetime: electricity. No more kerosene lanterns. No more buildings run on finicky gas-powered generators. Electric power that was constant and reliable. Months earlier, on a trip to Lansing, they went to a contractor's shop, where his father talked with a man about having their house wired for electric power. The man explained knob-and-tube installation, how the wires would be *fished* between wall studs and along ceiling joists. Jed imagined invisible trout and bluegills swimming about his bedroom. The man had a jovial confidence that made Jed suspicious, but then he showed them a selection of light switches, each mounted on an oblong brass plate in a display case. Some switches were knobs that were turned; others a pair of buttons, one above the other. The man said *Go ahead,* and Jed turned the switch, which lit the bulb at the top of the display case. Then he pushed the button, forcing the lower button to pop out, lighting another bulb. *Which one do you like, son?* Jed pushed the bottom button in, shutting off the light, and then he pushed the top button again, turning the light back on.

The combustion engine and electricity. Mr. Kehoe, his father, the Lansing salesman, they talked of the future as if it belonged to Jed, as if it were something for which he was already responsible. He excelled in mathematics, his teachers told his parents. When his father said he was good at figures, he might have been talking about a foreign language. He sounded both sad and proud.

▪ ▪ ▪

On the way to my class, I encountered Miss Weatherby in the hall. At the start of the day she often stood outside her door and greeted students as they arrived; it was a small, reassuring gesture: *We'll get through this day together.*

"Morning, Bea. You're leg's better?"

"Yes, Miss Weatherby, but . . ." I hesitated because I didn't want to sound as though I were complaining. "But everything seems more complicated." I explained about riding to school on horseback because my father's truck wouldn't start, and that Jed had to return our mare to the farm. "I just hope that Jed doesn't get in trouble for being late."

Miss Weatherby placed a hand on her small chin. She studied me for a moment, and once again I suspected she could see right inside me. She glanced down the hall, as though to be certain that we could not be overheard. "Well," she said, her eyes coming back to me. "What's her name?"

I felt caught. In a panic I thought she might be talking about a girl—a girl that Jed was interested in. "Who's name?" I whispered.

"Your mare, what's her name?"

"Oh." At this point, my full weight was on those crutches. "Her name is Daisy."

"How old?"

"How old?" I couldn't even think. "She's older than me, fifteen or sixteen."

"Excuse me?"

"I am . . . she's older than *I am.*"

Miss Weatherby smiled. "Ah. Now I understand." There was some commotion in her classroom. Voices were raised; there was high-pitched laughter. She turned and glanced through the window in the door. "I need to get their day started." Turning back to me, she said, "Everything will be fine, Bea. Now you should get along to your class."

"Yes," I said, out of breath. "I have an exam now. So—"

"Go now, with you," she said with a little shooing motion of her hand. "But don't try to walk too fast on those crutches." She began to open the door, but then turned to me once more. "I'm sure it's been trying, recuperation can seem tortuously slow." I nodded. "It's a matter of patience. Given time, in most cases, we are inclined to heal. Heart, mind, and body."

"Thank you, Miss Weatherby."

She gave me a smile, and a slight nod, and then went back inside her classroom, pulling the door shut behind her. I watched through the window for a moment. Her presence immediately brought calm and order to the classroom.

I was late. I would have some explaining to do. My excuse would be my leg, the cast, and the crutches, which again squeaked on the hardwood floor as I worked my way down the hall. They sounded like little animals, hamsters or mice, speaking in their own language.

▪ ▪ ▪

After leaving Daisy in her stall, Jed ran back to school. It felt good to run, to break a sweat. He jumped over ruts in the fields, leaped across puddles of standing water.

As he neared the line of trees just outside the village, he heard something.

A distant thud.

Birds in the trees flushed into the sky, screeching and cawing. He wasn't sure what direction the sound came from, so while still jogging he spun around and to the west he saw a column of smoke rising into the air. Whatever had happened was beyond the trees on the horizon. It could be a house or a barn. It could be someone's machine. It could be a farmer burning trash in his field, which was not uncommon. The railroad tracks ran out there, and it could be that something happened to a train, or the line gang had done something. Whatever it was, it was no small fire. The thud suggested an explosion.

Jed entered the woods, running faster. When he reached school, he would stop in the Main Office and tell someone about the explosion. They might already know what had happened. Or they might call the township's telephone switchboard office, which was in the Vail's house, down the hill on Main Street. When necessary, the operator Leonora Babcock sent out ten rings, the alarm signal, to all the phones in the township.

Jed emerged from the woods, and as he ran toward Main Street, there was another explosion—this time in front of him and its force knocked him down.

Lying on the sidewalk, dazed as he stared at the cloud of smoke darkening the sky overhead, an image came to him: he had once seen, from a distance across a field, a farmer shoot an old horse in the forehead, dropping the animal to the ground. The explosion was that sudden.

▪ ▪ ▪

When Harrington had arrived at school to inspect the generator, Frank Smith had taken him down into the basement. The school was actually two buildings: the north wing was the old school building, with a full basement under it; the new building, the south wing, had been erected over a crawl space no more than three feet high.

Harrington had just begun to inspect the water pump in the north wing basement, when there was an explosion, which threw both men against the stone foundation. Neither man was injured, though they were stunned and confused, and it was difficult to see through all the dust. The second explosion caused the entire structure above them to shudder, as though there were an earthquake, and then they heard and felt parts of the south wing collapsing.

▪ ▪ ▪

Since I'd broken my leg what had always been easy presented challenges. Stairs—I had to descend the stairs in the north wing. I took both crutches in my left hand so that I could clutch the banister with my right, and I found that first stepping down with my injured leg provided sufficient support while I then lowered myself with my good leg. I'd taken one step when the first explosion occurred behind me and I found myself lying on the landing halfway down the staircase. The air had turned to dust and smoke. I was covered with a white, gritty concrete powder. It reminded me of the sand that covered us after swimming in Round Lake. I don't recall hearing anything at first, probably because my eardrums had been concussed. For some time, the landing and the stairs above and below me continued to shudder, and I reached out and grabbed the nearest baluster, expecting everything around me to collapse at any moment. But it didn't. Things became still and I could barely see.

There was a sensation, a warm, liquid feeling inside my cast, and I wondered if I'd been cut, that I was bleeding. Sitting up, I saw that the plaster had cracked open—I thought of a clam shell, which I had only seen in books, the way the two halves can be forced apart—and I could see my leg. There was no blood. The skin was extremely white, though in places there were red creases, caused by tightness of the cast. When I moved my leg, the cast fell away, exposing my calf. (I had skinny legs at fourteen, and at this point the calf looked anemic.) I articulated my foot, proving that my ankle, which for some time had been held motionless in the cast, actually worked as it should.

Then I was standing. I don't remember getting to my feet, but I was standing, with both hands on the windowsill above the landing. The cast lay on the floor, two halves, opened on a jagged hinge. There was an indent in the plaster that I knew had not been there before, and something lay nearby on the floor, covered with dust. I didn't know what it was—I still don't, though I suspect that it might have been a right-angle piece of a pipe or a valve, perhaps from the plumbing or heating system. It appeared to be metal, and I began to recall that at the moment of the explosion something heavy had struck the cast, hard enough to crack it open. The projectile must have been ripped out of its proper place in the building—well back down the hall, I gathered, and been hurled at me at a speed I couldn't imagine. It was a piece of shrapnel. I understood then, and believe to this day, that had I not been wearing that cast my right leg might have been broken again or even severed.

The dust was getting heavier and, thinking the air outside would be cleaner, I leaned closer to the windowpanes, which contained shards of glass. The dust was so thick that I feared I was in danger of suffocating. I was careful of the broken glass, which covered the windowsill, and as I tried to breathe in air from outside the window, I saw a boy down below me. He was covered with dust, like he'd been rolled in flour. He lay face down in the grass, the white grass. He appeared to be asleep. I watched him, for I don't know how long, waiting for him to move.

▪ ▪ ▪

Jed lay on the sidewalk in front of the school. The first blast had knocked him down. It wasn't until later, much later, that he even realized that he had scraped his right elbow when breaking his fall. The second blast occurred as he was getting to his feet. This time he wasn't knocked down, but turned sideways so that he was looking north, down Main Street toward the village. In that moment there were only a few people on the sidewalks in front of stores. Jed had the sense that time had stopped. No one moved.

He was so close to the blast that his eardrums seem to have shut down in self-defense. The atmosphere about him had been transformed from the clear spring air he'd been breathing as he ran toward the village into something dense and thick with particles, as though a white cloud had miraculously descended on the school grounds. There came a series of thuds, which shook the ground, forcing him to spread his legs to keep his balance. He faced the school again. Smoke and dust made it difficult to see. The building—no, part of the building, the north wing—had collapsed.

There were bodies lying on the ground. Some writhing, some motionless. White, everything white. White bodies, making them unrecognizable, though Jed began to understand that they were children. Students from his school. All covered in this ghostly whiteness. He couldn't grasp how they got there, and wondered if they'd fallen from the sky.

No, they must have been blown out of the building, through windows, through walls as they exploded outward. One moment, in a classroom, sitting at their desks, standing at the chalkboard, and then here, flung into the yard, white.

There were sounds, loud enough to cut through his muffled hearing. Screams, shouts, cries. They came from some of the bodies on the ground, others from inside the building. Taking a few steps into the street, Jed could see them in the rubble that had been the north wing. He saw arms and legs—white, all white—sticking out from piles of brick, from between sections of plaster and lath walls, from a cockeyed window frame. Arms and legs that were black against the white, which he knew had to be blood. Arms and legs that were motionless, and some that wriggled in an attempt to get out from under the crushing weight of building material, bricks—so many bricks—splintered wooden two-by-fours, and electrical wiring, which lay in great serpentine coils, as though poised to strike.

And he saw heads in the rubble. One, a girl's face, trapped in a pile of bricks. Another, a scalp that seemed caved in on one side. A boy, who appeared to be asleep, his face lifted toward the sky.

Jed looked for crutches, for a leg with a cast on it. Not seeing any sign of Bea, he walked toward the building, but was stopped when a hand clutched his shoulder. More than anything, this sent a pang of fear through him, it was so unexpected. He looked up and a man was standing beside him. Jed knew the man, but for some reason he couldn't recall his name. "No, Jed. You keep clear now."

That's what Jed thought the man said. He could barely hear him. It bothered Jed that he couldn't think of this man's name—it just wouldn't come to him.

The man removed his hand from Jed's shoulder and ran toward the school building, fading into the cloud of white. Down the hill Jed saw them coming now, other adults, some running, others walking as fast as they could—help, adults coming to help, because something was happening to Jed's ears, he was able to hear better, or perhaps the screams and cries were getting louder, or they were coming from more children. They were shrieking, calling for help, calling for their mothers and fathers. They were begging for someone to come and get them out, to get it off them. They were frantic and frightened and their voices wouldn't stop, so that Jed could no longer stand there.

He ran across the street, into the white.

10.

As the entire Kehoe farm went up in flames, the heat intensified, forcing everyone to move farther back.

Then David Harte shouted, "*Nellie!*"

Others called her name as well, a keening, a pagan chant, a prayer: *Nellie Nellie Nellie!*

There was no sign of her. If she was in that house, she had to be dead.

Maybe she was still down in Lansing, at the hospital, or staying with her sisters, though Harte and his wife had last seen her Monday night, just the day before yesterday, when Kehoe brought her back from Lansing. She looked frail, needing help to climb the steps to the front porch.

■ ■ ■

Like a surveyor, Monty Ellsworth saw distances in rods. Sometimes he used the older terms of measurement, perch or pole, but it tended to confuse people. His farm was some 60 rods west of Kehoe's. When he heard the explosion, he was working in the melon patch in his garden. Black smoke rose above the Kehoe place; and then there was another explosion, farther east in the village, and then another, both louder than those that went off at the Kehoe farm. The sound frightened cattle grazing in nearby fields, causing them to scatter, and perhaps ten rods to the south, a horse that had been hitched to a plow broke free and ran across the field, its harness trailing behind.

Ellsworth's wife Mabel came out of the house screaming, "My God, the school is blowed up!"

He ran to his truck and started out for the village. He had the gas pedal to the floor, but the Ford wouldn't go any faster. The sky above the school was different, not black smoke indicating fire, but a white cloud rising up out of the trees. When he arrived on Main Street, it was what he imagined a war zone to be like. There were dozens of people on the hill, tending to the bodies—children mostly, caked in dust. Already they had begun to lay out the dead in a row in front of the school, covering them with anything that was brought from nearby houses—bedsheets, towels, curtains. Men and women stood and knelt over some of the bodies, crying, while others were in each other's arms. Dr. Crumm and his wife had come up from their pharmacy, and they appeared to be the only ones who could provide medical assistance to injured children. And young women, they were among the dead and wounded—though it was difficult to tell who they were because of the dust covering them from head to toe, they must have been the teachers. There was a great deal of blood.

Ellsworth approached the collapsed building, where the cries of other children trapped in the rubble could be heard. He had some experience with building structures. In fact, he'd purchased an abandoned tenant farmer's house from Kehoe some time back for $250, because he believed it was structurally sound, and moved it to his property. But he'd never seen anything like this. The vertical support of the building's walls—the bearing walls—had been destroyed by the blast, so that the roof and the second floor came down on the first floor. It reminded him of a stack of pancakes.

Ellsworth couldn't understand: How could a building, a brick building erected just five years earlier collapse like this? How much force did it take to cause such destruction?

He realized that the initial problem was that the roof was still largely intact, making it impossible to get at anyone who was trapped underneath—they were not going to get everyone out until they somehow pulled the roof away. Dozens of men and women were digging in the bricks with their bare hands. They were villagers, and there were also Consumer Power crewmen. Ellsworth joined them, tossing aside bricks and plaster and wood. No one knew what could be done about the roof. He said he had heavy duty cordage and block and tackle back at his farm. One of the power company crewmen looked down toward the village where they'd been working. He said they had cable, but it was already strung between the poles they'd erected. He looked at Ellsworth, as if to say you have to make the choice. Ellsworth didn't want to abandon the attempt at getting the children out, but the roof had to be moved.

▪ ▪ ▪

The boy lying in the grass didn't move. I kept watching him until I realized that he was dead.

I managed to get from the landing down the remainder of the stairs to the first floor, and was reassured to see that the hallway in the south wing appeared not to be damaged other than broken glass from some display cases glinting on the floor. Two teachers, Miss Sterling and Miss Gutekunst, had their students lined up in rows, everything orderly and quiet, the way they did during fire drills. I hobbled down the corridor toward them—without the cast, my right leg wasn't as strong—and got in line behind the children, who were all first and second graders. They looked up at me, confused and frightened. They understood that this was not just another drill. At the head of the column, their teachers told them to walk toward the door at the end of the hall, and not to run. I followed the children, herding a couple of girls ahead of me. Frank Smith, the janitor, was there, as well, urging them on, and the one-armed man who did repairs on the school generator, Mr. Harrington, held the door open. The children moved slowly but steadily toward the door and the dusty air outside. I expected there to be another explosion at any moment. I'm sure we all did—yet we didn't panic. We waited our turn to file through the open door. That's the way we were brought up in Bath. Think of others. Get in line. Wait your turn.

Ever since that day I've had dreams about that door. It's always held open by Mr. Harrington, there is a line of children ahead of me, and I can't walk fast enough with my bad leg and my crutches. My heart races because the door recedes, though sometimes the hallway extends, becoming longer and longer, making the light from outside smaller and farther away. When the children stop moving toward the door, I ask what's holding them up, and they turn around and speak in a foreign language, which I don't understand. But Miss Sterling interprets.

Didn't you take Latin, Beatrice? She pronounces my name *Be-ah-TREE-chay.*

Yes, but it was years ago.

The children all stand in line, staring up at me with abnormally big eyes.

Miss Sterling says, *Io fui gia quel che voi siete e quel ch'io sono voi anco sarete.*

Is that Latin or Italian?

You should be able to translate. Miss Sterling, never one to give you an answer, expects you to find it yourself. She turns and walks toward the door, the children following.

Wait . . . I know! It means: I once was what now you are, and what I am, you shall yet be.

She stops, and when she turns around, she whispers, *That's not what the children are saying, Beatrice.*

What are they saying?

They're saying that none of us deserves to get out of this building.

And then the dream always ends with an explosion in the distance that wakes me up.

▪ ▪ ▪

As Monty Ellsworth drove out to his farm to get rope, block and tackle, a Ford pickup passed him heading east toward the village.

Kehoe.

He raised his hand off the steering wheel—in greeting?—and he grinned.

At that moment, Monty knew something. He didn't yet understand it, but he knew it.

Kehoe.

Monty felt it had always been there, that he had always known it.

▪ ▪ ▪

Superintendent Emory Huyck had been in the assembly hall, overseeing an exam when two blasts jarred the building. Overhead, the hanging globe ceiling lights oscillated perilously. Cracks had appeared in the plaster, but the walls seemed to be holding. It was as though some great force were rotating the room. The sounds coming from the north wing had to mean that that portion of the building was collapsing.

The assembly hall windows were perhaps a dozen feet above the ground.

One of the senior boys climbed out an open window and, despite Huyck's admonishments, jumped. Huyck went to the window and put his hands on the sill, avoiding the shards of glass. The boy had landed on the roof of a shed below the window, and then he jumped again, sprawling on the ground and rolling across the grass.

Other high school students had crowded at the windows to each side of Huyck. "We should wait," he said in a loud but calm voice.

They began climbing out the windows and leaping to the shed roof, and then to the ground.

"*Wait,* I said. Someone will bring a ladder."

They kept jumping. Some got up off the ground, limping, but they all got away from the building as best they could.

There were now screams and cries coming from the north wing. When all of the students in the assembly hall had leapt to safety, Huyck brushed the glass off the windowsill and climbed out. He was a short, compact man in his thirties. He'd been a good athlete when younger, and when in the army had trained for combat. He jumped, landing on the roof, and then he dropped the remaining distance to the ground. In the effort, he felt his shirt tear under his suitcoat.

He ran around to the front of the school, where bodies littered the yard. People were already digging in the rubble. There were shouts and screams. He couldn't imagine the cause of such an explosion, other than the generator or the boiler, but it seemed inconceivable that either would cause such extensive damage.

A boy was lying in the grass, unconscious but alive. Because of the dust it took a moment to realize it was Carlton Hollister, a fifth grader. Carlton had a bruise above his left eye, and his hair was slick with blood. Huyck picked the boy up and began walking. He walked across the lawn and down Main Street, carrying the boy all the way to the Vail's house, where the Bath telephone exchange was located. The front door was ajar, and he went in and lay the boy on a couch.

Leonora Babcock was at the switchboard. She was still in her teens, and she'd left school to take this job. She was clearly nervous but looked resolute. "I've already sent out the ten-ring alarm," she said. "Next, I'll call Lansing." She looked at Carlton. "And I'll see what can be done for him."

"Right. We need help from the police and fire departments. Doctors, nurses. And ambulances." Huyck went to the door. Main Street was now filled with cars and trucks, and people swarmed up the sidewalks. The blasts had been such that windows were shattered throughout the village. "And call St. John's and see what they can send down." He went outside and began walking up the hill toward the school.

▪ ▪ ▪

As he drove toward the village, Kehoe passed Ellsworth's truck heading the other way. It was only the previous Friday morning that he had gone to Monty's farm, where they'd arranged to take some target practice. Kehoe brought cardboard targets, which they set up in Monty's pasture, and then they took turns shooting with their rifles, from first one hundred yards and then fifty yards. Kehoe was the better shot, and Monty was impressed by his bolt-action Winchester. After letting him shoot with it, Kehoe offered to trade his Winchester for Monty's rifle plus twenty-five dollars. The fool made a counteroffer of ten dollars, so they didn't strike a deal. Now the Winchester lay on the bench seat beside Kehoe in the truck.

His rifle to Monty.

His one-eyed horse to McMullen.

Try to give them something to remember him by, and they don't get it.

And they would never appreciate the planning that was involved. The trips to Lansing and Jackson to purchase the necessary ordnance, and stealing crates of dynamite and pyrotol from road construction sites in the middle of the night. The electrical installation alone was a first-rate job. Everything on the farm wired to go up, the house, the barn, all the outbuildings. And at the school, they would be impressed—no, stunned—by how many hours it took to plant that much dynamite. The problem was the new building, the north wing. The old building had a full basement, where it was easy to run wires high up along joists, placing them in the dark against the subflooring so they wouldn't be detected. You'd have to know what you were looking for, and few people other than Frank Smith spent much time down there. The new wing, however, didn't have a basement, just a crawl space. For all the money they spent on that building, you'd think it would come with a proper basement. In order to get the charges and the wires deep into the back corners of the crawl space, he used metal eaves troughs, running long sections back into that tight dark space. Then he inserted bamboo fishing poles to push the dynamite and the blasting caps, connected to the wiring, all the way down the eavestroughs until they reached the corners under the first floor. It took countless trips late at night to haul the materials into the school, all the while leaving no visible evidence around the workbench he'd set up in the basement. Just performing the usual maintenance jobs requested of him. No compensation other than four dollars a day. All that money going to taxes, and his labor thrown in for almost nothing. That's what they expected. And when he'd lose the farm, no one, none of them would connect it with those taxes. No, some would—he wasn't the only one close to selling or foreclosure. Plenty of other farmers around Bath were on the brink. He could see it in their faces. They'd been hopeful when he first got involved with the school board, when he stood up to the others and raised the issue of the cost of the school. The high contract bids, the nepotism, the overruns, the excesses. There were people about town who appreciated what he was doing. They'd give him a nod, or in private some would say quietly, *Glad you're speaking up—somebody's got to tell them what this is doing to us.* But where were they, where was his support when it came to these elections, last year for the treasurer's position, and then this spring for justice of the peace? Where were they? They don't vote their conscious, don't vote with conviction. The votes evaporated. That boy, Jed, he might get it. Could have used him to climb up in that crawl space and push everything through the dirt to the corners of the building. He would appreciate the work involved. Tell him about spark plugs and pistons and combustion and you can see that he's taking it all in. Heard from someone, one of the parents, he was good in math. He'd have done all right. Why? Because he listens. Keeps his mouth shut, watches and listens.

▪ ▪ ▪

After Floyd Huggett rang the gong bell to announce the beginning of the school day, he had walked next door to the Methodist church. As principal, he was responsible for organizing the commencement ceremony that was scheduled in the church for the next day, Thursday. He worked with two students, Thelma Cressman and Bertha Kumm, who were to give readings during the ceremony.

Standing erect behind the pulpit, Thelma read three stanzas of a poem, and then looked out at him.

"Very good, Thelma. You're enunciating every syllable. But we all have a tendency to speed up when reading in front of an audience. This time, read it slowly."

She nodded, uncertainly.

"And pause between phrases. Inhale. The secret to public speaking is remembering to breathe."

As she looked down at the sheet of paper in her hands, an explosion struck the school, shaking the church so that pews clattered as they tipped over. Then came the second explosion.

Huggett looked at the girls up by the altar. Bertha had fallen to the floor, while Thelma was gripping the pulpit with both arms. "Are you all right?" he asked.

Bertha got to her feet. "Yes."

"Stay here, please. Both of you."

As he ran down the aisle toward the front doors, screams and cries could be heard outside the church. He was one of the first to reach the school. One of the students, Jed Browne, the one Huggett had allowed to take Bea Turcott's mare home, was hurrying across the street toward the school. Huggett put a hand on his shoulder and told him to stand clear. The boy gazed up at him. He didn't appear to be injured, though he looked confused. Huggett left the boy, ran toward the school and begin digging through the rubble, his hands soon bloodied from the rough edges of the bricks.

▪ ▪ ▪

While Ellsworth went to his farm for the rope and block and tackle, men at the school considered the problem of the roof while they continued the process of pulling debris aside. They agreed that they needed leverage. A pole, a long pole might work.

Jay Pope and his son-in-law Lawrence Hart walked out to the street, where they saw Superintendent Huyck's wife Ethel, who taught music at Bath Consolidated.

"There are telephone poles nearby," Hart said to her. "We need to tow one up here."

Ethel looked at her sedan, parked at the curb. "You could take our car, but Emory has the keys and I have no idea where he is."

Hart took a jackknife from his pocket. "Mind if I try, Ethel?"

She nodded, and he got in behind the steering wheel. He reached under the dashboard, and when he found the ignition cables, he cut them and skinned back the insulation; when he connected the exposed wires, the engine started. He and his father-in-law drove three blocks to a pile of telephone poles that had not yet been installed by the Consumer Power crews. There were other men there and they helped get a pole tied to the fender of the car. Frank Smith's younger brother Glenn, who was the postmaster, rode with them back up the hill to the school.

▪ ▪ ▪

I've never felt such a sense of relief—the relief of finally escaping through the south wing door, of being outside, where I wasn't confined to a structure of walls and ceilings that threatened to crash down on me at any moment. Since that day, so many years ago, I've rarely felt safe being indoors, and have often looked at walls and ceilings—even this ceiling—believing they could cave in at any moment.

When I got outside the school building, my fear gave way to something else. I hobbled around the grounds until I could see the destroyed north wing. My stomach churned and I thought I might throw up. I felt woozy—even with the crutches I found it difficult to keep my balance. My recollections have distilled those moments down to a few images. Bodies motionless on the ground, their postures impossibly awkward. A boy, his eyes closed, moaning for his mother. A girl's body hanging upside down from the wreckage, her feet tangled in electrical wires. Two men were trying to get her down, as though by eradicating that one image they might eliminate the rest of them.

My hearing seemed impaired. I could hear some things, but not others. There was the sound of sirens—police cars and ambulances had begun to arrive. I heard voices, children trapped in the building calling out, some screaming. For moments, however, I became keenly aware of the birds high in the trees above Main Street. Black birds—starlings, I believe—and they put up a steady chatter, as though they were debating what had happened to all those people down there. I wondered what the birds made of this. I still wonder. What do they think of us, these two-legged beings that don't fly but build houses and drive machines and pour concrete and asphalt on the surface of the earth—what does this mean to birds? I suspect their thoughts are confined to the constant search for food and safe shelter. But somehow they must understand that a scene such as the one below them on that spring day was not the result of a species that is more advanced than they are—no matter what we tell ourselves.

A woman was speaking to me. I looked away from the trees. Her mouth was moving, but I couldn't hear her at first. I think I said, "What did you say?" I might have shouted. I don't know.

She was about my mother's age, forty, or close to it. As she placed her hand on my shoulder, I realized I knew who she was but couldn't recall her name. (This has been happening with greater frequency since that day, and I don't know if the school disaster is the cause or if it's just the natural deterioration of my memory.) The woman leaned down toward my face and spoke slowly. I suspected she was asking if I was injured. She might have thought I'd been hurt in the bombing and had somehow already acquired the crutches, as unlikely as that seemed. At that point nothing made much sense, nothing was beyond the realm of possibility. A phrase I often think about: *the realm of possibility.*

I glanced down at my pale, withered leg and said, "I lost my cast."

"Did you, dear?" She didn't know my name either, and I liked her all the better for it.

"I left it on the stairs."

"We'll get you a new one. Soon." Her hand was trying to guide me away from the building, from the crowd that by then had gathered at the edge of the rubble, sorting through the debris. When I resisted, she said, "Let's get you back this way, where it's safe."

"Safe? But I need to find him."

"Who?"

"Jed. He returned the horse."

"Did he now?"

"I need to find out if he got back here in time. Mr. Huggett told him not to dawdle, and that's not like him anyway. He's very responsible, you know. It's unusual in a twelve-year-old boy but it's true."

Her hand became firmer. But I resisted. She probably thought I was hysterical. Maybe I was, I don't know. I'm quite sure I shouted then, but I'm not certain. I might have screamed. After that, I don't remember anything.

■ ■ ■

As he walked back up Main Street, Emory Huyck saw two men carrying the limp body of a child into Frank Smith's house directly across from the school. Frank's wife Leone was holding the door open. Huyck went up the steps and followed her into the house. Villagers, mostly women, attended to injured children lying on blankets spread on the floor, on the sofa, and two stuffed chairs. There was a great deal of whimpering and crying.

"I'm keeping them here," Leone said, "until they can be driven down to the hospitals in Lansing. Word has gone out to come here with a car or truck."

"Good," the superintendent said. "We've put calls out to Lansing, St. John's, Dewitt. Ambulances should arrive soon. You have room for more?"

"Yes, I'm now putting them in the bedrooms. Neighbors are upstairs with them, and next door they're making sandwiches and coffee. This is going to go on for some time and people will need to eat."

"Thank you, Leone," he said.

She accompanied him to the front door. "Frank was in the basement when it happened. He and Harrington. He came over to tell me he was all right, and to get ready for the injured children. I saw the police arrive. I think some of them have gone down to inspect the basement in the north wing to see if they can determine what happened. Frank said it wasn't the generator or the boiler. If that's what caused this explosion, he and Harrington would be dead."

Huyck went out on the front steps and looked back at her. There was blood on her print dress. "I'm glad Frank's all right."

Across the street, Huyck's sedan pulled up to the curb in front of the school. But his wife wasn't in the car. Instead Jay Pope, Lawrence Hart, and Glenn Smith got out and began to untie a telephone pole that had been lashed to the fender. Glenn was Leone's brother-in-law. Jay was Lawrence's father-in-law. Other men came to help, including Glenn's father-in-law Nelson McFarren. Everything and everyone in Bath seemed connected one way or the other. When Huyck took the position as superintendent, he soon realized this about the town. Many of them were related by blood, by marriage. Recently he had informed the school board that he would be leaving at the end of the school year, moving on to another job. It had not been an easy decision. Maybe it was the wrong decision. Maybe, despite the devastation here, he was meant to stay. "What incredible people," Huyck said in wonder. He turned and looked back at Leone, who nodded once, as though she'd been expecting him to finally see it, come to this realization. "The whole town of Bath. Everyone's turning out to lend a hand."

▪ ▪ ▪

Jed had a brick in each hand when he saw the leg.

A girl's leg, caked in dust. Short white sock and a tiny shoe.

Too small.

It wasn't Bea.

A man climbed up toward Jed, his feet unsteady on the bricks and plaster. He shouted, "We've got one here!" Looking at Jed, he said quietly. "Good job, son. But you shouldn't be here. Whyn't you get back down on the grass with the others."

He got down on both knees carefully and began removing bricks around the girl's leg.

As other men came to help dig the girl out, Jed climbed across the debris to his right. He began again to pick up bricks and toss them on the grass below and behind him.

11.

Kehoe wanted to survey the result of his labors. He wanted to look them in the eye and see if any of them understood now. People will believe what they want to believe. The truth was another story. It's the last thing they want to know. You just have to tell them right. You have to demonstrate it to them before they'll believe it. All the lies, all the distractions are designed to keep them from the thing they fear most about themselves, about each other: the truth.

It's interesting how clear things become once you make up your mind. When he talked to Nellie's sisters on the phone last night, it was effortless.

"She's not here," he'd said into the phone.

"Nellie's not up there with you in Bath? Where is she?"

"She's visiting friends in Jackson."

"She's in Jackson? Today?"

"Yes."

"I don't believe it."

"Drove her down there myself."

She held the phone away from her stupid mouth and said to the other one, "She's in Jackson!"

The other one said something. It sounded like "I don't believe it. Nellie's so frail. She was with us, for I don't know how long, and she was so tired. Why would she go down to Jackson the day after she got home?"

"I told you," he said, careful not to raise his voice, "she's visiting friends, because she wanted to see them. Isn't that why you visit friends?"

Her silence on the line was skeptical. He decided not to fill it. They had a lot of nerve to even talk to him—they've been working on Nellie to leave Bath and come live with them in Lansing—but they don't have the nerve to challenge him directly. Their attorney Joseph Dunnebeck was hired to do that. This business about the mortgage. For years they expected him to pay for a farm that was grossly overpriced. All of them, the sisters and the cousins, sitting down there in Lansing, living off the reputation of Lawrence Price, a big deal in the state capital. Living off his money, what it was. They'd gotten to her. He'd seen it in her eyes as she sat in the living room. She didn't want to be there, she wanted to be back in Lansing, where her sisters would wait on her hand and foot. They said they felt guilty. (They never felt guilty about anything.) After their mother died, Nellie, the oldest sister, raised them practically on her own, so they felt they owed her. Leave your lawfully wedded husband, come back to Lansing, and we'll take good care of you. And we'll get the farm back, sell it, and get the money that's owed us. She believed them; it was for the best—that's what was in her eyes as she sat in the living room, the blanket over her lap. She drank tea. He sat, gazing out the window at the two horses that were left in his field. He'd have to do something about them, too. He waited, wanting to see how she'd approach it. She never came at a thing straight on. Not anymore. Always some roundabout way. Talk about this and lead up to that. She talked about the hospital, how well the nurses treated her at St. Lawrence. Then about how nice it was at her sisters', being close to the hospital and her doctors and all. These frequent trips between Bath and Lansing were so exhausting.

"I always drive you," he had said. "I take you to Lansing whenever there's the need."

It was like she didn't hear him.

"Since my last surgery, everything is more difficult now. Being closer to the doctors would be more sensible."

"Sensible. That's your favorite word."

"What? What are you saying, Andrew?"

"You don't know what sensible is. You never will."

When he stood up, there was the briefest moment where it registered in her eyes: alarm. Something about his movements, unexpected and abrupt, raised doubt.

"I'm just going in the kitchen for a moment." Reassuring. The truth. He was just going in the kitchen. As if he needed a reason to walk into his own kitchen. "Would you like me to make more tea?"

"No, there was plenty left in the pot."

"Would you like me to warm that up?"

"No, thank you, it's hot enough."

He paused in the doorway to the kitchen and looked back across the living room. She was staring out the bay windows that faced west. The sun was low enough that light streamed across her face.

▪ ▪ ▪

Leone Smith stood in her front doorway, watching Emory Huyck walk back toward the school. Frank had told her that Huyck would be leaving at the end of the school year. It wasn't public knowledge yet, but word was getting around, quietly. Frank was sorry the superintendent was leaving but not surprised. A bright young man like that; the kind who always thought that there was a better opportunity elsewhere. Leone wondered how his wife Ethel felt about it. She would have to leave her position as music teacher.

There was such a crowd now on the front lawn of the school. Some had brought wounded children to her house, while others had taken them down the street toward the village. The dead ones, she suspected. What they did with them, she didn't know, but she was thankful that they didn't bring those into her house. There was no organization, people just did what they thought best. One of the men who had brought an injured child to the house mentioned Bert Detluff, the widowed blacksmith. His daughter had a cut in her ankle. He had taken her home, made sure she was comfortable in bed, and then he returned to the school and got back to work digging other children out of the debris. Mr. Huyck was right; it was remarkable in its own way, how everyone pitched in. Tending to the injured. Driving them as quickly as possible down to a hospital in Lansing. Even making sandwiches and coffee.

Another explosion sounded in the distance. Someone said they were coming from the Kehoe farm. Leone couldn't believe it—the school, the farm, none of it made sense.

She needed to get back inside and help out. The children in the living room, their cries and moans. But she lingered just a moment longer, watching the crowd in front of the school, watching as Superintendent Huyck, approached them. He had an authority about him. He was not a big man, but there was something about his bearing. Impeccably dressed in a suit, white shirt, and tie. He strode across Main Street looking as though he were in charge. He nodded to people, said a few words, but keep on, moving toward the school. He was calm, composed. They needed that then.

Huyck stopped by his car, which the other men had used to drag the telephone pole to the school. He was right: so many of them were connected by blood and marriage. Frank's brother, Glenn, in his post office uniform, leaned against the car fender. Leone couldn't hear the men, but it was clear that they were discussing how best to use the pole to move sections of the roof that had remained intact. Monty Ellsworth had returned from his farm with rope and block and tackle. That roof was the biggest obstacle to getting everyone out from under that rubble.

As the men stood on the sidewalk, a Ford truck pulled up behind Huyck's sedan. There were so many Fords, cars and pickups; they were everywhere in 1927. It was hard to differentiate between them. Andrew Kehoe got out of the truck. It made sense to Leone: even if there was something wrong at his farm, he would be there at the school. A member of the school board, even though he and Nellie had no children, no loved ones attending Bath Consolidated School. Everyone was making sacrifices that day. He should be there. He was needed. Few people knew the school better than Andrew Kehoe. When the building required maintenance or repairs, he saw to it, either doing the work himself or finding someone who could fix the problem. *What incredible people.* Is that what Emory Huyck said before he left her front door stoop?

Leone watched the superintendent leave the group of men who were untying the pole from the fender of his car and walk over to Kehoe. They spoke briefly, standing next to his Ford truck. With people milling about in the street, it was hard for Leone to see them. For a moment she thought they might be arguing, she couldn't be sure. They must have been debating how to deal with this, how to get that section of roof pulled off the rubble. It was interesting, she thought, because everyone knew of the adversarial relationship between the two men. And Kehoe did seem agitated. Perhaps because of the problem, whatever it was, out at his farm. Perhaps because of something Huyck said. Leone just couldn't be sure, and the people and cars in the street kept getting in her way, blocking her view.

She turned to go back inside her house. As she began to close the front door it happened, another explosion, right there in the street. Her living room windows broke and she would have been knocked to the floor if she hadn't been holding on to the door. She leaned against the jamb and looked at the smoke and flames where Kehoe's truck had been parked on the curb.

▪ ▪ ▪

I must have fainted, there in front of the school. When I came to, I remembered her name, Mrs. Beamer. Edna Beamer. Lived on a farm east of the village. She was older than I'd first thought. She had just helped me to my feet, when it happened. An explosion changes the atmosphere. The air becomes a physical force. I was knocked to the ground again, and I discovered the woman lying next to me, one arm draped over my shoulder protectively. My hearing was terribly muffled. The blast had come from the street, not the school. Mrs. Beamer lay still, and I thought she was dead. I moved her arm carefully and got to my feet. I wanted to hear clearly. It was all a pantomime. People were tending to the fallen. Fear, horror, shock, agony, all acted out in the swirling dust.

Mrs. Beamer shifted on the ground, reaching for her leg. Something was embedded in her calf. I helped her stand up, and we began to walk, our roles reversed—I had my arm about her thick waist and she favored that leg. It didn't occur to me until much later, but I had left my crutches behind on the grass. I never went back to retrieve them. Never used crutches again, never bothered to have the cast replaced. I didn't know where Mrs. Beamer and I were going, we were just walking, dazed, when a man I didn't know came and helped her to an ambulance that had just arrived on Main Street.

I stood there between the school and the sidewalk. More people were injured. More people, apparently, had been killed. The smoke made it difficult to breathe, but my hearing had improved enough that I heard a woman ask if there were bombs falling from the trees or out of the sky. A group of people had gathered around a man lying near the smoldering remnant of the truck that had been the source of the blast—it was the postman, Glenn Smith, who was the brother of Mr. Smith the school's janitor. Other vehicles parked nearby were damaged, windshields shattered, roof fabric in tatters. Some were on fire. There was that smell of burning rubber, and something else I couldn't identify. A car headlamp hung by its wire from one of the power cables that had been strung between telephone poles. And there was something else hanging up there. I stared at it, trying to comprehend what it was, but then I knew and I couldn't look at it any longer.

It occurred to me that before I fainted I had been searching for Jed. I turned toward the school, where several men were carrying a body out of the wreckage of the building. It was a boy. It might have been Jed. I couldn't be sure. Despite the ache in my leg, I ran toward the men as they lay the boy on the grass.

The boy's face was covered with blood, but it wasn't Jed. I kept searching for him. Everyone was dazed. Some people moved slowly, as though they'd just awakened, while others rushed about, seeing to the injured. And then I saw him, lying on his back on the white grass, close to a pile of bricks.

▪ ▪ ▪

When Jed opened his eyes he stared up at Bea's face.

"*You're not dead!*" she shouted.

"No, I guess not."

"*Are you hurt?*"

"I don't think so. When it went off, I was knocked down."

"*You're sure you're not hurt?*"

"You don't need to shout."

"*What?*"

She was about to shout something else, but hesitated when he raised a hand, indicating she should wait. He placed his hand on his chest . . . *I* . . . then made an OK circle with his thumb and forefinger . . . *am all right.*

Though tears welled in her eyes, she smiled. But then her face darkened, and she said, quietly, "My sister. We have to find Alma."

He nodded and got to his feet. They began to walk. The yard in front of the school was crowded. There were nurses now, in white uniforms and caps, and a number of police and firemen in uniform. The uniforms were reassuring. They were attempting to usher the crowd back toward the street and to cordon off the lawn in front of the school. Sirens sounded near and far.

Jed and Bea must have drifted among the crowd, asking people they knew if they'd seen Alma. No one had.

"You're sure she got to school on time?" Jed asked finally.

"Yes. She was nervous about the exams and she left very early. The exam was going to be given by Mr. Huyck in the assembly hall."

"That part of the building didn't come down."

They worked their way out to Main Street, which was thronged with people and vehicles, many of them ambulances being loaded with the injured. After crossing the street, they saw Alma sitting on the stoop in front of a house, holding a glass of water. They rushed across the trodden grass.

"You're safe," Bea said. She wasn't shouting now but her voice was breaking.

Alma stared up at her younger sister, and then at Jed. "Warren."

"Are you sure?" Bea asked.

"I'm sure."

"You saw him?"

"Yes. They dug him out."

Bea sat down on the stoop next to her sister. Until that moment Jed never saw much of a resemblance between them. Though she was younger, Bea was taller, her hair, cut just above her shoulders, swirling around her face as a breeze came along Main Street. Alma had thick darker hair, and she was fleshy like a grown woman, or so it seemed to Jed. But the jawline and the set of the eyes, angled to each side of their nose ridge, they were definitely siblings.

Alma gazed down into the glass, held with both hands. "Isosceles triangle."

"What?" Bea asked.

"On my exam, there was an isosceles triangle." Alma took a sip of her water and stared into the glass as though she didn't know how it got into her hands.

12.

The three of us sat on that stoop for what seemed a long time. We learned things from overheard conversations. People were beginning to piece together what had happened, how it had happened. And to this day, I'm still trying to piece together what happened.

Andrew Kehoe had packed his truck with dynamite. The air reeked of it—that was the sweet odor, which some say smells like almonds. The explosion was so powerful that it drove screws out of the door lock in a house across the street. Not only had his machine been rigged out as a bomb, he had loaded it with boxes of scrap metal: nuts, bolts, nails, screws, empty bullet casings. Shrapnel struck people more than a block away from the truck. Down Main Street in the village, Anna Perrone, the wife of the rail gang foreman, had been holding her infant Rose in her arms, with her toddler Dominic next to her, when a piece of metal blinded her in one eye. Her children weren't injured. Cleo Clayton, an eight-year-old boy who had survived the collapse of the school unharmed, had a bolt rip through his stomach and break his spine. The father of three students, F. M. Fritz, was hit by a bolt that entered his chest and deflected off of bone until it worked its way down into his left bicep. Like a worm boring blindly through an apple. The bolt was removed and he survived, though his daughter Marjory had been killed when the school collapsed. One of the men closest to Kehoe's Ford, Nelson McFarren, who had been assisting with the telephone pole tethered to Mr. Huyck's car, was found dead, his body hurled against a tree trunk. His son-in-law Glenn Smith, the postmaster, took the blast on the left side of his body, causing severe burns, and his leg was severed at the thigh. One of the electric company crewmen tried to use his belt as a tourniquet, and our veterinarian, Dr. Rice, attempted to save the postmaster, but nothing could be done. Skin and muscle hung from branches and power lines. The truck's steering wheel was draped with intestines. One man cut some of the flesh away and placed it in a jar of alcohol, presumably as a souvenir.

Two hours after the school explosions occurred, the police cleared the area in front of the ruins. In the basement of the south wing, they had discovered more dynamite, which for whatever reason had not detonated. They brought out long sections of eaves troughs and bamboo poles, two hot shot batteries, and massive tangled coils of wire and crates of explosives.

It was becoming clear that this was not some freak accident, was not, as many suspected, some kind of gas-related ignition, but the work of one man, Andrew Kehoe, a member of the school board, who must have worked for weeks, perhaps months, at this murderous project. He had been methodical, thorough, and exacting. In the aftermath, we began to recall things about Kehoe, which at the time seemed, if not entirely innocent, certainly not threatening. He bought a lot of explosives, which was not uncommon for farmers who wanted to clear the land of trees and boulders. He once explained to his neighbor Job Sleight, who on more than one occasion had driven him to Lansing and Jackson where Kehoe made some of his purchases, that he'd could sell his surplus ordnance to other farmers for a bit of a profit. Kehoe had only bought his own Ford pickup about a year earlier, so he'd been stockpiling explosives on his farm for years. When Sleight made the connection between their trips together and this result, he was physically sickened. People who lived on Main Street now recalled seeing on more than one occasion a pickup driving around behind the school late at night. They didn't think it unusual or worrisome, but now understood that Kehoe had set up the explosives while Bath's children were asleep in their beds.

We were in awe of the amount of material that the police removed from the basement. Kehoe's handiwork, the police had to admit, was impressive. The wires connecting the blasting caps to the batteries had been fed along beams and joists in places where they would be difficult to detect. Kehoe had stapled the wires every three feet. The day of the bombing, police retrieved more than five hundred pounds of unexploded dynamite and pyrotol, leading us to speculate how much had been installed throughout the structure with the intention of bringing the entire building down. Some of the dynamite crates were labeled *Bureau of Public Roads,* which suggested that they'd been stolen from state road construction crews.

Once the police determined that the building was safe from further explosions, the efforts to find buried victims resumed. As more people arrived in Bath, there was the need to control the crowd and traffic. Busloads of men were driven in from the Oldsmobile, Reo, and Fischer Body plants in Lansing; likewise, students in the ROTC program at Michigan State College. The Red Cross opened a clinic in Dr. Crumm's pharmacy and a temporary morgue was established in the town hall. Journalists set up a press room in a shed behind the telephone exchange; others occupied the train depot, sitting on wood benches as they pounded out reports on typewriters. Police and fire officials imposed greater order to rescue efforts, but there was an increased sense of urgency as time was running out for possible survivors who were still buried. It took dozens of men, using heavy cables, to pull a section of the roof away. Freed, two ghostly boys caked in white dust rose up out of the rubble and ran off, like cats scattering before danger.

■ ■ ■

At about eleven o'clock Leone Smith was exhausted and needed a breath of fresh air. She stepped out her kitchen door—she was wary of using her front door. Staring across the backyard at their garden seemed an absurd consolation. She and Frank had turned the soil, which after the rain overnight was black and rich, and this weekend they intended to begin planting. Frank's brother Glenn had promised to stop by to lend a hand. Leone's favorite time of year, planting season. Lettuce, tomatoes, rhubarb. She'd been thinking maybe a row of melons this year. She loved the new grass and budding trees, and then the flowers. It would not be long before the fragrance of lilacs filled the air.

Leone turned to go back into the house when something caught her eye, and she walked across the yard. She didn't know what it was, an article of clothing? As she made her way into the garden, dirt filled her shoes, and she tried to step carefully.

There was a jacket in the dirt and she began to take deep breaths.

Not just a jacket. It was a body—part of a body—encased in a suitcoat. The face had been driven into the dirt, and the hair on the back of the head was matted with blood.

Something protruded from the side pocket, and she bent down and removed it—a bank book and a Michigan driver's license. She didn't have her reading glasses with her. Even holding the documents up close to her face, she couldn't read the print.

She walked out of the garden, planning to return to the house for her glasses, when she looked up the side yard to the street, where a car just pulled over to the curb. Printed on the door:

Sheriff
Clinton County

▪ ▪ ▪

The older of the two men who got out of the car was Bart Fox, the sheriff from St. John's, some twenty miles to the north. The other man, the driver, William Searl, was younger and he immediately rushed across the street toward the crowd.

Bart Fox stood with his suitcoat thrown back and his hands on his hips as he stared at the damaged vehicles and the demolished school. He needed to talk to police already on the scene to get a read on what had gone on here. It was a war zone, with an audience.

"Sheriff Fox?" A woman's voice, behind him.

He turned and watched her cross the yard to the sidewalk. She walked uncomfortably, as though her feet hurt or she had something in her shoes. Her print dress was smeared with blood.

"I'm Frank Smith's wife, Leone."

Her husband Frank had dealt with Fox's office occasionally in matters pertaining to the school, inspections and such. "Yes?"

"I don't have my spectacles." She handed something to him. "I can't read this."

It almost sounded like it was his fault.

"Well." He opened the bank book in his hand. "The Lilley State Bank, in Tecumseh. That's way down by Ann Arbor." He read the typed name, ink blotting the half-circle in the top of the *P:* "Andrew P. Kehoe." Studying the driver's license, he said, "And this is his license, issued just last year . . . February 17."

He gazed at Mrs. Smith. She appeared exhausted but agitated.

"Would you accompany me to my garden, just down back this way?"

Without waiting for his response, she turned and began walking down the side of the house.

Bart Fox felt a growing agitation himself. There wasn't the time for someone's garden. He looked across the street at William Searl, whose bright red hair was easy to spot in the crowd. The county prosecutor was eager, too eager, perhaps, but he was sharp. Ran in the family—his father was Judge Searl, down in Lansing. The school building was half collapsed, and there was wreckage from a second incident, an explosion, here on the street. People were gathered around the smoldering frame of what must have been a Ford pickup. Bart looked for a police uniform, someone with rank, but only saw patrolmen and a few state troopers attempting to control the crowd in front of the school.

He turned toward the backyard, where Mrs. Smith was waiting by an oblong patch of dirt, seeming not so much impatient, for she was someone who ordinarily respected authority, but piqued that he did not comprehend her mission. "Yes, coming," he said as he started across the new spring grass.

Beyond her there was nothing but an oblong garden patch, perhaps twenty yards long and half as wide. She walked on, stepping over the uneven soil in shoes with low heels.

He saw it: at the far end of the garden something lay in the dirt, not exactly buried but seemingly driven part way into the ground, as though it had been dropped from some great height. The colors had nothing to do with flowers, vegetables, or gardens.

▪ ▪ ▪

Shortly after arriving at Bath Consolidated, William Searl, Clinton County's prosecutor, walked down into the village, where he was told he would find the telephone exchange. There were reporters all about, most of them behind the house because extra phone lines had been set up for the press. The young woman at the switchboard, a teenager named Leonora, got him settled in a relatively quiet corner out of sight of the journalists, where he could use a telephone.

He called his father, who had been practicing law in Lansing for as long as Bill could remember, and now also served as a district judge. Nothing ever seemed to surprise his father, though when his secretary put Bill through to his office, his deep voice sounded a bit curious—Wednesday morning, when they were both busy with their respective duties, wasn't ordinarily a time when they'd phone each other.

After Bill explained where he was and why, his father said, "Bath? This happened up in Bath?"

Since he and Sheriff Fox had arrived, Bill's stomach had become increasingly sour. It started as soon as they were in sight of the school and the damage to vehicles and surrounding houses. Bill had immediately waded into the crowd—leaving the sheriff behind—and sought information from members of the state police, the fire marshal, anyone who was there in an official capacity. What they told him had caused his bowels to churn and he felt lightheaded. Walking down to the telephone exchange, he hoped would allow him to collect himself. Along with the row of bodies in front of the school, he'd seen that a number of spectators had fainted. It wouldn't do for the county prosecutor to pass out.

"Yes, this morning. There must be dozens dead, most of them children. And there are sure to be more buried in that school building."

"A bomb?" his father asked. "Are you sure?"

"The police came up from the basement with wires and more dynamite than I've ever laid eyes on." Bill hesitated. He could see his father sitting in his office in downtown Lansing. As a boy, he was sometimes allowed to visit him there, and the shelves of law books were both intriguing and intimidating—when he was young he thought of their uniformity, lined up row upon row, as soldiers standing shoulder to shoulder. As he got older, particularly when he began his legal studies, he came to think of the law as a form of defense, the only means we have of fighting against tyranny and chaos. "Dad," he said quietly. His father waited. There were times when he could expound—that was the only word for it—but he also knew when it was essential that he just listen. Bill could hear his shallow breathing, the result of too many years of pipe and cigar smoking. "I can't say this with certainty at this point, but there are indications, clear indications, that we know who did this."

His father's breathing halted.

"Andrew Kehoe."

Bill waited as his father inhaled slowly.

"My client?"

"'Fraid so. Not long before Bart Fox and I arrived, Kehoe drove into the village in his pickup and blew it up, right in front of the school. People were killed. Maimed. And he took the school superintendent with him."

After a moment, his father cleared his throat.

"Kehoe wired the entire school," Bill said, "but fortunately only part of it went up. His farm, they've had a series of explosions out there as well, and the entire place is burning to the ground. It's too hot for anyone to do anything." He knew what was coming, so he said, "We don't know. No one has any idea where his wife is."

His father seemed to hold the phone closer to his mouth as he whispered, "This . . . it's so . . . but in this profession one comes to realize that we never know what a person is capable of."

"You're not surprised, not entirely?"

"No, Bill. I can't say that I am. Kehoe was . . ."

He left it at that.

The two men, father and son, maintained silence for a good while, until Bill said, "The police and fire chiefs, Bart Fox, all those who are taking charge of this—I'm younger than they are."

"You're the county prosecutor. You have a job to do."

"I've never dealt with anything like this before."

"No one has."

"I suppose. Help is pouring in from all around. I should get back out there. Much to do. We have to get a positive ID on every one of them."

"All right, then." His father had never been one for goodbyes, something that often pained and sometimes irked Bill's mother. He was more inclined to conclude a conversation as though there were nothing more to say. Or, perhaps, as though this was only a brief hiatus, and the thread of the discussion would be picked up in the future. But this time his father cleared his throat once more, and said, "You'll be fine, Bill. Let me know what I can do." He hung up.

▪ ▪ ▪

As they worked their way across the garden, Sheriff Fox had taken Leone Smith's arm, but when they reached the middle of the plot, she hesitated.

He removed his hand from her elbow and continued on until he reached the back of the garden, where he bent over, his hands on his knees. Without turning, he said, "Do you recognize him?"

"I didn't see the face, just took the documents from the pocket."

He reached down with one hand and cleared dirt away from the head.

She looked away. It was like those embarrassing moments during a doctor's appointment, which seemed unendurable and overly long, and then the examination was completed.

As the sheriff came back toward her, he brushed dirt off his hands. "He must have been right by the truck. It's a fair distance from there to here. I don't know if we'll find the rest of him."

"Our superintendent, Mr. Huyck, he was there, too."

The sheriff looked about the yard. "We'll have to keep an eye out for him."

"And the postmaster, my husband's brother . . ."

It was clear to Leone that Sheriff Fox must have spent much of his career dealing with violent crime, with accidents, with the injured and the dead. Now, as he gazed across the street toward the school a moment, he appeared incredulous, baffled. "I've never . . . I mean, nothing like this. I'm sorry."

Leone wanted this over; she wanted to get back inside her house and tend to the children. She began walking back toward her house. When he tried to come up beside her, in fear that he would touch her elbow again, she said, "*Don't.*"

He remained in the middle of the garden. When she reached the grass, she looked back at him. "I'll need to find someone to give a positive ID," he said apologetically.

"There's plenty of people in this village who can help you." She climbed the stairs to the back door. "Get your positive ID. Then you get *that* out of my garden."

In the living room, children were being attended to by her neighbors. They were cleaning wounds, ringing out cloths in bowls and pans of water that were pink with blood. Leone went up to the second floor, where a nurse was just coming out of the bedroom. A tall woman, with wire-frame spectacles. The blood on the skirt of her uniform made Leone think of the butcher down at the grocery.

"I'm afraid that one didn't make it. I'll have someone take the body out."

"How long have you been here?"

"We were driven up from Lansing as soon as we got word. There are more coming."

Leone didn't know if she was referring to more nurses or children. She was too tired to ask. There were injured and dying children in every room now. No place to go. She sat down on the top step of the staircase. "My husband, he's the janitor at the school. He was in the basement at the time of the explosion."

The nurse sat next to her. "He's all right?"

"Yes, he's over there helping dig them out. His brother Glenn died right across the street. We were going to plant the garden this weekend. Glenn offered to help out. Now, I don't know that we'll plant anything."

"You're very kind to do this."

Leone removed one of her shoes and tapped the dirt from the garden out on the step. Ordinarily, she would never pour dirt on her floor. Her house would never feel clean again. "Kindness has nothing to do with it."

In the distance, there was a sound, an unfamiliar noise, which seemed to be coming from the sky.

"It's the airplane," the nurse said. "Some of the reporters were talking about how a Chicago newspaper was having a plane come over from Detroit. It'll pick up the photographers' negatives, and then fly on to Chicago. The pictures will be in newspapers across the country by the evening edition." The nurse removed her glasses and wiped them with a handkerchief. "Everybody's caught up with this race," she said. "New York to Paris. Nonstop. Can you believe such a thing?"

Leone had seen the photographs. She couldn't think of his name. A tall young man standing by his plane. Blonde, absurdly handsome, wearing leather jacket and boots; jodhpurs and a helmet with goggles on his forehead. Why couldn't she remember his name? At breakfast yesterday or the day before—yes, the day before—Frank had looked up from the *Lansing State Journal* and said, "All the students are excited about this. They want to know if someone can actually survive such a thing. What's the world coming to—flying across the Atlantic Ocean, nonstop from New York to Paris?"

Leone turned to the nurse, who despite an officious appearance had compassionate eyes. "Lindbergh. His name is Lindbergh. These children, they'll never know if he made it."

13.

Alma sat between us on the front stoop of the house two doors down from Frank and Leone Smith's. Some man, a stranger, had come up Main Street, carrying a wooden crate of Vernor's ginger ale. He opened a bottle for each of us. Said they were from the grocery and then moved on to another group of children. He might have been distributing a sacrament.

We nursed our Vernor's, spectators watching the spectators. A constant line of vehicles crept through the throng that crowded Main Street. Uniformed state patrolmen tried to direct traffic, and eventually roadblocks were set up at both ends of the village. The proximity of curiosity and anguish created a strange relief as out-of-town gawkers mingled with people from Bath. From the school came the sound of bricks being tossed—the inexorable sound of brick striking brick, an oddly fragile sound, not unlike Aunt Ginny's china teacups being placed in their saucers.

Alma was gripping my hand as though she feared I'd let go. A few hours earlier this would have been unthinkable. We had always been adversaries. She was the older sister, the presumptive leader. She often reminded me that in the alphabet *A* comes before *B;* that she deserved to be served first, to get the bigger portion, the newer article of clothing. It was her birthright. I must wait my turn and be thankful for leftovers and hand-me-downs. In the past year, as I grew taller, she treated me like a usurper and a cheat.

What we had in common was Warren. Each in our own way, we wanted him. But Alma actually loved the boy and desired a life with the man he would become. My desire for him—if that's even the word—was far more abstract. I didn't want to love Warren so much as the *idea* of being in love with Warren. Alma loved his bold, daring antics. She believed he would never become dull or boring. Even at that moment, with this tragic pageant playing out before us on Main Street, I could imagine Warren and Alma as an old couple who still shared inside jokes and a lightness in their voices when they replied *Yes, Dear.* I sensed that my sister was not just hurt but damaged. As we held hands, I began to realize that what had happened that morning would change our lives.

There came a strange noise—at first I couldn't place it—a sound that seemed to transform the air, grew louder, a sputtering noise that overwhelmed the sound of the tossed bricks, and then everyone was gazing up at the sky. How remarkable: a biplane flying above Bath. I tried to imagine what it looked like down below, our fields, our houses. The plane carved a low arc above the village, and we could see the pilot's helmet, his goggles, a pair of disks glinting in the sun.

Jed raised his arms as though holding an imaginary rifle and, following the plane's flight path, mouthed what sounded like gunshots.

▪ ▪ ▪

Sitting on the front steps, nursing our Vernor's, we continued to learn things in stages, by word of mouth. With all the reporters and photographers swarming the village, it was clear that this was news that was going out to the rest of the world by telephone, telegraph, and broadcasts on the wireless. Photographs were picked up by a World War I pilot ace in the biplane that soared overhead, and they were flown directly to Chicago. In some ways, this seemed more unreal than the actual incidents. It wasn't just that it happened, but that it happened in Bath. In the newspapers and radio broadcasts, we were described as a small farming community. A quiet village. A place where people work the land, tend to their livestock, and nothing ever really happens. As though something like this should only be possible in a city, not here in the countryside of Michigan. By early afternoon, the news reports attributed these heinous acts to Andrew P. Kehoe. His head and torso, found in the Smith's garden, had been identified by a neighbor, Sydney Howell, and one of Kehoe's adversaries during his confrontations with the school board, Mel Kyes. Kehoe was described in headlines as a monster and a maniac. The day before he had been a neighbor.

There was speculation and rumor about Nellie. The Lansing Fire Department's chemical truck was sent to the Kehoe farm. The house, the barn, and all the outbuildings, except the chicken coop, had burned to the ground. Only the brick chimney remained standing, straight and erect. All of the shade trees around the house had been girdled, a deep swath having been cut in the bark around the base of each trunk. The grapevine roots had all been sawed off at the ground, the roots then carefully placed on the stumps to conceal their destruction. Electrical wires ran from batteries in the house to all the outbuildings, but for some reason the connection had failed in the henhouse. The carcasses of Kehoe's two horses, one of them the one-eyed Kit, were found in the charred remnants of the barn. Their hooves had been bound with wire so they couldn't escape their stalls.

Firemen poured two sixty-gallon barrels of fire-retardant chemicals on the smoldering ruins of the farmhouse in an effort to reduce the heat, but there was no evidence of Nellie.

They did find a hand-painted wooden sign Kehoe had hung from a fence post:

Criminals are made, not born.

▪ ▪ ▪

After attorney Joseph Dunnebeck finished lunch at the Olds Hotel in downtown Lansing, he saw a special afternoon edition of the *State Journal,* which identified Andrew P. Kehoe as the perpetrator of the disaster in Bath. He returned to his office and was not surprised to find Nellie's sisters, Elizabeth, Genevieve, and Loretta, waiting to see him. He'd represented the Price family for years. They told him they'd spoken to Andrew by phone only the night before; he had said Nellie was visiting friends named Vorst in Jackson. Dunnebeck located the Vorst's address, and during the forty-mile drive south, the sisters discussed how they would break the news to Nellie, considering her fragile state. They noted that Andrew had originally planned to pick Nellie up at the hospital this past Sunday, May 15, which was their wedding anniversary. But because of the damp weather and how it might affect her lungs, her doctor suggested that she remain in the hospital until Monday.

▪ ▪ ▪

By afternoon, Prosecutor William Searl's stomach went from bad to worse, when Bart Fox told him that Kehoe had shipped a package from the Bath train depot early that morning. Sheriff Fox got this from a trooper, who had first spoken to the agent in the depot office. Searl and Fox were standing outside the town hall, where the deceased had been brought for positive identification. Though some people cried and wailed, Searl had come to realize that many of the parents showed little or no emotion when identifying their child. They would stare and nod, or say a simple *Yes, this one's ours.* In some ways, it was more difficult to deal with people in such a state. When asked questions about age and addresses, they didn't seem to hear you. They appeared to stare into a place where no one else could go.

Fox said, "State police are conducting a search of the stations along the Michigan Central line between Bath and Lansing."

"Another search." Searl shook his head. "How're you fixed for butts? I'm running low."

Fox took from his coat pocket a pack of cigarettes and a box of matches. "They're not looking for a *package.* Christ. It was a wooden crate—with the word *dynamite* stamped on the side." He offered Searl a cigarette and struck a match.

"And it was shipped?" Searl leaned into the flame.

"Yes. The agent said he thought it was just an old crate. He didn't think—well, who would?"

Searl drew in on his cigarette. They were all smoking constantly, as though it would keep the worst of this at a distance. "He knows where it was shipped? I mean, they keep records of that."

Fox gazed across Main Street. Though there were roadblocks set up outside the village, the town was full of people who just wanted to walk by the school and see what had happened. They were quiet, even respectful, but there were so many of them now that more of the police and state troopers were needed to keep them from interfering with the rescue efforts.

"The package was addressed to Lansing. To a law office. I have it here." Fox took a notebook from his coat pocket and began to flip through the pages. "Yes, it went to an attorney named . . . Clyde Smith?"

"I know him," Searl said. "Kehoe used to be my father's client, but since he'd become a judge, Clyde has been Kehoe's lawyer. We have to get in touch with him immediately."

"I just came from the telephone exchange," Fox said. "Already called there. The package hasn't arrived at his office. It was supposed to go on a train from here to Lansing. It should have gotten there around midday. Nobody has a clue where it is." He took one last deep drag and dropped his cigarette on the ground and crushed it with his heel. "Funny. All day I'm dealing with people named Smith. It's a common name, but what are the odds?"

"Odds?" Searl said. "There are two families that have lost loved ones—named Hart and the other Harte, one ending with an *e*, the other without. I'm not sure but I think they're related by marriage. The Harte's—with an *e*—live right across the street from Kehoe's place. It's hard to keep it all straight, but I think their daughter-in-law taught at the school and was taken to the hospital. And they had a grandson in the school. . . . I'm just not sure."

"Smith and Smith. Hart and Harte," Fox said. "Here, there are no odds."

▪ ▪ ▪

Pa found us sitting on the stoop on Main Street. He tried not to seem upset, but he wanted to know where my crutches were, and the cast on my leg.

"I'm fine," I said.

"I still can't get my truck started, so I went across and borrowed the Traver's. I'm parked several blocks away—the traffic coming in here, I've never seen anything like it." He was watching Alma, and when he looked at me, I shrugged. "We need to get you home. Your mother is in a state. The only way I kept her from coming was by saying that she should be there in case you got home on your own."

"I don't want to go," I said.

Hands shoved in the pockets of his overalls, his way of exercising authority. "Bea."

"No."

He looked across the street toward the school. He didn't like confrontation, least not with his girls. It was as though that was Ma's job. "You can't walk home. Can you even walk to the truck?"

"With dead children over there, how can you ask if I can walk?"

Immediately, I regretted saying it. It was as though I were blaming Pa, when I knew none of this was his fault. "I can walk fine," I said. "Take Alma home." She was still holding my hand, and when she squeezed my fingers, I realized that she didn't want to be separated from me. More than anything that happened that day, this seemed the most incredible thing—Alma had spent her life keeping above and clear of her little sister.

Pa could see there was something going on here that he had no experience with, no answer for, and he turned his attention to Jed, who was trying not to be a part of this. "We spoke to your folks on the phone," Pa said. "Told them I'd find you and get you home, too."

Jed was not a boy to defy an adult. None of us was, usually—we weren't raised that way. But he stared up at my father and said, "I'll stay here with Bea, sir. We'll find our way home all right."

Pa stared at the three empty bottles of Vernor's lined up on the bottom step. "Your mother," he said, "she'll have my hide."

"No, she won't," I said, though I knew he was right. "Pa, please, just take Alma home." For a moment I thought I might cry, but pleading was the last thing I wanted—if I pleaded with him, I would have lost and we'd all be on our way home. "They're not all out of it yet. We need to stay."

Jed added, "I'll try to find her crutches."

Pa seemed at a loss. Distraught. I didn't realize then how this was affecting him, or Ma, or any of the parents. It wasn't until years later, when I was a parent myself, that I knew the constancy and depth of their anguish. At the moment, Pa seemed unable to move as he gazed at the crowd and the demolished school. I know he wanted to go across the street and help out, but he had been sent to collect us and bring us out of the village.

Alma let go of my hand and, standing, stepped up close to him, so he put his arms around her. "You want to go home, sweetheart?" he whispered.

She lay her head against his forearm. I always loved Pa's forearms; she did too.

"Okay." He looked at Jed and me with a new resolve. "You two stick together, hear?"

Jed and I nodded.

Once more Pa looked across the street, incredulous, shaking his head, and then, taking Alma's hand, they started to weave through the crowd that had gathered on Main Street.

▪ ▪ ▪

Nellie was not at the Vorst's farm in Jackson, and she had not visited them as her husband had said. Dunnebeck drove her sisters back to Lansing. They were inconsolable. When they reached his office, he made phone calls, talking to the police, the Lansing fire department, and hospital administrators. According to a woman named Abrams, who was a case worker for the Social Services Bureau, which had been given the task of confirming the dead, there was still no clear accounting of who the bombing victims were, and more were being found beneath the rubble. He talked to the county prosecutor Bill Searl, Judge Searl's son, who was up in Bath along with Sheriff Bart Fox. No one knew where Nellie Kehoe was, and word came back from the farm that the destruction there was so complete and still so hot that it was impossible to thoroughly search the ruins.

Nellie's sisters sat in Dunnebeck's office, not touching the coffee his secretary had brought in; they had been animated in their alarm during the drive back from Jackson, but now they barely whispered to each other. Dunnebeck frequently dealt with survivors, people who sat in his office while he read the contents of a relative's will. He'd seen remorse and sorrow; he'd seen the guilt and shame, and the anger, that often followed a death. This was something else. Though the sisters had said they still couldn't believe that Andrew was capable of such a thing, Dunnebeck believed that they actually knew he was—still, they were unprepared to acknowledge it. The range of emotions expressed did not include surprise. However, Nellie's fate—the not knowing—was far more devastating.

He was about to suggest that he drive them home, where they might rest, when the phone rang.

▪ ▪ ▪

Bill Searl was smoking his last cigarette when Dunnebeck answered his call. From the telephone exchange in the Vail house, Searl could look down Bath's Main Street. The sidewalks were crammed with people. It was clear that most weren't from the town by the way they gawked, staring in windows of the shops, an implements store, a barber shop and pool room, the pharmacy and ice cream parlor, the People's Bank, the DeLamarter Hotel. Even the cucumber brine station was regarded as significant in the light of such unimaginable tragedy.

"Are Nellie Kehoe's sisters still there?" he asked.

"They're sitting right here across my desk." Dunnebeck kept his voice neutral, calm, certainly with the intention to not excite the women.

"Tell them that we still have no news of their sister."

Dunnebeck's receiver was muffled—he must have covered the mouthpiece as he spoke to them. Searl inhaled slowly on his cigarette, trying to make it last.

"They understand that everything is being done there in Bath," Dunnebeck said.

"We are getting more help from outside. Doctors, nurses, ambulances. It's quite remarkable how everyone is pitching in. But I'd like you to convey a question to them."

"Of course."

"There was a package," Searl said. "Andrew took a wooden crate to the train station here early this morning, to be sent down to his lawyer's office—Clyde Smith."

"Yes, I know Clyde."

Searl hesitated and decided not to mention that the crate had originally been used to store dynamite. "It hasn't arrived in Lansing. Not at the station, nor at Smith's office. There's no sign of it, and Smith says he wasn't expecting any package." Searl took a deeper drag, feeling the heat of the tobacco on his fingers. "We don't know what's in the crate. Ask them if they have any idea what Kehoe might have sent to Smith."

Again, Dunnebeck muffled his phone, and the conversation that ensued, which went on longer than Searl expected, sounded as though it were conducted under water.

Finally, Dunnebeck said, "They have no idea."

"Not surprised, but I thought I'd ask. Tell them that we're still looking for their sister."

"I will." Dunnebeck rang off.

Searl stubbed out his cigarette in the ashtray that was full and got to his feet. Earlier he had thought that eating something might help settle his stomach, and he'd had half a chicken salad sandwich offered by a woman who'd come into the town hall with a basket of sandwiches and a thermos of coffee. The sandwich tasted fine, but if anything, Searl's stomach was in greater distress.

He went outside and walked down to the town hall, where Bart Fox was coming down the front steps. He lit a cigarette. "It's getting a bit ripe in there."

"I'm out of butts."

Fox offered him the pack, which was nearly full. "That's it. I got the last of what the pharmacy has in stock."

Searl lit his cigarette, letting the smoke linger before exhaling. "How can someone mail a crate marked dynamite and no one take notice? How can such a thing just disappear?"

Fox shrugged. "He could have put a timer in it. His work may not be finished. Out at the farm, the only thing that didn't burn down was the chicken coop. For some reason it didn't go off. The ground is still too scorched—they probably won't be able to conduct a thorough search till tomorrow. But they did find a device that Kehoe had made. Quite ingenious. A tin pan with a glass jar standing in it upside down. The jar was filled with gasoline, and there was a spark plug, which was attached to a wire that ran from the coop to the house, where there was a battery. The best part is there was not one chicken in that coop. Still, he wanted to blow it up." He glanced at Searl as if to prepare him because there was more. "There are rumors going around the locals here."

"Rumors?"

"The way this was done, they wonder if he's not alone in it. They have a point. Just look at the wiring job on the school—one man got all that stuff into the basement and rigged it up? They think he might have accomplices who are planning to blow something else up. People are checking their houses, looking for wires, anything suspicious. Cops are starting to help out." Fox flicked his cigarette into the street. "If I lived here, I'd be looking too."

■ ■ ■

The traffic was so bad that it took Joseph Dunnebeck several hours to drive the Price sisters the ten miles up to Bath. When they finally arrived at Clark Road, the farm where the sisters had been raised was a smoldering ruin. They briefly visited with David and Lulu Harte across the road, learning that they had lost a grandson and that their daughter-in-law, Blanche, who taught at the school, was in a Lansing hospital with injuries they'd been told were grave.

■ ■ ■

By late afternoon, volunteers digging in the rubble at the school had filled five-gallon pails with fingers, hands, feet, human remains that could not be identified with certainty.

They found Heather Weatherby beneath a pile of bricks. She was sitting in her desk chair, a child in each arm.

■ ■ ■

Late in the evening Searl learned that Kehoe's crate had been discovered at the train depot in Laingsburg, about ten miles from Bath. Apparently, the address had been misread at the station in Bath, and the parcel had been shipped north instead of south to the law offices of Clyde Smith in Lansing. The return address was merely *Andrew P. Kehoe.*

Police put the crate on a truck and drove it to Lansing—at twenty miles an hour, the road ahead being inspected for bumps and ruts that might jostle the cargo. When they arrived at the state police barracks, the crate was left overnight in the parade grounds, a safe distance from the barracks, to await inspection by bomb experts.

Searl remained in Bath until after midnight. He had spent much of the day making arrangements for identifying bodies. His stomach only got worse. Tomorrow he would begin to organize the inquest, which he feared would be a drawn-out affair involving depositions and the impossible task of reconciling contrary facts and information. He would be responsible for compiling a record of these events, an official accounting that would become history in which statistics would replace blood.

■ ■ ■

I don't remember how Jed and I got home. Though so much about that day is still vivid in my mind, some things have just disappeared, and no matter how hard I try to recall them they're just gone.

I know it was after we learned that Miss Weatherby's body had been found. When I heard that, I said to Jed that it was time for us to leave. I remember holding his hand as we were led to someone's Ford. But I don't recall much of the trip or who drove us. It wasn't Pa, and it wasn't Jed's father. I was so exhausted I fell asleep in the back seat. I believe there were two men sitting in the front seat, and I vaguely recalled being lifted out of the car. The last thing I remember of that night was being in Pa's arms as he climbed the steps to our front porch.

14.

Jed couldn't sleep. Sometime after midnight he climbed out his bedroom window and lay on the shallow-pitched kitchen roof that ran off the back of the house. Wrapped in his blanket, he could lie comfortably on the roof, still slightly warm from the day's heat, and stare up at the sky. He loved the smell of cedar shingles and he could use the Big Dipper to find the North Star. He was facing north, which allowed him to imagine himself as the needle in a compass.

He couldn't stop thinking about Mr. Kehoe. At first, there was doubt, and then disbelief among most of the villagers, but after the explosion of Kehoe's truck, there seemed to be no question that he was responsible for all of it. Jed believed that Mr. Kehoe could do such a thing. He didn't know *why,* but there was something about the man that seemed at odds with the world. The way he surveyed his land that lay fallow. The thorough way he examined the damage after they'd blown up another tree stump. The way he sucked on his cigar, making the end glow a bright color that might be a small circular piece of hell.

Jed's classmates were dead. Miss Weatherby and Mr. Huyck were dead. Mr. Kehoe was dead. He had wanted to kill them all but had failed. He had explained to Jed how spark plugs and pistons work. He talked about the nature of a criminal. He talked about the future—told Jed his future was electricity and the combustion engine. He could have killed Jed in the woods, blown him up with one of the tree stumps. But he didn't—he wanted to blow him up in the school with the others. Jed was supposed to be in school yesterday morning, but he had returned Daisy to her stall. The old mare had saved his life.

He wondered where his classmates and the others were now. In church they spoke of heaven. Jed wondered if it was really up there, beyond the stars. And hell—wherever that was—Mr. Kehoe might be there now, burning eternally, like the ash on his cigar. Jed wanted to know why he was lying there, wrapped in his blanket on the kitchen roof. They also talked in church about God's purpose, as though that explains everything. What was the purpose of any of this? He wanted to know why he wasn't dead like the others.

▪ ▪ ▪

Police and fire departments from around the state were sending help. Early Thursday morning two men from the Saginaw Sheriff's Department drove down to the Kehoe farm. Ray Cole and John Ward had heard about Nellie Kehoe's disappearance and the anguish it had caused her sisters. The search on Wednesday had ranged far and wide, without any result. Cole and Ward wanted a look at the farm once the heat from the fires had subsided. The state police had placed two young troopers on guard at the farm during the night. When Cole and Ward arrived, they told the troopers to take a cigarette break while they inspected what was left of the farmhouse. The ruins were cool enough to traverse but they found nothing.

One of the troopers, George Carpenter, called to them. They walked across the barren earth to the back of the chicken coop, the only structure that hadn't been consumed by fire. Carpenter had found the charred body of a woman lying beneath the axle connecting two large metal wheels. She was on her back, her right arm raised up and draped over the axle. The left arm had broken off, and the right leg appeared to be broken. Corset stays protruded from the torso.

"A wheelbarrow," Cole said. "Everything but the metal burned."

"It's a homemade job," Ward replied as he picked up a nearby stick. "Could have been a hog chute."

He positioned himself so he wouldn't disturb the corpse and with the stick prodded the box that was partially buried in the ashes beside the woman's torso. It was a metal treasure chest, the paint peeling. "Looky here," he said, as he raised the lid with the stick. Using a handkerchief, he began to remove the objects from the box and lay them on the ground. Silverware. A woman's wristwatch. A set of teaspoons with *K* etched in the handle. Two rings. A brooch on a chain. A pair of earrings. A pin from the organization called The Maccabees.

Then Ward reached inside the box and removed the last items, badly singed paper. A roll of money, or possibly World War I Liberty Bonds—it was impossible to tell. There were also medical bills from hospitals in Detroit and Lansing. Finally, the Kehoe's marriage license.

Cole shoved his hands in the pockets of his trousers. "Ground was so hot, they didn't find this yesterday. I'd say she was laid in the barrow and wheeled out here from the house. Look at the crack in the skull. The heat from the fire could have done that. Or a blow to the head with a blunt instrument. No knowing if she was dead or alive when she burned."

Ward folded up his handkerchief as he stood up. "Family heirlooms," he said. "Almost like a ritual, sacrificing the dead and sending them off with their valuables."

Cole looked at the young state trooper, who was still smoking his cigarette. "Nice work, son."

Carpenter seemed uncertain how to take this; he dropped his cigarette butt to the ground and crushed it with his boot.

Cole stared at the farm on the other side of Clark Road. There was a large coop, and he could hear chickens. Wires led from a telephone pole to the house. "They have a phone."

Both men walked toward the road, working their way around the charred remnants of the Kehoe farm.

▪ ▪ ▪

David Harte held the curtain aside in the front-door window and watched them coming. Two men in suits and fedoras going over the ground until one of the young troopers who'd been there all night found something back near Kehoe's chicken coop. As they crossed the road, Harte saw something in their gait. Slow, resolute, but urgent. He opened his front door and stepped out on the porch.

The smaller of the two men glanced at the name on the mailbox, then looked up at the porch, "Mind if we use your telephone?"

"Police?"

"Yes, sir. Ray Cole and John Ward. Down from Saginaw."

"You find her?"

The two men exchanged a look, as though to debate whether they should answer. The bigger fellow, John Ward, said, "We've found remains over there."

"Nellie. You found Nellie Kehoe."

Cole said, "There'll have to be an examination to determine the identity."

"You better come in then. My wife's still in bed, and I hope she's able to get some sleep." He stared across the road a moment, not sure how to say it, not sure if he could say it. "We lost family yesterday," his voice sounding strained as it came up out of him. "And our daughter-in-law, who taught at the school, was taken to the hospital in Lansing."

"We understand," Cole said. "Sorry to trouble you."

They climbed the porch steps and removed their hats as they entered the house. Harte pulled the front door shut carefully and then led them down the hall to the kitchen. "Phone's there on the wall," he said. "I just made the coffee."

Cole went to the phone and took the receiver off the hook.

"Much obliged," John Ward said.

Harte poured coffee into three mugs. Cole spoke quietly, leaning so that his mouth was up close to the hand-crank phone on the wall. Harte came to the kitchen table and sat across from Ward.

"Milk? Sugar?"

"Black's fine. Thanks."

Harte added two teaspoons of sugar from the bowl in the center of the table. From Cole's conversation, he assumed that he had called the county prosecutor's office. He said the name William Searl, which Harte had heard several times the day before.

"There will be a lot of activity over there today," John Ward said. "The place'll have to be cordoned off while they conduct their investigation." He took a sip of his coffee. "You been neighbors long?"

"Years," Harte said. "Farm belonged to Nellie's family, and then she and Andrew bought it nearly a decade ago." Ward's gaze was even, noncommittal. He looked like a man who had done police work for a long time. "There were signs, I guess. Nobody could deny that Kehoe was peculiar. But this—something like this: never. Even when he shot our dog some time back, there seemed some logic to it. But I thought it strange the way he was letting the land go, and taking out the trees at the back of the property. Then he started selling things off. Chickens, livestock—everything but the two horses that burned up in that barn. He tied up their legs so they couldn't escape." Harte took a sip of his coffee. "What's that tell you about a man?"

■ ■ ■

Lulu Harte lay in their bed on the second floor. The men in the kitchen were trying to be quiet, speaking softly, but their voices came up through the heat grate that was directly above the stove. There was a moment during the night—she'd not slept at all—when there was absolute silence. It had a weight to it. As she'd gotten older, she'd become increasingly sensitive to sound. A lot of folks her age were hard of hearing, some plain deaf. Lulu sometimes thought she could hear everything all at once. During the day, their house was rarely without the sound of the chickens out in the coop. Their chatter became like the air, constant, enveloping. But other sounds—the Michigan Central trains in the distance, livestock in the fields, dogs barking, a passing machine on Clark Road, the clatter of plates and utensils during meals in the kitchen—they made her want to clap her hands over her ears until there was quiet.

But tonight she thought the silence might kill her. She needed sound. She'd always been so busy with living, the constant work of the day, that she never realized that silence was the sound of death. In the silence she imagined that she heard the voices of all those children, and the teachers who were killed. It was difficult, remembering a voice.

As Lulu got out of bed she heard the mattress and box spring. She pulled on her bathrobe and stepped into her slippers. She went down the stairs, careful to avoid the left side of the third step from the bottom, which had creaked for years, an ascending groan that reminded her of a nail being yanked from a two-by-four. Light came down the hall from the kitchen. She could hear the three men, could smell their coffee and cigarettes. She opened the front door and stepped out onto the porch, leaving the door ajar—she knew that closing it would rattle the window because of missing putty. Three steps down and her slippers were in new spring grass. She walked, the cool mist of dew on her ankles and shins. Walked past the chicken coop, which was silent at this hour. The road and the Kehoe farm were to her right. There was the smell of charred wood. There was no breeze and the air was warm. She walked out into the field, soon to be planted with corn. Walked back away from the road, from the smell of fire, walked across acres of dirt. David called it good Michigan dirt. Walked out where the darkness seemed more complete, where the only light came from the kitchen windows in the house. Walked the land that swelled and rolled to the south tree line. Walked on deeper into the silence.

▪ ▪ ▪

Andrew Kehoe's package had spent the night sitting in a field, well away from the state police barracks in Lansing. No one approached it until Thursday morning, when two men, T. E. Trombla, an inspector from the explosives unit of the Interstate Commerce Commission in Detroit, and Lieutenant Lyle Morse of the Michigan State Police walked across the field. Trombla stopped some ten yards from the wooden crate and took a drag on his cigarette.

"Look at that, *dynamite,* written right there on the box," he said. "What are the chances there's dynamite in there, Lieutenant?"

"I don't know, but I'm not willing to bet against it."

"You want to go back to the barracks with the others?"

Morse stared at the crate. "I was up there in Bath yesterday. We pulled a lot of dynamite out of the part of the school that didn't go up. If this stuff was going to kill me, yesterday would have been the day."

"The crate was meant to be delivered to a lawyer's office. Most folks don't think much of lawyers."

"I have a cousin married to a lawyer," Morse said, "and I don't think much of him."

Trombla chuckled. "Would you send him a bomb?"

Morse considered this a moment. "No, there are other ways. But if it weren't for the kids sometimes I think my cousin might."

"Well, all right," Trombla said, flicking his cigarette in the grass.

Both men walked slowly toward the crate and knelt down in the grass. The box was bound with twine. Trombla took a penknife from his pocket, opened it, and cut the twine. They both sat back on their haunches and waited. Then they began pulling the twine away, carefully, until the box lid was free. There were two hinges on one side, a hasp on the other. Trombla lifted the hasp and paused. He looked at Morse. "What's your favorite thing to eat?"

"Excuse me?"

"What do you like to eat?"

"I don't know. Bacon and eggs."

"How do you like your eggs?"

"Not picky. No, poached, I like them poached, three of them laid out on toast."

"Good," Trombla said. "Poached eggs and bacon, very good."

"Why'd you ask?"

"Anytime I'm about to handle something that might blow me to kingdom come I like to think about a good meal."

"I see. So what's on the menu?"

"I'm thinking my grandmother's *pasta e fagioli.*"

"What's *fagioli?*"

"Beans. For her *zuppe.* Nonna added thyme and rosemary from her garden, some onion. And *guanciale.*"

Morse was mystified but reluctant to ask.

"It's pork jowls. *Guancia* means cheeks. Not everyone uses *guanciale,* but Nonna did. While she was cooking, the house would have this aroma. Morse, I want to cry just thinking about Nonna's *zuppe* simmering on the stove."

"Now you're making me hungry."

"Works every time." Trombla lifted the lid and both men held still for a long moment. "So far, so good."

"Are those what I think they are?" Morse asked.

Trombla leaned down for a closer look. "Think so."

A stack of leather-bound books lay in the bottom of the crate. Trombla reached inside with both hands and removed the books—they were ledgers, the kind used for accounting.

"So this is what Kehoe sent to his lawyer?" Morse said.

A folded sheet of paper stuck out of the ledger on top of the pile.

Trombla took a pair of reading spectacles from the inside of his suitcoat, moving slowly, a man who appreciates that a good soup requires time to simmer. After putting his glasses on, he removed the sheet of paper from the ledger, unfolded it, and cleared his throat:

> Dear Sir,
>
> I am leaving the school board and turning over to you all my accounts. Due to an uncashed check, the bank had 22¢ more than my books showed when I took them over. Due to an error on the part of the Secretary in order no. 118,

dated November 18, 1925. He changed the figures on the order after the check had been sent to the payee—the bank gained one cent more over my books, making the bank account show 23¢ more than my books. Otherwise I am sure you will find my books exactly right.

Sincerely yours,

A. P. Kehoe

"So," Trombla said, "this fella Kehoe, he's formally resigned from the school board. And here are the accounting ledgers." He sounded disappointed. "What does that tell you?"

"Everything neat and tidy, down to the penny." Morse stared at the ledgers. "It tells me we'll never understand, never grasp why. A man who keeps impeccable records, a man who is logical and organized, some might say to a fault, and he's capable of blowing up a school full of children and their teachers. Apparently because he believes the taxes on his farm are too high."

"Because of the school—it was only constructed a few years ago?"

"Right," Morse said. "But that's only part of it. There must have been things—don't ask me what—that had been working on him for a long time. A long time. This wasn't some spur of the moment thing. It wasn't your crime of passion. He planned it and spent who knows how long to set it up. Just like these ledgers, he was proud of how exact everything was—the school, the farm, even his truck, loaded with dynamite and enough shrapnel to create a battlefield of dead and wounded."

"Shrapnel?" Trombla said.

"He packed the truck with nuts, bolts—hundreds of bits of metal. We dug them out of the ground, out of the trees, out of the bodies."

Trombla closed the lid of the crate. With effort, both men got up off the grass.

Morse brushed off the knees of his trousers. "This wasn't just about taxes, this was deep and goes way back to a place we'll never find. You can't tell me what goes through the mind of a man like that."

▪ ▪ ▪

The cracks in my ceiling play games with me, with my failing eyesight. The lines tend to shift and move, they suggest phantasmagorical images, like those advertisements that ask you to find the hidden figures in a sketch: a tree, a dog, a woman, a man, a child. Thursday, May 19, the Bath school bombing was on the front pages of newspapers across the nation, and beyond. Thirty-eight children and four adults were killed; the number of injured was more difficult to determine, but most sources put the number at fifty-eight. Many newspaper stories had inaccurate figures regarding the dead and injured. Such statistics don't go beyond physical injury.

All day long families went to the school to retrieve clothing and books that had belonged to students. A line of machines streamed through the village. It took some vehicles over four hours to make the trip from Lansing. One policeman counted 2,750 cars passing the school in two hours. Estimates of the number of machines to drive through Bath vary, but all are in the tens of thousands.

It was odd: the more I read and heard about Bath the less I believed it was true, let alone possible; if anything, these accounts made it all seem more remote and implausible. There's a reason why we say *beyond belief.* Reality lay not in the statistics and the news reports, but in those articles of clothing retrieved from the bomb site. One girl's bloodied coat hung from a tree limb for hours before it was claimed. What do you do with a dead child's coat? Preserve it as a talisman, or fold it up and hide it away in a drawer? Or do you destroy it in an effort to obliterate the memories it brings to mind? We did all of these things, and more.

What couldn't be anticipated was that after only a couple of days of being the headline story in virtually every newspaper in the country, the Bath school disaster would be forgotten once the world learned that Charles Augustus Lindbergh had landed his plane the *Spirit of St. Louis* in Paris, where he was greeted by a crowd of over one hundred thousand. The world forgot, but we had to live with what happened in Bath, Michigan.

III. Michigan Dirt

15.

A mass funeral was considered, but that proved too complicated and many families wanted their service (or services) to be private. Friday, Saturday, and Sunday following the bombings there were funerals practically on the hour, many in Bath but some held in nearby towns and down in Lansing. During these first days the town was still overrun with sightseers. Strangers would walk up to the houses of grieving families and stare into the windows. People occupied yards and lawns, some spreading out blankets for a picnic. Crowd control at the funerals overextended the police. Some residents claimed they didn't mind the intruders, understanding that people were just curious, and that in many cases they came to express genuine sympathy; other locals wanted to declare open hunting season, threatening to take up sniper positions on their front porches and attic windows and pick off gawkers. It wasn't just strangers, though; by the weekend postcards depicting scenes of devastation at both the school and the Kehoe farm were on sale in local stores.

Nellie's remains, which simply disintegrated once authorities tried to move them, were buried at the Price family plot in Lansing, her sisters and relatives in attendance. Everything in Bath seemed fair game for press photographers, but remarkably no pictures of the graveside ceremony appeared in the newspapers.

Andrew Kehoe's remains were collected by his sister Agnes, who came up from Battle Creek. Her first intention was to bury him in the family plot in Clinton, but that plan was abandoned and he was interred in the pauper's section of a cemetery in St. John's, north of Bath. To thwart the curious and the press, two graves were dug. When Kehoe was buried no minister was present, no prayers recited. Only Agnes and one brother, Lewis, were in attendance as the grave diggers lowered the coffin into the ground.

Death leads to financial burdens. Some families of the deceased didn't have sufficient funds to cover funeral costs. Michigan's governor Fred W. Green promised to provide financial assistance, and he issued a proclamation to all the towns and cities in Michigan, imploring them to help out. The town of Bath itself had less than $200 in its education fund, so we had no idea how or when a new school might be built. The first of many attempts to raise funds for a new school in Bath occurred Sunday afternoon, when a benefit baseball game was played between a group of military veterans and a team comprised of employees from the Lansing Oldsmobile plant.

The days immediately following the bombings are difficult for me to recall. More so as I've gotten older. Not a day has passed—perhaps I should say not an hour, if not a minute—when some image, some recollection hasn't surfaced in my mind. Something like this never leaves you.

I know that during those spring days in 1927, when the ruins of the school and the Kehoe farm were still visible reminders of what had transpired, we managed to go about our business—that's what we often called it, *our business.* We ate and slept and worked, and the chores never ended. We did the things one has to do to get through the days, but of course none of it was the same as before the bombings. Everything we did was tinged or tainted. I can remember once leaning over and tying my shoe—it was morning and there was the smell of rain coming through my open window—when I stopped and sat upright on my bed. Shoes. Shoelaces. They were things of this world. I had an image from perhaps a week before the explosions: during recess, one of the students, a girl in the first grade, was sitting on the back steps of the school. She was busy tying her shoes. It took all her concentration. She couldn't get it right and she was on the verge of tears. I thought that I might help, a big eighth grader showing her how to tie the knot. For some reason I didn't go to her but watched as she tried over and over, getting it wrong until finally she got it right, pulling two large bows out and saying triumphantly (and mimicking her parents, I assumed): "Like butterflies!

You make them like butterfly wings." At the time, watching the girl—her name has long ago escaped me but I know that she was one of the children killed in the bombing—I thought it silly, equating a shoelace correctly knotted with the wings of a butterfly. But years later, when I was a mother with small children who were trying to learn how to tie their own shoes, I told them to think of butterfly wings. Sitting there on my bed in the spring of '27, staring at the rain soaking the fields outside my window, I thought about shoes and laces, and I could not arrive at any conclusion. This happened often in those first days. I would think of something, try to make a connection between things that ought to be related, but I would find the effort futile. That morning I made the decision to remove my shoes and socks and went barefoot, long enough that my mother finally said something about it. Still, I refused to put anything on my feet.

And the days became weeks, and then months; and the years became decades. What happened to us is what happens to everyone. We grew up. We became adults. We lived our lives. We got old. I am old. So old I now sometimes find myself doing the math on a slip of paper—or in the margin of a newspaper. I'll see the date and I'll write down the year, and then subtract from it the year of my birth, 1912. It takes a long time to get to that point. We don't grow old overnight. I often think and feel that, other than physical decline, I'm no different from the girl who decided to go barefoot. The girl who brought tea and oatmeal-raisin cookies up to Nellie Kehoe's bedroom. The girl who couldn't connect things. The girl who survived, and who never could understand why.

Many of us naturally thought God had a hand in the bombings. Andrew Kehoe was an agent of evil—the newspapers often described him as such. I was suspicious of such conclusions, and still am. They seem convenient, too neat and tidy. They avoid notions of culpability, of responsibility. Such acts drive many people deeper into their religion; they will tell you they are closer to God. They equate the death of innocent women and children with the will of God. It's a sign, it's a warning, it may even be considered a blessing. Though I've never felt that far from God, I came to think of religion as another matter: God and religion are separate, two different things. This is a notion that makes some people uncomfortable. At times I've gone so far as to suggest that religion moves us further away from God. And I know in this I'm not alone. I'd see it in the faces of others. During Sunday sermons or just conversation around the dinner table. Skepticism is a religion unto itself. The barefoot girl became skeptical about everything: shoes, shoelaces, butterflies, the nature of God's will. I just didn't know how anyone could be sure of anything. I wallowed in doubt. Uncertainty was my only refuge.

I had no answers except in my dreams. Miss Weatherby's funeral was in her hometown, Howard City, north of Grand Rapids. I still have dreams about Miss Weatherby. Sometimes she speaks to me while sitting at her desk, a dead child, caked in white dust, in each arm. Other times I am in the back of her classroom and all the children are alive. There is a tacit understanding between Miss Weatherby and me. She would write a question on the blackboard and ask who knows the answer. I did, but I would wait, letting other students raise their hands. If no one gave the correct answer, Miss Weatherby would eventually glance at me, and I would stand up and give the answer. Only in my dreams do I possess such certainty.

▪ ▪ ▪

There was no graduation ceremony, no official end to the school year.

Instead, Jed attended several funerals of his classmates. The coffins were different sizes and he realized that someone must have used a tape measure on each child.

At every funeral they spoke of Jesus. His love for us. Our faith in Him.

They talked of Jesus, who will return once again, and all our souls will be delivered.

Jed wanted to ask a question. He wanted to stand up during the funeral ceremony and ask, *What if Jesus had already returned?* He wanted to ask what if Jesus came back and we didn't pay attention. Maybe we didn't notice. Maybe Jesus looked around and saw how things were and left this earth for good. We know what we believe. Do we know what Jesus believed? Maybe he came back and believed that we could not be saved, from evil, from the forces of nature, from ourselves.

But Jed remained silent at the funerals, couldn't wait for them to be over.

His father took him to the benefit baseball game Sunday afternoon. It was intended to be a reward for Jed's good behavior during the past few days. There was a large crowd at the game, but many of the spectators weren't from Bath. They seemed to be enjoying themselves, standing and sitting around the baseball diamond on a spring afternoon. The ballplayers weren't particularly skilled at the game, but no one seemed to mind. Jed didn't understand how many of the batters would swing when they should take a pitch, and then not swing when they were ahead in the count and got a good pitch to hit. After several innings he asked his father if they could go home.

They didn't speak as the truck rolled down back roads that cut through the fields, until his father said, "We won't need to do chores for a day or two, all right?"

Jed didn't respond. Ordinarily, he looked forward to summer. Swimming up at Round Lake. Wetting a line in Looking Glass River. Playing pickup ballgames. And even chores, which he was expected to finish before he could go off to swim or play ball. But the thought of summer meant nothing somehow. It loomed, dark and empty. He didn't know how he would fill all that time. The mathematics of the clock hovered over his thoughts. He often calculated how many hours and minutes had passed since the bombing.

When they reached home, his father did a rare thing as they walked across the barnyard. He placed his hand on his son's shoulder. Jed swiped it away with his hand. Inside, he went straight up to his room.

▪ ▪ ▪

After the weekend of the funerals I spent a lot of time riding Daisy. Bareback, barefoot. We shared apples. I'd take a bite out of a Granny Smith and watch her ears twitch, then take the piece of apple from my mouth and hold it out so she could nibble it from the palm of my hand. Little things, like eating an apple with Daisy, seemed important all of a sudden. The stream of vehicles from out of town evaporated and Bath made an attempt at a return to normalcy. Stores opened for business, farmers worked the fields. Every day I rode Daisy by the school. More than anything, that old mare got me through those first days.

Bath organized a number of work bees. We'd gather at the school to clean up the bomb site, and the women would lay out lunch for everyone. In retrospect, it was the best thing we could do. It said something about the people of Bath. I recall joining women who were pulling nails from lumber. While they labored, they talked about how certain families were holding up—that was the phrase often used, *holding up*—and then they would go on about someone's pie crust or recipe for fried chicken. The sound of the nails being pulled from wood—a groaning, screeching noise that for some reason I found reassuring—punctuated conversation. Sometimes I felt that the women avoided talking about certain things when I was present, but I felt I knew what was really on their minds. None of us, it seemed, knew what to do other than what we were doing, which was clearing the rubble that had been our school. Bricks were stacked and carted away; boards and lumber were stripped of nails so they could be reused. *Waste not, want not.* (And this was a few years before the Depression—when it came, some people said Bath had long been prepared.) In order to rebuild, it was first necessary to complete the destruction. I remember thinking of the words *construction* and *destruction,* how they complemented each other. I remember having conversations in my mind with Miss Weatherby about how certain words were natural opposites. I remember how my fingers hurt and bled when they were pierced by splinters from the wood. I don't remember any of us, women or girls, wearing gloves while we pulled nails.

One afternoon I rode over to Jed's house. I hadn't seen him in days. Mrs. Browne let me in the kitchen door, and she had a look on her face. I wasn't sure what it meant but clearly she was worried.

"He's in his room," she said.

I thought she would go to the stairs and call up to him so he'd come down—she often used his full name, Jedidiah, which I rather liked—but she made a motion with her head that it was all right for me to go up to his room. I'd been there before, but always when there were other children, boys and girls. She was indicating that I could go to his room alone and I was tempted to ask if she was sure.

But I climbed the stairs, steep and narrow in the Browne farmhouse. Jed's room was at the end of the hall, the door closed. I knocked and there was no answer.

"Jed. It's Bea." Foolish to say my name, but somehow I thought it necessary.

After a long moment of silence, I heard him get up from the bed and walk to the door. He let me in, returned to his bed, and lay down on his back, hands clasped behind his head. I stood in the middle of the room and looked at the walls—Jed's Wall. He'd always tacked up photographs from magazines and newspapers. Baseball players. Flying aces. Western movie stars. Hogs. Cows. Horses. Dogs. Locomotives. Cars and trucks. Tractors. The walls were now bare. I could see the pin holes where the tacks had been; in some cases, I could see the faint outline of a photograph that had occupied the space a long time. Then I turned toward the closet door. One of the panels had a wide crack.

It was the ceiling that caused me to sit in the chair at his desk. Above the bed there were short gray lines in the plaster. At first I thought they'd been drawn with a pencil, but then I realized that they were thin cuts. I didn't know how they got there, until I saw the knife on his nightstand, which was an apple crate turned on its end. It was a big knife, with a blade at least eight inches long. I'd seen it before; he kept it in a leather sheath on his belt sometimes when he was doing chores—he liked to whittle sticks. All the cuts in the ceiling were above the bed, where Jed now lay, staring straight up.

"How do you do that?" I asked.

"Bounce."

"On the bed. You bounce and stab the ceiling."

He didn't say anything.

"Why?"

He stared at the ceiling.

"What's your father say?"

"Nothing." Then he thought something was funny. "He didn't say anything. Mom said if I did it again I'd sleep in the barn."

"And the door?" I said, looking toward the closet. "What you hit it with, a baseball bat?"

He shook his head.

"Your fist. You cracked the door with your fist?"

He continued to stare at the ceiling.

I'd never seen him like this and I decided it was best to leave him alone, but when I got to my feet, I just stood there. Outside the open window we could hear the birds in the fields. Several minutes passed. I went over to the bed and sat down. With my elbow I nudged him in the side until he moved over. I lay down on my back beside him. I was fourteen, he was twelve. We gazed up at what he'd done to the ceiling. I found his hand and held it. We'd held hands before, particularly when we were younger, as children do. This was different. I wasn't sure how, but I knew it was different. He didn't pull away and his hand was lifeless, inert in mine. I don't know how long we lay there. It was a hot afternoon and the room was close, the oblong of sun illuminating dust motes above the floorboards. We didn't move, didn't speak. Eventually, I fell asleep.

I've always wondered why we say *fall* or *fell asleep.* As though it's a descent into another realm. Sometimes I think of sleep as a kind of ascending, a rising up into a higher plane. I often find sleep the best refuge. Over the years there have been times when I would become overwhelmed, some might say overcome;

these days, people call it depression. I won't argue the semantics. I have known depression, yes, and often the safest place, the only respite, can be found in sleep.

When I opened my eyes the shaft of sunlight had moved across the floor and fell across the desk and chair. I wondered what Mrs. Browne must have been thinking downstairs. She hadn't come up; she hadn't said anything. I suspect she was afraid to interfere, possibly because she knew that what was happening to Jedidiah was beyond her. She understood that, though he was still healthy and alive, she was in danger of losing her son.

I got up and went to the door. Before opening it, I looked back at Jed, who was now lying on his side, staring at me. The sunlight in the room illumined the down on his cheek, and his eyes, usually a stony blue, were the color of the ocean, or what I thought of as the ocean, which at that point I had never seen. He stared back at me, unblinking, as I let myself out of his room.

16.

The inquest was held in the town hall, conducted by the Clinton County prosecutor William Searl. Ma and Pa attended; others stayed away. Some thought there was an inquest simply because the authorities believed that such events required one.

Lieutenant Lyle Morse gave testimony regarding the dynamite found at both the school and the Kehoe farm, as well as the accounting ledgers Kehoe had tried to ship to his lawyer's office in Lansing. Attorney Joseph Dunnebeck attested vehemently that, though Andrew and Nellie had long been delinquent in their mortgage payment, the Price family had no intention of evicting them from the farm. Mrs. Perrone, who had lost an eye while standing on the Main Street sidewalk with her two small children, submitted to questioning, though she spoke little English. Evidence was offered regarding Nellie Kehoe's corpse, confirming that it was impossible to determine the exact nature of her death. The medical examiner could not ascertain that her cracked skull was the result of a blow with a blunt instrument; more likely, the extreme heat from the fire turned her brain to gas, which expanded, causing the fracture.

The findings, in essence, were that Andrew Kehoe was not insane and that he acted alone.

Yet there still lingered the fear that he had accomplices, thus homes and buildings received thorough inspections.

■ ■ ■

The first was a boy named Bobby. He and Jed got into a fight up at Round Lake not a week after the bombing. Afterward, Jed couldn't remember why. He took a good licking. Bobby was older, taller, his belly big, and Jed's fists seemed to just get lost in all that soft flesh. He walked home with bruises on his face, skinned knuckles, and sore ribs from being kicked after he'd been knocked to the ground. His mother washed the bruises with a towel dipped in hot water and Epsom salts. At dinner, his father didn't remark on Jed's injuries until he pushed himself away from the table. "Boys after a certain age tend to scrap," he said. "You best learn to defend yourself."

The next boy was someone's cousin visiting from Grand Ledge. Then there was Ronnie, after a disagreement over an inside pitch during a pickup baseball game. By June anyone who looked at Jed wrong was fair game. Some boys came looking for him. Often they were slightly older, a little bigger, but they recognized that he had established himself as a challenger. He fought them all, never once backed down. Lost his share, but he learned to defend himself, limiting the damage.

His mother claimed he was sprouting overnight. She altered his shirts and pants, saying she couldn't keep up with his legs and arms. His voice cracked and dropped, and he discovered pubic hair. Work on the farm hardened his back, and once while stacking hay bales his father commented on his shoulders being firm as a hog's butt. He won fights; only occasionally there would be what amounted to a draw. Some boys shied away, not wanting to mix it up with him. He could freeze them with his eyes, staring at them until they looked away.

The Dempsey-Tunney heavyweight championship bout was scheduled for September 22 at Soldier Field in Chicago. Jed pinned just two photographs on his wall, above his bed: Gene Tunney in the ring; Gene Tunney in a double-breasted suit. Tunney was quick, shrewd, his defense flawless. Dempsey was slower, a true slugger. Though Tunney had won their first fight a year earlier, the odds were on Dempsey, but Jed believed the well-read gentleman who wore fine suits would win again.

He remembered how careful Mr. Kehoe was of his suits. If the ground was muddy, he'd wear rubber boots and tuck his cuffed trousers inside. Often when they were preparing to blow up a tree stump, he would remove his jacket, fold it neatly, and lay it out on the seat of the Ford. When they worked on farm machinery, he'd hang the jacket from a hook on the shed door. Jed could see Mr. Kehoe, sitting on a handkerchief spread out on a rock in the woods. While Jed gathered the splintered wood after a stump had been blown up, Mr. Kehoe would smoke his cigar. He was planning on killing all of them, every student in Bath Consolidated School. He knew Jed would be one of them—should have been one of them, if he hadn't returned Daisy to the Turcott farm. Despite his explanations about how combustion engines and electrical circuitry worked, despite his references to Jed's future, Mr. Kehoe was planning to make sure that there would be no future. Somehow the suits and white shirts and ties were the key. Jed remembered studying the lining of one suitcoat—a white satin material, the likes of which he'd never seen before. Why would a man wear such clothing while working on his farm? Jed studied men's suits in magazines and newspapers. Suits came to him in his dreams. He believed that if he could understand why Mr. Kehoe wore a suit every day he could understand why the man blew up the school. But he couldn't get there. He couldn't figure it out. He was good at figuring things out—told so by his teachers, and he knew it to be true, especially when it came to mathematics. But this, he could not fathom. In his dreams he was sometimes wearing a suit—it was both too large and too tight, the sleeves and pants confining his arms and legs as though he were tied up with rope. Often he woke up in a sweat, struggling to get out of the suit, only to find that he was tangled up in his bedsheets. Some nights after such a dream he could only get back to sleep by lying on the pinewood floor with a pillow under his head.

▪ ▪ ▪

Alma seldom left the farm, never on her own. Ma and Pa took her to doctors in Lansing, but no one could do anything for her. When she and I went into the village, she'd hold my hand. People were kind. They spoke slowly to her, and usually too loud as though she were hard of hearing. Often she would not respond, and would look to me—I would never try to speak for her, but for both of us. *We would like a bag of sugar,* I'd say. *We need five pounds of galvanized eightpenny nails for Pa.*

Despite attempts at normalcy in the village, grief and tension were in the air. We'd pass certain houses, knowing they'd lost a child. Some families lost more than one. It was not uncommon to see someone on a porch, bandaged or leaning on crutches. Schoolmates. Children who no longer looked like children. They didn't exactly look old, but as though they'd been to a place that was haunted and beyond belief, a place they could not forget. They stared out at me, astride Daisy's back, with hollow eyes.

More dynamite was found in the section of the school that had not blown up. Some, including Ma and Pa, believed the entire structure needed to be torn down, but there was the fear of what may be found in the walls. The fear that this was not finished lingered throughout the summer. We looked at each other, searching for accomplices. Rumors spread that the police were investigating certain people. An employee at the Peoples' Bank was questioned but nothing came of it. Though there was never any proof that Kehoe had collaborators, for decades after the explosions, the Bath public schools received bomb threats, often on the anniversary of the 1927 tragedy.

Strangers—sightseeing tourists from out of town—infested the village. They picked through the rubble in search of souvenirs. We hated them for it. Perhaps Kehoe's accomplices were not one of us but from somewhere else. An out-of-town woman discovered more dynamite in the ruins, which led police to find even more: 244 sticks, weighing over 200 pounds, neatly wrapped and stuffed into cavities beneath the subflooring. It seemed inconceivable that one man could acquire and hide so much explosive material.

Bath was confronted with the problem of what to do about the coming school year. Senator James Couzens committed his own money for the construction of a new school in Bath. He had amassed great wealth during the years that he helped establish the Ford Motor Company. After a falling out with Henry Ford, Couzens embarked on a career of public service, first as mayor of Detroit, and then in the US Senate. He and his wife had lost one child soon after childbirth, and their teenaged son was later killed in an automobile accident. Senator Couzens offered Bath $75,000, which was more than twice what the Consolidated School had cost to build in 1922, but his donation came with conditions. He wanted the new building erected on the site of the old school, and architecturally it had to be virtually the same design. This created much discord in Bath; many wanted the new school built down the hill to the east of the present school, and they believed a memorial should be established on the

"Here we go with your big words."

"Pugilism. You didn't put up your dukes?"

"No, I didn't."

"Oh. I heard that's your new means of communication."

"Byers was just wild. I can tell when someone's trying to bean me. He apologized and threw another ball way outside giving me the walk. I stole second and third, and then came home on a blooper to right. It was pretty funny—Snooky was coming in on the ball and might have had a play at the plate, until he stepped right in a cow pie."

"Ha. I stepped in one when I was about four. I was—"

"Do you know what Jack Dempsey's reach is?" Before I could tell him—of course I didn't—he said, "Seventy-seven inches. And Tunney's? Seventy-seven inches. Know what Dempsey weighs? One-ninety-three. Tunney? One-ninety-two. And they're both just over six feet tall. Dempsey has a quarter inch on him. So what does that tell you? Right. They're even-steven. But. Tunney is quicker."

It went on like this all the way to Browne farm. He moved from the Dempsey-Tunney bout, scheduled for September, to Charles Lindbergh, who was in the newspapers daily. The *Spirit of St. Louis* was a "flying gas tank," carrying over 450 gallons of gasoline. So Lindbergh figured he had a range of 4,200 miles. The plane had a 223-horsepower radial engine. Did I know where the term horsepower came from? (I did not, or so Jed presumed because I was given no opportunity to answer.) It came from an estimate of how many horses it would take to pull a Model T out of the mud. Jed laughed then, and at first I suspected that he'd made that up, but then I realized that he'd read it somewhere. Lindbergh's nonstop flight took thirty-three and a half hours, New York to Paris. The plane averaged about ten miles to the gallon. Much of the time while he was over the Atlantic, he flew through snow and sleet. "But what's incredible," Jed concluded as we were crossing the field behind his house, "is that during the entire trip he couldn't see where he was going!"

"Really. How could he get to Paris without seeing where he was going?"

"The engine. It was so big, attached to the front of the plane—he couldn't see out the front. He could only look out the side windows. He used a compass and made calculations in a notebook. Over Ireland he dipped low out of the sky, and people in a field pointed toward Paris!"

Even Daisy's ears were turned oddly, as though she'd heard enough.

"You believe that?" I asked.

"What?"

"Do you know what *apocryphal* means?"

"You're the one with the big vocabulary—you tell me."

"It means they sound like stretchers, but people tend to believe them," I said. "Do you believe that they did that in Ireland? And that that's where horsepower comes from?"

"What are you talking about?"

"No. What are *you* talking about, Jedidiah Solomon Browne? I know that brain of yours is a sponge. How many facts can you store up there?"

"I don't know. You think your brain ever fills up?"

"Beats me. But I suspect yours has sprung a leak."

"Ha-ha, very funny."

"You're right," Bea said. "It's not funny. For days—weeks—you hardly say a word. And then all this stuff just pours out of your head. Boxers' reach and height and weight, and Lindbergh's flying gas tank, and not being able to see where he's going."

"But it's all true!"

"It may be. I don't know. That's my point."

"What *is* your point?"

We had nearly reached the barnyard behind his house, and Daisy's head was bobbing with the effort, though I thought she might be nodding because she agreed with me.

"You know the other day Pa used this term I never heard before," I said. "Haywire."

"Yeah, for bailing."

"But that's not what he meant. You know how bailing wire tends to get tangled, so tangled you can't sort it out?"

"Yeah."

"Pa said that's what happens to some people. To their brains. They go haywire."

Daisy stopped when she reached the hard-packed earth before the porch.

Jed didn't say anything.

"Haywire," I repeated. "He was talking about you know who."

Jed's arms let go of my waist, and he slid down off Daisy. As he went up the steps, I said, "Don't go haywire, Jed. You hear?"

He paused on the top step but didn't turn around.

"I said, you hear? It's enough to see what this all has done to Alma."

He looked back at me then. I couldn't tell what he was thinking. He looked alert, pleased even, as though he'd just figured something out.

"There are some things," I said. "Things we can't know, things we can't comprehend."

I could tell he didn't believe me. Or didn't want to even hear me say such a thing. He opened the kitchen door by shoving it with his shoulder, the way he always did.

17.

Nobody wanted to admit it but you kept an eye out for souvenirs. During the community work bees, you'd find something and slip it in a pocket or a purse. Though the demolished school was disappearing, slowly, methodically, it was sacred ground. You wanted a piece of it. Nothing of real value. A pair of scissors probably from the home economics class. A tattered Latin grammar. Even a portion of a brick, plucked from the rubble. Both locals and tourists (who continued to stream through Bath months after the disaster) spirited away bits of the school building. You'd think there was a fear that there'd come a day when the events of May 18, 1927, might be forgotten, that some remnant of the Bath Consolidated School would be necessary to recall such a tragedy.

But this was different.

A finger.

By the time it was found, by a girl who wasn't yet ten years old, it had turned stiff and brown. At first sight it resembled a twig. But it was a finger, separated from a hand at the middle knuckle. Small, and for some reason it was presumed to have belonged to a girl. Something about the tiny, perfect fingernail.

The child who found it wrapped it in a handkerchief and took it home. She hid it in her room. She feared getting in trouble. It couldn't be put on display, and if she showed it to her parents they would question her about why she had gone near the school when she had been forbidden to do so. The finger remained hidden in the box that held her toys in her bedroom.

Until one day when her mother was cleaning her daughter's room. The room was a mess, as usual. Toys littered the floor—dolls and a teddy bear. She picked them up and put them back in the toy box, but as she began to close the lid she noticed the crumpled handkerchief partially hidden by a wooden horse in the back corner. She picked up the handkerchief and at the sight of the finger the woman sat down on her daughter's bed, her free hand placed over her mouth. They had been fortunate. Their two children, though both attending school on the day of the bombing, had escaped injury. Both children had nightmares. The girl frequently wet her bed. Her mother kept the finger and handkerchief for a number of days, unsure what to do about it. She noticed something about her daughter's behavior—the girl pretended nothing was the matter, but clearly she knew that the finger was missing from her toy box and she was afraid her parents had found it.

Finally, her mother showed the finger and handkerchief to her husband. It was at night, after the children were asleep. They were in bed, both lying on their backs, whispering. They didn't know if they should confront their daughter about the finger or continue to pretend that nothing was amiss. They agreed that attempting to find out whose finger it was would be as impossible as it would be hurtful. Though they ruled out taking the finger to the police, they considered taking it to the minister—but he and his wife had suffered the loss of their child in the bombing. They lay in bed deep into the night, unable to decide what to do.

▪ ▪ ▪

Hay wire.

Bea had meant haywire.

She was particular about words: she was talking about people like Mr. Kehoe.

Standing on the porch, looking up at her astride Daisy, Jed had thought *hay wire.* It was an answer, a solution.

That night he slipped out of his open window and walked east across the fields to the Fagan's barn. Rance Fagan and his father sometimes sat in the barn, to get out of the sun or the snow or a downpour. They got what Fagan called Religion. The old man kept a jug on a shelf with some paint cans. Claimed it was from a good still up in St. John's, so he referred to it as the Saint's Blood. Jed knew that Fagan also had large coils of hay wire hanging from beam pegs, and that on the shelf above the paints and turpentine, he kept a detonator. Years ago, after Jed's father had cut down the elm that was dying in the front yard, he and Fagan blew the stump out of the ground. Jed must have been about five or six.

When he entered Fagan's barn, Jed struck a match, which gave enough light for him to see his way to the shelves. He used a stool to reach the top shelf. The detonator was still there, along with blasting caps and a coil of rubber-coated wire. He took them down, and as he was leaving the barn, he heard footsteps crossing the yard from the house. He hid in an empty stall just as lantern light illuminated the barn, casting long shadows. A horse paced in the stall next to Jed's. The light came nearer, and Jed could see a hand stroke the horse's nose.

"Thought I saw something out here," Fagan said to the horse. "Just a critter? Or you be gettin' ornery?"

Fagan left the barn, walked back across the yard, and entered the house. Jed remained in the stall for he didn't know how long—a half hour, at least. Fagan had a suspicious nature and was the kind of man who would remain at his window and watch the barn for a good while. Finally, Jed hung the coiled wire over his shoulder and shoved the blasting caps in his pockets. He picked up the detonator, a metal box of considerable weight with a plunger handle on the top, and went to the open barn doors, where he could look across the yard at the house. One window upstairs was illuminated by a flickering light. Widowed, Fagan was the kind of codger who might refuse to have power lines run into his house—he was even suspicious of electricity. Everyone talked about the power company coming to Bath, and earlier in the spring Fagan had expressed his doubts to Jed's father. *Don't know what this electricity business will do to you. Can't see it, but there's something there in that invisible power that will bring a body to harm.*

Jed stepped out into the yard, walked quickly around the corner of the barn and out of sight of the house. He kept to the tree lines that bordered fields, heading west, until he came to the back road that ran behind the Kehoe property. When he found the tree stump, he began digging in the soft earth beneath a large exposed root. The dynamite sticks he'd found in the basement of the school were still wrapped in wax paper, and he'd put them in a burlap sack. The detonator and the blasting caps fit inside the sack, but the wire coil was too big. He dug with both hands, making the hole deeper and wider. After placing the wire in the bottom of the hole, he laid the burlap sack on top of it, and covered everything up. When finished, he tamped the dirt with his feet and then spread pine needles on it. He walked home at first light, using a matchstick splinter to work the dirt out from under his fingernails.

■ ■ ■

We all reacted to Kehoe's malice in our own way, and I know I wasn't the only one plagued by nightmares. This old woman still is—and now it seems, I don't even have to be asleep to have them. There are times when I drift into a state of exhaustion, and my mind just goes wherever.

The months after the bombings I had many a sleepless night. I was afraid to go to bed. Before electricity the world was so dark. I never minded it, but that summer I feared the dark. It was as though I were waiting, for what I don't know. I was not alone. We all felt that way, Alma and Jed and all of the children who had survived. For me, it manifests itself as fear. For Jed, it took the form of anger. Often at night I'd hear Alma crying and moaning in her bedroom. But worse was the night silence of my bedroom, which I found terrorizing. I'd lie in bed waiting for something, a sound, a voice, a sign. I can remember one night when the outhouse must have been left unlatched, and the wind slammed the door shut. It sounded like a gunshot. After a painful jolt to my heart, I lay trembling in the dark for hours.

Sleep, if it arrived, often came in the early morning. But it wasn't restful sleep, and I'd often drag myself about during the day (my leg still bothered me at times). An afternoon nap lying in the shade of the trees on the west side of the house, or sometimes dozing on the porch glider, helped; but upon waking I knew I was in for another difficult night.

When I couldn't sleep, I sat up and read. Words on a page look different in lantern light. The paper and even the printed letters have texture. That summer I read (and reread) fairy tales, by both Hans Christian Andersen and the Brothers Grimm. And I read the Bible, though the print was so small (and the paper so thin!), I had to hold the book right up to my face as I lay in bed. I think now that the nightmares were often fed by images from fairy tales and the Bible. A few have remained with me all these years: grotesque creatures, ogres, fallen angels. The places in my nightmares were most vivid, often causing me to wake up in a sweat, and more than once I must have cried out in my sleep because Ma would be there leaning over my bed when I opened my eyes. Some places in my dreams might have been right out of Dante's *Inferno,* portions of which I'd read, but the one that came to me most frequently was the graveyard. It was quiet and dark, the ground covered by a low fog. The rows of headstones were ancient and crooked, reminding me of rotten teeth. I would walk among the graves, waiting, and I'd become increasingly afraid. Until I'd wake up shaking. The graveyard nightmare has never left me. But something has changed as I've gotten older. I now believe that death will be a sweet respite. When they say Rest in Peace, it's an expression of faith. I'm no longer so sure about any of that afterlife business, but my hope is that they are right about there being peace.

Though Alma stayed close to home, sometimes she'd wander off without leaving our sixty acres. I'd go looking for her and learned her habits. She tended to cross the fields to the south stand of trees because she was drawn to a creek there, so small, winding through the woods, that it didn't have a formal name. We just called it South Creek.

When I'd find Alma there, she'd often be sitting on the banks staring at the water. Sometimes she'd collect rocks or she'd build things out of mud, castles and walls mostly. Once, after several days of rain which caused the creek to rise and spill over its banks, I found Alma in the water. Her clothes were hanging from a tree branch. She had her back to me, her hands below the surface, and the water about her was agitated. She was whispering, pleading really. I knew what she was doing.

I walked out of the woods and waited at the edge of the field. When she came out her hair was matted, her wet shirt clinging to her. I told her if she went home like that Ma would have a conniption. So we both lay on our backs in the grass so her clothes could dry in the sun.

"Where is he?" she asked.

"Warren?"

"Do you know?"

"I don't, Alma. Nobody does."

"You think he's in heaven?"

After a moment, I said, "I suppose." I sat up and spread her hair out on the grass so it would dry faster.

"We were going to get married."

"Alma, you're not old enough. He wasn't even eighteen."

"So. Rachel and Pete Weiss married before they graduated."

"Alma."

"We were going to get married. He promised. So it was all right."

My hands stopped fussing with her hair, which when wet was glossy black. "You aren't—" I couldn't even say the word.

"I don't know," she said. "I haven't had my period."

Maybe I didn't know what she was doing in the creek.

All I could say was, "Oh, Alma."

I was sitting in the grass behind her. She raised her eyes to look at me. "If I am, I hope it's a boy." She seemed to find this funny. "His name would be settled right off." Then, worried, she said, "You won't go telling Ma and Pa."

I shook my head.

"It's our secret. Promise."

"Promise."

I lay back in the grass so that my head was next to hers. I hadn't slept much the night before and closed my eyes. There is a difference between being tired and being exhausted. At that moment, I realized that I was exhausted, and that I had been since the bombing. I was grateful for the warmth of the sun on my eyelids and could have fallen right asleep.

▪ ▪ ▪

Billy Cox was three years older, and his punches left Jed dizzy and nauseated. Walking home afterward, he staggered until he fell to the ground. The knuckles of his right hand were swollen, and he lay in the dirt trying to remember what had caused the fight. Something Billy had said? He couldn't remember.

When he got home, he stopped at the rain barrel under the eaves at the west corner of the chicken coop and plunged his head in the water. He held his breath for as long as he could and then pulled out. The cool water helped the dizziness, so he soaked his fists as well.

"Lose this one?"

His father had come out of the barn and was crossing the yard, chickens scurrying out of his way. "Let me see."

Jed kept his arms at his side, the water soaking his shirt sleeves. His father grabbed him by the wrists and lifted his arms. As his fingers probed the knuckles, he concluded, "Don't think anything's broken."

Jed yanked his hands away and expected to be slapped for his defiance.

Instead his father leaned against the rain barrel and pulled his pack of

Chesterfields from his overalls. Jed watched him tap one out and light it. When he exhaled smoke, Jed inhaled.

Watching him, his father said, "You've started already?"

"Sometimes. Yeah."

He couldn't read his father's face. Concern. Indecision. Until he held out the pack and the small box of matches. "Just don't tell your mother. She'll kill me."

Jed lit a cigarette and inhaled deeply. "She can't see back here."

His father almost smiled. "Sometimes I think she can see through walls."

Jed took another drag on his cigarette and somehow the smoke made his dizziness more tolerable. His head, which was sore around the cheek bones, seemed to float above his shoulders. He took another cigarette from the pack and pushed it through a small knothole in the side of the coop.

"What was this fight about?"

"Nothing." He gave the pack to his father. "They're all about nothing."

"Not much point then, fighting over nothing."

"Sometimes it's what you have to do."

His father accepted this with a nod. "I got in a scrape with a fella once. I was your age, a little older. He was much bigger." He dropped his cigarette butt and ground it out with the heel of his boot. "Beat me. Bad enough that I didn't go looking for fights no more." He took his weight off the rain barrel. "Now you stay here and finish your smoke. Then you come in the house for supper. Don't be too long. You know how she don't like her meals to get cold."

"It wasn't about nothing."

"Really?"

"He said something I didn't like."

"What was that?"

When Jed didn't answer, his father said, "Well, it's your business." He walked around the side of the coop, heading up toward the house.

Jed took another deep drag on his cigarette, remembering Billy Cox's eyes and that grin. It was for all the boys, standing around waiting to see what was going to happen. He said it for them. The knowingness there, when you knew he didn't know a thing. Except he knew what would get Jed's goat.

I tell you—them Turcott sisters. The tits on that Alma. And your girlfriend Bea, she's coming along too.

▪ ▪ ▪

It was the girl's idea. Her mother and father couldn't decide what to do about the finger. They worried about how it would look, if people learned that their daughter had brought it home. One night at dinner, she said, "Can we give it a funeral?"

They looked at each other and then told her and her brother that that's exactly what they should do. But they weren't to tell a soul. It was a secret.

On Sunday after returning from church, while still in their good clothes, they walked out to their east pasture. The girl carried the coffin, a cigar box she and her brother had wrapped in yellow paper before their mother tied a neat bow with some green ribbon left over from the previous Christmas. When they reached the hole that her father had dug the night before, the girl got down on her knees and laid the box in the grave. She wept and her mother picked her up and brushed off her knees. They each tossed a handful of dirt on the box before her father took up the shovel and refilled the hole. After a moment of silence, they started back toward the house. Thunderheads were looming on the horizon, and the first drops of rain splattered on the tin porch roof just as they climbed the steps to the back door. The girl only stopped weeping after her parents assured her that the finger had gone to heaven and found its owner.

18.

One night Alma didn't come downstairs for dinner.

"Where is she?" Pa asked.

"In bed," Ma said, "with the hot water bottle."

This was our way of referring to what Ma called women's ailments. Just the mention of a hot water bottle embarrassed Pa.

"I'll go look in on her after I've eaten," I said, knowing that if I didn't Ma most likely would—and she nodded as she cut into her potato.

Conversation at the dinner table was not encouraged. I knew some children in Bath who were forbidden to speak during meals, other than saying grace. That wasn't the case in our house, but it turned out we had little to say to each other. Perhaps Ma would mention someone she saw in the village or Pa would talk about tomorrow's chores. Since May 18, we had been even more reluctant to talk, particularly because of Alma. She maintained a silence that made any attempt at conversation seem awkward and forced. If Ma or Pa asked her a question—something simple like *What did you do today?*—Alma would usually stare at her plate. I don't know if it was a matter of her having difficulty recalling what she'd done, or if she was concerned about what she had done. Which was not much at all. Many days she would spend hours merely sitting.

If the weather was poor, she'd stare out a window. On good days she might go out to the glider on the porch, and only occasionally wander off on her own, though never leaving the farm. If Ma told Alma to help her with some chore around the house, she would do so but eventually she'd simply stop whatever it was—cleaning or scrubbing—and stare off into the distance that she'd discovered since everything went haywire. Before May 18, Alma was chatty, to the point where I tired of listening to her. The more she talked the less she said. But now her mind was elsewhere, as Ma would say. And none of us knew exactly where that was or how to bring her back.

But since the day at South Creek, I knew what was weighing on Alma's mind. I ate faster than usual because I wanted to go upstairs and check on her.

"When you go up," Ma said, "bring her a plate. She needs to eat."

"I will."

Something about Pa's hands, the way they hovered over his chicken. Ordinarily, once he commenced eating, nothing stopped him.

"What?" I said. "What is it?"

"You've been very good to her ever since . . ." Ma left it at that. No need to identify what was always on our minds. "The way the two of you used to bicker, but now—well, if there's any silver lining, it's that you and she are closer. She relies on you."

I busied myself by wiping my plate with the last of my bread. My parents weren't given to compliments. There was something else. "And?" I said finally.

Pa could only clear his throat.

"We're taking her to a . . ." Ma seemed at a loss. "To a place. A house. It's in Detroit."

"What do you mean, a *house?*"

"It's a home."

At that moment, I thought they knew that Alma was—or might be—pregnant. My face must have flushed as it often did because Ma studied me in that way that suggested she could read my mind. "What kind of home?" I asked, my voice rising. "*This* is her home."

"Of course, it is," Ma said, speaking in an unnaturally (for her) gentle manner. "But the last doctor who saw her recommended this place."

"She's going to stay there?"

Pa shifted in his chair. "For a while."

"A while. How long's that?"

"The doctors at this home," Ma said. "They'll determine when she's ready to return to Bath."

I placed the rest of my bread on my plate. "It's for crazy people. A loony bin."

Ma now looked desperate. "We wouldn't do this if we didn't think . . ."

"You're going to stick her in an institution."

"We want to help her, Bea," she said. "Sitting here day after day, it's just not . . ."

I suppose I had tears in my eyes by then, or I looked like I was on the verge of crying.

"Nothing's been decided yet," Pa said. He hated to see either of his girls cry.

"You're just saying that."

He looked chagrinned, caught in a lie. Ma, I could tell, was ready to slap me.

I pushed away from the table and took the plate and silverware at Alma's place to the stove, where I served up a chicken leg, and the biggest baked potato left—Alma liked potatoes. I took the plate upstairs, where she was sitting on the old milking stool she kept in her room, staring out the window.

"I know you're hungry," I said.

The hot water bottle lay on her bed, which had come down from our mother's grandmother. We'd been told that every child in the family since then had been born in that bed. "Is that hot water bottle for real or just for show?" I asked.

She only shook her head as I handed her the plate. I sat on the windowsill and watched her eat the potato. I knew she wasn't going to touch anything else, so I picked up the chicken leg and began eating it. Nobody cooked chicken like Ma.

"This place in Detroit," she said. "What are they going to do to me there?"

"I don't know."

"They'll get rid of it."

"It's not that kind of a place." I didn't sound too sure, and Alma glanced up from the plate balanced on her knees. "I don't know what they do. It's a 'home,' whatever that means."

"For—what do they call them?—wayward girls," she said. "Remember that girl, Iris something? Got in trouble with that boy from Ovid. They did nothing to him but they sent her to one of those places. I heard she had the baby and then they gave it away lickety-split. But sometimes they just get rid of it, and you're lucky if you don't bleed to death."

"You're not going to any home."

"Really?"

"No."

This was the most extensive conversation we'd had since the bombing. It seemed to exhaust Alma. She picked up her baked potato with her fingers and gazed at it as though it were medicine. "If I don't have my period soon," she said, taking a bite out of the potato, "I'm going to have to go somewhere."

▪ ▪ ▪

Jed took the cigarette from the knot hole in the back wall of the chicken coop and started out across the fields toward Kehoe's woods. Lowering clouds above the fields. It was beginning to rain, again.

Sunday night, relations came to dinner, and Jed's Uncle Garland had looked out at the rain and said that a lot of farmers in Bath were one failed crop away from being put off their land. The other adults at the table fell silent; they seemed to know where this was going. Uncle Gar was the one who wasn't afraid to speak what was on everyone's mind.

"Fear and despair drove him to what he did. Wasn't right, but what people don't want to admit is he's not the only one that's afraid of losing everything."

Then Aunt Eunice: "Those little ones, and the others, they're all with Him now. Sitting by His side. That's got to be some comfort."

And this was followed by another silence, reverential and solemn.

Jed had wanted to say *They're not with anybody. He's not out there waiting for them. They're all dead and gone. Just gone.*

But he didn't.

▪ ▪ ▪

When Alma and I were out riding Daisy, we often passed by the Kehoe place on Clark Road. I suspect most of us did. We couldn't help it. All that was left standing was the brick chimney. Most of the charred wood and rubble had been carted away, much of it by souvenir hunters, same as up at the school.

A fine mist was angling across the fields. Alma must have seen him enter the woods, too. "Isn't that Jed?"

"I believe so."

I pulled on the reins and reluctantly Daisy turned off the road and started across the muddy field. By the time we reached the woods, the rain had let up—it had been like that for days, on and off—and I tied Daisy to a tree. Alma held my hand as we entered the fogbound woods. When we saw him, sitting on a large tree stump, his head appeared to be on fire, smoke drifting up into the damp air.

"He's got a cigarette," Alma whispered.

"I knew it. I've smelled it on him lately."

I led her over felled tree trunks and around bushes, and he stood up after a twig snapped beneath Alma's feet. When he saw that it was us, he didn't look guilty but defiant.

"Stunt your growth," I said when we reached him. I held out my hand until he gave me the cigarette. I took a drag and fought to hold it down. I'd tried them before and didn't like what the smoke did to my throat. Jed stared at me, angry. Either because I was taking his cigarette or because I wasn't supposed to smoke it. "What's the matter?" I asked, exhaling as I handed the cigarette back to him. "Don't think girls should smoke?" He just glared at me. The remnant of a shiner darkened his left eyelid. "You haven't seen Betty Compson in the Lucky Strike advertisements? You know, 'It's toasted.'"

"What about me?" Alma said.

Jed considered the cigarette between his fingers.

"No. She doesn't like it," I said. "Finish your cigarette."

He took a drag and held it in expertly. His hair matted to his scalp by the rain, the man he was becoming was evident in his hairline and the angle of his jaw. The boyish flesh was giving way to something pared down and chiseled.

"You come all the way out here to hide while you smoke?" I asked.

His eyes, which had always seemed to look for an answer, now offered none. He was smoking a cigarette, so what?

Then his attention was drawn to Alma, who began to wander around the tree stump, drifting away as she often did now. Jed didn't like it, for some reason. He turned and said across the top of the stump. "What are you doing?"

"Nothing."

He looked back at me, calculating, maybe nervous. "Why can't she have a puff?" He looked at Alma again. "You want one?"

She came back around the stump, twigs and pine needles clinging to her leggings. He handed her the cigarette, which she considered fretfully. Then she placed it between her lips, inhaled, and coughed, exploding smoke on us.

I laughed. "See?"

Jed took the cigarette back. Something was up with him, I could tell. I walked around the stump, and he watched me as he took a last puff and then crushed the cigarette out in the ground.

I thought I understood, and said, "This is where he did it. This is where you helped him blow up tree stumps."

"Yeah," he said.

"What about this one?"

"What about it?"

"He didn't blow it up. Too big?"

"Maybe."

"He didn't get to all of them. Suppose he just gave up?"

"Maybe. Now let's get out of here before it rains again." He walked off through the woods, and we followed.

When we reached Daisy at the edge of the field, we all climbed up on her back, and she started along the dirt road that split the fields. In the distance, a long Michigan Central train passed slowly on the way down to Lansing. As we neared the tracks we saw a thin column of smoke rising out of the woods.

"Hobos," Alma said in my ear. "They build camps in there."

"How do you know?" I asked.

"I've seen the ashes from their fires."

"You've been out there?" I said. "Alone?"

"Once. Or twice."

"They leave behind tin cans and bottles, junk from their bindles," Jed said. "They stay in the woods near the tracks, where they can catch a train coming through. The Michigan Central line will take you anywhere. Detroit. Chicago. St. Louis. Eventually you could get to San Francisco."

"San Francisco?" Alma said.

"I've looked at the rail maps," he said. "You can go anywhere."

"Would you like to live in San Francisco, Alma?" I asked.

"I'd like to live anywhere but here."

"Jed, how 'bout you?" I said over my shoulder. "What's your destination?"

He didn't answer.

"Rather go east?" I asked.

"East? Sure, Toronto, or maybe all the way to New York," he said. "Doesn't matter."

Over the years, this exchange has come to mean something very different to me, but then, as the three of us straddled Daisy's withered back and the rain began again, it was just kids dreaming of escape from a small town in Michigan.

19.

Our house was small, the walls thin. I knew when my sister shut a door, when Ma and Pa argued. Their recent silence was suspicious. They were talking when Alma and I weren't around. I felt it: they were planning on taking her to Detroit soon—in a matter of days—where she'd be placed in her new home.

Alma and I were in the village one afternoon in early September. Hot and humid. So, we went in the train depot, to get out of the sun. When I was a girl watching trains come and go was a source of entertainment, mysterious and enlightening simply because we could observe people going about their business. It was like spying: two girls nobody paid any mind. We sat on one of the long oak benches while Alma finished the chocolate ice cream cone we'd gotten at Crumm's Pharmacy. In less than a week, school was going to start again. There was no school building, though. The coming year classes would be held here in the village. A new principal and superintendent had been hired. The hope was that a new school would be built in time for the following school year. In the meantime, it was the village. I hated the idea; never realized how much I loved being in the Consolidated School building.

Alma methodically licked her ice cream while I studied the train schedule on the wall above the ticket window. She wouldn't return to school this September, and I realized then that Ma and Pa wanted to get her to this home—whatever it was, wherever it was in Detroit—before the fall semester began. She would sit in a room somewhere, wondering what had happened to us, not understanding why she was there. She would feel guilty, as though she were being punished. I would be in the temporary classrooms here in the village, and all of us would be aware of the children who weren't in school with us. Others, the ones who had been injured, would come to class on crutches or wearing slings and bandages. The teachers would try to make things seem normal. No one would believe them.

As I stared up at the train schedule, it came to me. We could hop a freight train. If hobos did it, why couldn't we? We could be in Chicago within a day. We'd find jobs—I imagined waitressing in a restaurant while Alma worked in the kitchen. I'd never been farther west than Kalamazoo, which was less than a hundred miles away. A life in Chicago seemed exotic, sophisticated. We'd live near Lake Michigan.

"I have an idea," I said.

Alma gazed at me, melted ice cream running down her fingers.

Overhead mourning doves perched on the rafters of the train station. I imagined that some of them lived their entire bird lives up there in the dark. I didn't know if they did so because they didn't want to get out of the station or they didn't know how. I quite envied their living in the shelter of those wooden trusses. They might be listening in on our Chicago scheme, but I couldn't tell whether their cooing was a sign of warning or approval.

"It's time," I said, getting up off the bench.

As we rode home on Daisy, I told her my plan.

"What about the baby?" she said.

"The baby. Well. You'll have it, and we'll take care of it."

"If it's a boy, I want to call it Warren."

"Fine. We'll raise Warren in Chicago."

"Where in Chicago?" she asked.

"People in cities live in apartments."

"An apartment?" You'd think I suggested going to Paris. "With wallpaper?"

"With wallpaper."

"Blue. I want blue in Warren's room. But yellow in the living room."

"Of course."

It went on like this all the way home. Alma rarely expressed enthusiasm for much anymore, but now she determined the colors in every room in the apartment. While we were putting Daisy in her stall, Alma asked, "Can Ma and Pa pay us a visit?"

"Someday. Eventually, we'll tell them where we are, and they can visit. But for now, we don't say a word about this to Ma and Pa. Promise?"

"Promise. It's a secret." She put her hand on her stomach. "Like this."

■ ■ ■

After dinner Jed's parents went to a meeting in the town hall to elect new members to the school board. After they left, Jed lifted two of his father's cigarettes from his overalls hanging in the bedroom closet and walked across the fields. He followed a deer path through the woods smoking the first cigarette.

He wanted to know how Kehoe decided on a target. He wanted to know why he had returned Daisy to the farm when he was supposed to be in school. He knew it was because Bea had a broken leg, but it was more than that. It had to be. He was supposed to be in that building when it blew up, but instead he was on the sidewalk across the street. The blast shook the ground so that he was knocked down. In that moment his classmates died. Their bodies were torn apart so fast they wouldn't have felt a thing—so Jed's parents had said. Or they were killed by the weight of brick and timber and plaster, crushed in their seats. But two kids had been found sitting in Miss Weatherby's arms, so they must have had time after the blast to run to her in fear, moments before the building came down on all of them. Some got up and some didn't. Jed was almost there, but he wasn't. Another minute and he would've been inside the building. But he was late. Late because Bea had a broken leg and late because her father's truck wouldn't start that morning. Late because they had to ride old sauntering Daisy into the village, and late because the principal Mr. Huggett said that Daisy could not remain tied to the tree in front of the school all day because everyone knew what would happen: you can't have manure on the school lawn.

Who needs school? Henry Ford, *the* Henry Ford, didn't. He was suing the *Chicago Tribune* for libel because they said he was an "anarchist" and an "ignorant idealist." During the trial he testified that he'd heard of Benedict Arnold but thought that he might be a writer, and when asked about the American Revolution, he said it began in 1812. The man couldn't graduate from the fourth grade. Yet the jury, comprised of a dozen Michigan farmers, found in Ford's favor, awarding him damages from the Chicago newspaper: six cents.

Jed had seen one movie that summer, when his parents took him into Lansing where he had a dentist's appointment. Afterward, they took him to see *Wings,* starring Gary Cooper and Clara Bow. The Fox Movietone newsreel that preceded the main feature showed film of Charles Lindbergh and President Calvin Coolidge. Fame was curious. Lindbergh was world-renowned because he had survived. Other planes that had attempted to fly nonstop from New York to Paris kept falling out of the sky. Some disappeared, their crews never found. And there was a film of President Calvin Coolidge, taken while he and his wife vacationed in South Dakota, where he celebrated his fifty-fifth birthday on Independence Day. The president posed in his cowboy hat, scarf, holster and gun, chaps, boots, and spurs, which had been a gift from a local Indian tribe. The theater audience laughed: Coolidge was famous because he was the president and he looked foolish dressed up as a cowboy.

Kehoe had asked, *What's a criminal?*

Jed didn't know. It was a good question.

Hobos were treated like criminals, but all they did was live by the railroad tracks and go from place to place. One even helped Bea when she broke her leg. A criminal sees things others don't see. A criminal understands something's wrong. Kehoe was a criminal. Nobody knew it until it was too late. Jed should have known; he should have figured it out. When they were out in the woods, blowing up tree stumps, when Kehoe would settle himself down and begin working on his stogie, and he'd start talking about things in that way of his, Jed should have seen it; he should have done something. He felt it, but he didn't realize it: the man was a threat. He'd gone haywire and he was dangerous. Both to himself and to others. He was looking for a target. It had to do with the school board. Jed didn't understand it all, but from listening to his parents and other adults, he knew that Kehoe's problem stemmed from disagreements with members of the school board. If he needed a target, why didn't he blow them up? Go to a school board meeting with a few sticks of dynamite?

Because Kehoe wanted to hurt them. The adults, the parents, he wanted to hurt them but not kill them. Because once you're dead there is no pain. Unless you believe in hell (many people believed Kehoe was there now). He wanted to do something that would hurt the people who opposed him, and that meant making their children his target. Kill the children, maim them, wound them. Destroy everything the parents had done for their children, the Consolidated School that was the pride of Bath. A small, rural community with a future, a future represented by the children attending a fine school. Blow up the school, destroy the future. Kehoe was a criminal. It made perfect sense. But maybe he wasn't a criminal. Maybe he was an anarchist. Jed had looked the word up but still wasn't sure what it meant. They simply wanted to destroy the way things were. They believed that then, and only then, could a person be truly free.

Jed should have seen it and done something to stop it.

Or he should have been in the building with the others so it wouldn't matter to him now.

And there was this: *Admit it, having the dynamite, the wire, the blasting caps, and the detonator, it gives you this feeling of power. You could blow something up. You only need to decide on a target.*

He lit his second cigarette with the first and began walking back along the deer path toward home. It was getting dark but he knew the way.

▪ ▪ ▪

Alma was having another nightmare. This was not uncommon; we both had them. I heard her in her bed, whimpering. I went into her room, and she sat up, talking about the man, not making any sense. I got in bed with her and she lay curled against me like when we were younger, before we became such adversaries, and shared the same bed. I stroked her hair, her back, and asked her about the man.

Between sobs she whispered, "He's in the woods."

"What woods?"

"By South Creek."

"You saw a man by South Creek?"

Exhausted, she drifted into sleep, and soon I followed.

In the morning light everything seemed different. More rational. The remnants of my graveyard nightmare haunted me as I ate oatmeal for breakfast. Then we went out to do the milking. Sometimes Alma and I sang together while we filled our pails. Lately, we liked to sing "Ukulele Lady"—but this morning we were silent.

Until she said, "When do we leave for Chicago?"

I leaned over on my stool until I could see around the udder. Alma's back was to me and her right shoelace was coming untied. I was having second thoughts about Chicago. I knew how to set a table, but I'd never actually waitressed. "I don't know," I said as I resumed pulling. "What if we can't find jobs? How would we afford an apartment? Maybe it's not the best idea."

"But I want to go," she said. "Won't you take me?" When I didn't answer, she said, "I've kept my secrets," she said. "You haven't told anyone?"

"No, I haven't, Alma."

"I want to go soon. I heard Ma and Pa talking."

"You did?"

"They want me to go to Detroit with them. Soon. Can't we take a train to Chicago? You said we could."

"I know I did, I know. It's just that I worry that it won't be that easy. We don't know anybody there. It may be hard to find a place to live by the lake. And the train, how will we know which one goes through to Chicago? And there are men called yard bulls who throw you off trains if you shouldn't be there. And then there's getting on the train—even when they're moving slowly it's dangerous."

"The train is not a problem."

"It's not?"

"No. You just climb on board, up into one of the boxcars. I've seen hobos do it."

"I have, too. But what if we get in a boxcar with some hobos. They may not like a couple of girls being on their train."

"No, they're nice. He always is."

"Who? The man in the woods?"

"Yes," Alma said.

"He's a hobo."

"He's very friendly. I brought him some bread and cheese."

"Alma, I don't know if that's the best idea, either."

"If you had seen him eat it, you'd understand. He was hungry, very hungry. And he thanked me. And then . . . and then he . . ."

"He what?" I waited. "Alma, after he ate the bread and cheese, he what?"

She got up from her stool and took her pail over to the canister we had been filling. Though my pail wasn't full, I went over to the canister as well. We both poured our milk out. I put my pail down, made her do the same, and took her by the wrist and walked her out the back of the barn. "Alma, what did the man do?"

Since the bombing, she'd developed the habit of tugging on the ends of her hair, her fingers clawing at snarls, making them worse.

I took hold of her hand and pulled it away from her face. "I have to ask you, Alma. Who's the baby's father?"

She looked hurt, hurt and confused. "Warren."

"Warren is. So what about the man in the woods? What did he do?"

"He asked about you."

"*Me?*"

"Yes." She was staring out at the fields. "He if your leg was better."

"That man? The one who carried me into the village after I broke my leg?"

She stared out over the land. "We could find him at one of the camps in the woods and ask if he will take us to Chicago."

"How?" I asked. "How does he know?"

"Know what, how to get to Chicago?"

"That we're sisters."

"He watches us."

She nodded toward the woods beyond the field as though he were out there now. I scanned the woods but didn't see anyone, just trees.

"Come," I said as I took Alma by the arm and led her back inside the barn, where we continued our milking.

When you do chores about the farm, the repetition, the monotony lend themselves to a form of contemplation that I have always thought one of the true benefits of rural life (so distant and lost now—staring at this ceiling is not the same as milking a cow). When I sat down on my stool and resumed filling my pail I thought about the night I broke my leg. It occurred to me then that we kids had gone up to Round Lake to spy on the dancers at Lovings Dance Hall. I remembered how we crept across the cool spring grass toward the lights of the roadhouse, how exciting it was to sneak about in the dark. Voyeurism, certainly one of the Other Sins, needed to be added to my list. The vicarious pleasure of observing others who are engaged in what some may consider illicit activity—dancing, drinking, smoking, the forbidden romance of adulthood—that's what lured us to Round Lake that night. And then seeing Alma's misaligned shirt buttons, suggesting that she too had been doing something forbidden, it was all too much. So I ran, I ran in the dark, through the woods, down that field until my leg found that hole in the ground which sent me sprawling, overcome by the most sudden and intense pain I had ever experienced.

Was Alma saying that this man was also subject to the same voyeuristic tendencies? All the hobos who came through Bath, riding the rails, camping out in the woods, stealing chickens and eggs and pies, and seeking shelter in a hayloft or a caboose abandoned at the end of an overgrown siding, what would these men see in a town such as Bath, Michigan? Were there vicarious pleasures to be had, witnessing us as we went about our chores? Perhaps they find in their observations the reasons why (or how) they came to be hobos? Homeless. Drifters. Did they flee wherever they came from, or were they forced to leave? Were they ostracized? (A practice I had learned about in my Greek class, how in Athens and Sparta an individual who somehow had failed to conform to public expectation could be ostracized for ten years—ten years!)

As I pulled on those rubbery teats and filled my pail, I thought about a man, the man, observing me in my daily rituals. It was frightening but also thrilling. What seemed mundane routines to me, he might find of interest. He might find it revealed something about himself—why he left his own home, why he did not return. And when my pail was full, I merely sat there on my stool, the heat from the cow's belly warming my forehead, realizing that when I fell in the field that night, when I was writhing on the ground in agonizing pain, he was the one who emerged from the dark, picked me up, and carried me to safety.

▪ ▪ ▪

Jed thought it interesting. Fear, fear of the unknown, spread like a disease. Since May 18 farmers searched their cellars and barns and outbuildings, looking for any sign, any evidence that Kehoe had accomplices who might have wired up some explosives. There was no rhyme or reason why a particular house or building or farm would be targeted. That was the maddening thing about it. Utterly random. It wasn't against someone in particular. It wasn't because of a grudge; it wasn't a response to some specific act, some harm or slight. It was against *us.* Once the seed of fear was sown, it would not go away. That was Kehoe's point. It was him—or them—against *us.* But what was truly frightening was that it caused *us* to watch each other with suspicion. We were on the brink of losing all trust, all sense of civility. Anyone of *us* could be his accomplice.

▪ ▪ ▪

Several times a year Aunt Ginny came to dinner. It was usually a Sunday, or a holiday, Thanksgiving or Christmas. It required Pa driving out to her place and picking her up so she could come back to the house for the afternoon. The last Sunday in August she brought two blueberry pies, which we consumed after Ma's ham. There was a point, usually after Alma and I served the coffee, when we were dismissed from the table. (Ma sometimes referred to Aunt Ginny—never to her face, of course—as "our magpie" because of her tendency to gossip.) When we were younger, the rumors that Aunt Ginny brought to such occasions was of no interest to my sister and me. After Alma had gone out on the porch to sit on the glider, to my surprise Aunt Ginny suggested that I remain at the table to hear what she had to say. My curiosity was tempered by a sense of discomfort; I felt as though I were being admitted into a secret society that required unmitigated allegiance and unquestioning loyalty. A society that was as invidious as it was dangerous.

As was often the case, Aunt Ginny took her time getting to the goods, explaining how she came by her information—the more circuitous the path, the more enticing and, seemingly, verifiable the gossip. In this case, though, it came to her in a rather straightforward manner; instead, time and distance were the elements that gave her news the weight of veracity. Emmet Saunders and his wife Iola had been visiting her relations down south of Ann Arbor, in a place called Tecumseh, which everyone knew was named for the famous chieftain. Iola's cousins went back a fair distance in Tecumseh, three generations. Because of the Bath Consolidated School bombing, one of them told her and Emmet about the Andrew Kehoe who was raised on his family's farm in Tecumseh.

"They were Irish," Aunt Ginny said, stirring sugar into her coffee, "Catholics, of course, who had come from somewhere back east. Andrew's father had a reputation for contrary opinions and hard bargaining. He was particularly aggrieved with the taxes he had to pay, so right there you can see that the apple doesn't fall far from the tree. The man was known to become not just vocal but outright belligerent when the subject of taxes was raised.

"He had a large brood of children, being Catholic, and it eventually killed his wife. Not long afterward he remarried, taking a woman who was much younger than he, as is so often the case. Was a time, long ago, when the Captain took me as his new young wife." Aunt Ginny paused long enough that I feared she might be having one of those moments when her mind drifted off from the present. But then, a slight, ironic smile before she went on. "Kehoe's new wife was so young that she was not much older than his son Andrew, who was then in his thirties. Andrew was still living on the farm, a situation that didn't sit well, evidentially, and it is an understatement that he and his stepmother held little regard for each other.

"Now realize," Aunt Ginny said, holding her coffee mug with both hands, "that this is all speculation, but it has carried weight in Tecumseh for decades, and has been raised again since news of what happened here in Bath. One day Andrew's stepmother set out to prepare dinner for the Kehoe brood, but when she went to light the kitchen stove, it blew up. She was covered with kerosene, and the poor woman's body was engulfed in flames. There must have been quite a scene there, as you can imagine, and I don't need to go into further detail, certainly not here at the dinner table. The woman was burned terribly, and Andrew was sent to a neighbor's who had a telephone. The neighbors were close friends of Iola's family. After all was said and done, what they couldn't forget was how nonchalant Andrew was about the entire episode. Evidently, he sauntered up to their door, with no urgency in his step, and with remarkable calm he informed them that his father's wife was lying in bed, burnt nearly head to toe. He asked if they might phone the doctor. The doctor arrived and did what he could for the woman, but she succumbed to her injuries that night.

"Now Iola couldn't say with certainty what the authorities made of the situation, but it was clear that that stove had been tampered with—exactly how and by whom, no one could say. But there were suspicions about Andrew, based on the difficulties he was known to have with his stepmother, and that he had already proven to be handy with machines and such. Iola says that many people in Tecumseh to this day are convinced that Andrew was responsible for the woman's death, and it was confirmed by the fact that not long afterward he quit the farm and left the town for good."

Aunt Ginny finished her coffee. Looking from Ma and Pa to me, she said, "Whatever possessed that man to do such a thing as he did to the people here in Bath, it went back a long way. Such people live among us, harboring fear and hatred, capable of bestowing incomprehensible affliction on unsuspecting innocents." She smiled and took my hand, her fingers frail but warmed by the coffee mug. "I know Nellie Kehoe was fond of you, dear. She told me how you'd sit with her and converse when she was feeling poorly. God bless you, child."

Without looking at Ma or Pa, I whispered, "May I be excused."

Before they could answer, I got up from the table and went out to the porch. Alma was curled up on the glider, dozing. Though it was a warm summer evening, I felt a dark, ominous presence hovering about me. I sat down on the bottom porch step and slid off my shoes so I could feel the tamped earth under the soles of my feet. And, to this day, that's what I believed saved me from despair, from the abyss: Michigan dirt, smooth as skin.

20.

I often rode Daisy to and from the village along the path that bordered the railroad tracks. Late one afternoon in August as I was returning to the farm, I saw smoke rising through the trees beyond the caboose. There was the smell of cooking, something charred, which caused Daisy to want to stop, ever hopeful at the scent of a meal. I heeled her and reluctantly she continued on, but pulled up at the sight of the man. He stepped out from the far end of the caboose and came down the path toward us. Despite the heat, he wore a soiled tweed coat and a fedora. It looked like he'd had that beard his entire life.

"How's your leg?"

"Better," I said.

He was eyeing the sack draped across Daisy's withers. "Glad to hear."

I could hear the low mummer of men's voices, back in the woods. "I thank you for helping me that night," I said.

His acknowledgment was the slightest dip of the head. He kept looking at the sack, but then he stepped aside, indicating he didn't want to keep me from continuing down the path. Daisy proceeded, slower than usual, her head turned toward him and her ears back. From the woods came a terrible hacking cough, one of those uncontrollable things that pains the ribs.

I pulled up on the reins till she stopped. "Sick?"

"He's been feeling poorly." He was standing next to Daisy now. "Them's victuals?"

"Beans." I had another sack hanging crosswise from my shoulder. "And some canned goods for Ma." He kept staring at the sacks. He had bright eyes. But sad, tired. "I could give you some beans," I said. "She'll count the cans and know some's missing. Want some beans? You'd have to soak 'em first."

"Thank you kindly."

I lifted the sack off Daisy's withers and handed it down to him. His hands were so large, broad, with dark hair on the back. And he was missing two fingers on his right hand, the ring and pinkie.

"Could you take him to Dr. Taggart? He'd have something for that cough."

"I reckon. But no, thank you." He untied the sack and with his left hand removed a fistful of beans and stuffed them in the pocket of his coat. "Most likely, he'll be dead in a day or so." He said this with a casual certainty, as though he were predicting rain.

"I'm sorry." I didn't know what else to say.

He dug into the sack one more time. Some of the beans fell on the packed earth at his feet.

I reached into the sack slung from my shoulder and removed a can of peaches. He hesitated when I held it out to him. "I'll tell Ma it was my fault, I miscounted the cans."

He took the can with the hand missing fingers and put it in his other pocket. "Your name," he said, "It's Beatrice."

"How'd you know that?"

He looked away down the path, and then up at me. "You heard of Dante?"

"The poet."

"That's the one. He was infatuated with a girl with your name." He must have seen that this made me uncomfortable because he took a step back. "It's just a bit of history, is all." Touching the brim of his hat, he said, "You best be on your way before it gets dark."

I didn't want to go. I wanted to ask him if there wasn't something that could be done for the man with the cough, other than feeding him some beans and canned peaches. I wanted to know where he came from and what he did before he started riding the rails. I wanted to know why he was a hobo, living here in the woods on the outskirts of a small village in Michigan. I wanted to know why he didn't simply go home.

But I said, "My friend Jed, he thinks you're free."

"Does he now?" I couldn't tell if he thought this was humorous or not. Then that hand with the missing fingers came up, and he stroked his beard a moment. "I suppose, in a way. But then you might say we all are."

I wanted to tell him things. I wanted to ask him what my sister and I should do. I wanted to explain about my parents' plans to take Alma to Detroit, and my idea about running away to Chicago. But I said, "I'm not free. I don't feel free."

"It's that business with your school. But you survived. There's a reason."

"What's that?"

"So you can live. What more reason do you need?"

I wasn't sure I understood what he meant. Since then, sometimes I think I do, but I'm still not sure. But right then I believed him. I needed something, something to believe, and this man who lived by the rails, who had missing fingers, who had nothing other than pockets full of dry beans, had given me what I needed.

I looked toward the woods beyond the caboose. "What will you do, you know after?"

"We'll bury him. It's all you can do."

"Where? Out here, in the woods?"

"Think of a better place?"

"Well, no."

"Lots of souls buried out here in these woods," he said. "It's as good a place as any, maybe better."

I lifted the reins and was about to heel Daisy, but he said, "It's Alma, your sister, right?"

"What about her?"

"I talked to her once or twice. She mentioned going away. You're going to take her away from here, away from your home, your mother and father, and your friends. And this fine old mare. You think you can run away from it all."

"She told you that?"

He nodded. "Don't go," he said. I was startled by his sincerity. "Nothing out there you can't find here, and there are things here you'll never find nowhere else."

"You don't understand," I said. "There are circumstances."

"There always be circumstances, Beatrice. Pay them no heed. Circumstances become an excuse. Don't let them dissuade you." He nodded. "Now you best head on home."

He took another step back, and I gently heeled Daisy. As she walked down the path toward the darkening woods I looked back and saw him standing there. He watched me, the pockets of his coat bulging with dry haricot beans. I rode on into the woods, and when I looked around again he was gone. Nothing but the caboose, surrounded by tall grass and weeds.

▪ ▪ ▪

Jed was walking out near the tracks when he heard the slow clop of hooves behind him. He knew it was Daisy so he didn't turn around but just kept walking.

"I went by the field again where the boys play baseball." Bea's voice came from above and behind him. "They said you don't come and play much anymore."

He shoved his hands deep in his pockets as he walked with his head down.

"Why is that, Jed? You love to play baseball. I've seen you shag flies and steal bases. You have a good swing and a strong arm."

"Been busy."

"Yeah, me too." Sarcastic. He hated it when she did that. She seemed to know and she changed her tone. "You going over there, Kehoe's woods?"

He kept walking.

"I'll bet you got a cigarette on you."

He craned his head around so he could glance up at her. A sack hung from the pommel, another over her shoulder—she'd been to the village.

"Hey," she said. "You climb on up here, and Daisy'll get us there before Christmas."

Jed stopped walking.

"Hear about Beatrice Gibbs?"

"Yeah," he said. "She died a few days ago."

"In the hospital in Lansing. They think she may be the last one. There are not enough girls named Beatrice in this town anymore." He didn't know whether she was being sarcastic or not. She didn't look it. She was staring down the dirt road toward Kehoe's woods about a half mile away. "I don't know about you, but I could use a cigarette."

He climbed up on Daisy's back. Placing his arms around her waist, which he'd done so often, seemed dangerous. He was aware of her breasts touching his forearms as Daisy moved on down the road. He'd never thought about that stuff with Bea before, but it was getting difficult to ignore.

They didn't speak until Daisy reached the edge of the woods. Across the field they could see the brick chimney rising above the scorched land where the Kehoe farmhouse had been, and beyond that the Harte's farm. After Bea tied Daisy to a tree, he led her into the woods, where it was cooler in the shade. Bugs hovered about their heads as they made their way to the clearing, and when they reached the stump in the center, he took his pack of Chesterfields from his pocket.

"Where'd you get that?" she asked, though she didn't sound surprised.

He tapped the pack and offered her a cigarette.

"My very own? Such a gentleman."

"The smoke keeps the bugs away."

"And so practical."

He lit their cigarettes and they both sat on the stump.

"I'll bet you stole that pack, Jedidiah Solomon Browne."

"What if I did?"

"It's theft. It's dishonest."

"Then give back the cigarette."

She shook her head, exhaling. She was getting good at it, cigarettes. The way she held it between her fingers, periodically tapping the ash.

"So why no baseball? I bet you'd know if Babe Ruth hit one yesterday."

"Homer number forty-one off the Browns' Ernie Nevers."

"Think he'll hit sixty?"

"Yes. And Nevers should stick to football. They call him Big Dog."

"So, he should never have tried to play baseball."

"Ha-ha. That's a pun, right?"

"Sort of. Seriously, Jed, why no baseball? I was over there earlier, and I saw a grounder that went into left field. You would have had it and pegged the runner out trying to stretch it into a double." She waited, and then got off the stump and turned to him. "What's going on?"

"Dunno." Then he said, "Sometimes they come to watch the games."

"Who does? Oh, you mean those boys with the crutches. And the slings. And the stitches. And some still have bandages. Two of them were there today."

Jed nodded.

"You feel guilty, running around the field when they can't? That it? Okay. I feel guilty about Beatrice Gibbs, which is probably why I'm smoking this cigarette. Because I can. I'm not going to *not* smoke it because she died. You understand?"

Jed crushed out his cigarette on the stump, on the same place where he'd done so before, adding to the black smudge in the wood as big as his hand. "Suppose I died," he asked. "What would you do?"

"What would I *do?*"

"Would it change anything?"

"Sure it would."

"Like what? You'd still smoke cigarettes when you could get them. I know some of the older boys who play ball, they've got a stash of booze somewhere."

"I suppose someday I'd try to drink liquor," she said, "though it doesn't smell too good on Pa's breath. He doesn't think we can tell but we can."

"And what about boys?"

"Boys?"

"Kiss any yet?"

"*No.*"

"You will. And other stuff, too."

"So what's your point?"

"I dunno. There is no point."

"Is that the point, Jed? There is no point?"

"I don't want to talk about it anymore."

Bea came closer so that his feet, dangling off the tree stump, were touching her knees. "You think I'm going to do these things whether you're here or not, is that it? You think I'd forget." She looked about ready to slap him. "You think I'd grow up no matter what?"

"What's to stop you?" He got out his pack of cigarettes.

She grabbed them from him. "I don't like you talking that way."

"What you going to do about it? And give those back."

She put her arms behind her back. He looked down at the way her green blouse was tight across them. She was giggling now. "Say, please."

He tried to reach around her with his right arm but she turned sideways, and then he tried with his left, causing her to dance away from him. He got down off the stump. "Come on, give 'em."

"Say 'pretty please.'"

When he lunged toward her, she ran and he chased her around the stump, once, twice, and halfway around the third time she tripped and sprawled on the ground. He fell on top of her, both of them laughing. They wrestled, winded and sweating, until he pried the cigarette pack from her hand. He wanted to roll off her, but her arms came up around his neck and she pulled him to her hard. He held still, feeling all of her against him as something began to happen. She was quaking and holding him tighter, and she began to sob and then she just cried, holding him. He put the cigarette pack down in the pine needles and with one hand stroked her hair. Never done that before and he realized he'd always liked her hair, the way it tended to fly away as though each blond strand was lighter than air. Her cheek pressed against his, warm and wet from tears.

▪ ▪ ▪

I could not stop crying. It was as though I'd been storing it up since May 18. There had been a few times previously when I became weepy, particularly at the funerals, but also just all of a sudden it would come on me and my eyes would water up. But this was crying to beat the band. My entire body convulsed with it, and I didn't know what else to do but hold on to Jed. For dear life, that's what we say. I held on to him for dear life.

I was two years older than Jed. To children, it seems such a great distance. He would never, he could never catch up to me. But something happened there on the ground by the tree stump. Neither of us understood it then. Things like that you don't; they don't come to you all of a piece. It's something you learn along the way, in stages. I gather he was as confused as I. In his awkward, boyish way, he stroked my hair. A sign of affection, like petting a dog. But our bodies against each other like that. It was strange, like the time Pa had me push my arm up a cow, which was hot and moist and tight until I felt the calf's hooves, and he said *pull.* This was stranger than that, brand new. It frightened me and I didn't want it to end. I think it confused him. When I finally stopped crying, he rolled off me and lay on his back.

I tried to wipe my eyes and face with my hand. "I have to tell you something."

"Okay."

"It's a secret. Actually, it's two, or it may be two, I'm not sure."

"Okay."

"I'm leaving Bath. I'm taking Alma with me. She's—you know how she's been since it happened. Ma and Pa are going to put her in some home in Detroit. I think it's for crazy people."

"Really?"

"And then there's the other thing. She may be having a baby. We're not sure."

We both continued to stare up at the trees overhead, the late-summer sky beyond. We were silent so long I began to wonder if Jed understood what I'd told him.

But then he said, "Warren."

"Yes."

"He's why she's the way she is."

"I think so."

"He's lucky in a way."

"How's that?" I asked.

"He was loved. Not just by his family. She loved him."

"I suppose he is lucky, then."

"Where you going?"

"I was thinking Chicago."

I glanced at him and he was nodding. This was sensible, a fourteen-year-old takes her pregnant sister to Chicago, a place they'd never been to, a place where they didn't know a soul. I felt the need to justify my decision. "Detroit is too close. They'd find us in Detroit. But Chicago, no. We wouldn't be ourselves there. We could become someone else."

"Right."

I felt the urge to touch him, not like we'd just done, but hold his hand. We'd done that for as long as I can remember, but now it wouldn't be the same and I was afraid to reach out to him.

"When?" he asked.

"It's got to be soon, next week, I think. They want to take her to Detroit before school starts."

"School." He said it like he didn't know what the word meant.

"I know, it's going to be horrible. Classes in all those different buildings in the village, seeing all the kids who have spent the summer lying in beds. I guess I know why you've avoided the baseball games."

"School," he repeated, now sounding as though he'd made up his mind. "I don't think I'll be going to school this fall."

I sat up. "No? What are *you* going to do?"

He looked up at me with eyes that wouldn't let me in.

"I see, it's a secret." I reached across him for the pack of cigarettes. For a moment my face was close to his. I thought about it then and I think he did, too. "Where are the matches?"

Thankful for the activity, he dug the small box out of his pocket. He sat up then, and we both turned so we could rest our backs against the tree stump. We lit our cigarettes and looked at the woods around us.

"I hate secrets," I said finally. "Where you going?" He didn't answer, so I said, "Want to go with us to Chicago? We're going to hop a train, ride the rails."

He smoked his cigarette. I thought he was trying to figure out the best way to tell me that hopping a train was a bad idea. When he finished, he crushed the butt out in the dirt. "I can't."

"Why? You got someplace better to go?"

"No. I just can't."

"Right. It's a secret."

21.

Alma was packed. Though I continued to have misgivings, I was, too. We kept our suitcases—mine was a small valise Ma had given me to play with years earlier—in their usual places, on the shelf in our bedroom closets, hoping she'd never think to look inside them. Alma showed me the contents of her suitcase. I removed things. You won't need this; you won't need that. She looked at me in that way she had, lost, desperately confused. I told her she might have to lug that suitcase through the streets of Chicago. You take only essentials and forget about the rest. She seemed about to cry, so I told her they have stores in Chicago, where she could buy new things after we found jobs. A blue sweater? Yes, a blue sweater.

We'd visited the train depot several times so I could memorize the schedule. There were six passenger trains each day—we didn't want one of those. There were also unscheduled freight trains. We'd hop a freight train at night. The problem was leaving the farm. Our routine was strict: in the kitchen by six o'clock or else no supper. Or so Ma decreed, though she usually relented. After dinner Alma and I were expected to clean up, and after dark we rarely left the farm unless granted permission or on occasions when we were accompanied by

Ma and Pa—which happened only a few times a year. Evening was for reading, occasionally a card game, and during the school year for homework. In the summer, we might sit out on the porch glider if the bugs weren't too bad. Everyone went to bed early because farm chores began at sunrise.

Wednesday, the last day of August had been warm and humid, the ground muddy from a morning shower. At breakfast Ma informed us that she and Pa were going into the village that evening for another town meeting. She would prepare dinner and leave it on the stove. We were expected to serve ourselves and clean up afterward, as usual.

There was a westbound passenger train that came through at 5:32 p.m. After that, there was silence. I stood on the porch listening to the birds, the cows in the fields, while Alma sat on the glider (I had insisted that we eat early, as soon as Ma and Pa disappeared down the road in the Ford). If you're not listening for it, a train will seem to arrive all of a sudden. But if the wind is right and you pay attention, you can hear it coming from miles off. There it is, passing through Bath as though it had wormed up out of the ground. At first you're not sure; the rumbling could be anything, distant thunder, a truck or a tractor several miles across the fields. But then there's the moment when you're certain: it's a train, the sound could only be a train approaching. And then the sound becomes distinct and you feel you can hear the entire train: the clatter of the rails, the stuttering chuff of the coal engine, the wheels squealing around a bend in the track. And then the whistle as the locomotive approaches the village, assuring us of its presence, as if it feared it might pass through town unnoticed. Who doesn't love the sound of a train?

Late August and the days getting shorter. At dusk the day's heat gives way to a hint of fall. Trees and grass smell different. Plants and flowers are beginning to wither, filling the air with the sweetness of garden rot. But I heard no freight train. Tonight might be our only chance before Ma and Pa took Alma to Detroit (perhaps the next day or the day after, Friday—before the new school year began the following Tuesday, the day after Labor Day). What would they tell her? Would they say they were taking her to another doctor for a second opinion? How would they explain that they wanted her to pack her suitcase? Would I be allowed to go with them? Or would I have to say my goodbyes here?

"Alma," I said, turning toward her on the porch swing. "*Alma.*"

She opened her eyes and stared out at the world as though she'd never seen it before.

"I want you to get your suitcase and take it out there—to that place I showed you, where the track curves and the trains slow down."

"Now? Is the train coming?" She scanned the yard as though she were trying to find the train.

"Not yet. But soon, within the next hour or so a freight train is bound to come through. We have to be ready for it. Ma and Pa will be back no later than 8:30. It has to be tonight. Just go up and get your suitcase and wait for me out there."

She got to her feet and smoothed her skirt, running her hands over her abdomen. I'd noticed that she did this often, checking to see if she was showing yet.

"Nothing," I said. "It's too early."

"Are you sure?" she said, her fingers kneading her belly.

"Yes." I wasn't sure about any of that. "I'm sure that if we're going to get to Chicago it has to be tonight."

She went in the house and I listened to her climb the stairs. She was going to do as I said, no questions asked. Before May 18 this would not have been possible. In a sense, I loved her more at that moment, knowing that she trusted me, relied on me in a way neither of us had ever expected. But with that love came the weight of responsibility. I knew I was choosing between two disasters, Detroit and Chicago, and I was so afraid as I stood there on the porch listening for the train that might not come.

■ ■ ■

Dear Mother and Father,

By now I will be gone. I have just felt that I can't stay here any longer. I do not deserve to be here. I am supposed to be somewhere else. It is where I belong. Not back in school. I cannot go back there knowing that the others should be sitting at their desks too. I hope you do not get too mad at me.

Your Loving Son,

Jedidiah Solomon Browne

Jed folded the sheet of paper in half and placed it on the kitchen table next to his dinner plate. He considered adding to the letter a note about why he didn't eat any dinner—wanted to make sure his mother understood it wasn't because he didn't like her chicken casserole. He usually had two or three helpings, and often he and his father ate until the baking dish was empty, and then sometimes he would work the crusty parts loose from the bottom of the pan and eat them. But he wasn't hungry. There was something about an empty stomach that made your head clear. He'd felt clear for some time now. Since he had decided. Things seemed simpler. He knew what he needed to do, and he would do it and not worry about anything else.

He had come to understand that about Mr. Kehoe. The man was clear. Those days they had spent in the yard working on the tractor or in the woods blowing up tree stumps, it was obvious now that Mr. Kehoe was working toward it. He saw the direction he needed to take, and it was only a matter of going ahead with it. He was clear and nothing got in his way.

But there was a difference. Mr. Kehoe was afraid, afraid and angry. Jed wasn't sure he knew everything that made the man that way, though he suspected it had to do with Mrs. Kehoe, who was in poor health, and the fact that they didn't have children. And it had to do with money. Since the bombing, the way adults kept talking about the school board and the infighting that went on between the members, he realized that Mr. Kehoe felt that he could not be understood. It was an awful thing, to not be understood. When he'd talk to Jed while smoking a cigar, explaining pistons and spark plugs, asking what a criminal was, he had already made up his mind. He was just being clear. But he shouldn't have done it to the school, shouldn't have taken the children and the teachers and the superintendent and the postmaster and his father-in-law with him. Better to go alone. But he resolved to do Bath harm.

Jed set out from the house, crossing the fields. His wool jacket and pants were hot and the necktie tight around his throat, but he had to wear the suit. At the funerals he had heard how parents had dressed their children's bodies in their Sunday best. It was the decent and honorable thing to do. He wore his suit because it felt defiant. The nightmares had only gotten worse. Always there was the suit, confining him, inhibiting his movement, until he woke up in a sweat. He knew he would grow up and have to wear a suit. He would become Mr. Kehoe, wearing a suit every day, angry and afraid. So he put on his Sunday suit. Though it was heavy and made him sweat, it was the right thing to do. He had to do this right. He was clear about that.

▪ ▪ ▪

I had written Ma and Pa a letter and put it in an envelope, but I decided not to leave it. I tucked it in the pocket of my dress, planning on mailing it to them later. Maybe not from Chicago, but from Lansing or Kalamazoo. I would add some things to the letter, things that let them know that we were all right. I'd already tried to explain about Alma, how I couldn't let them take her to the home in Detroit. I just didn't know what to say about the other thing. I guess they would have to know some day. They deserved to know they were grandparents. But that would have to wait until Alma and I got settled. I needed to first prove to them—and myself—that I could do this, take Alma and find a life away from Bath. This is what people did. They went off and they led lives. *Led.* I don't know why we say that. It sounds like something you have trailing behind you on a leash. Life isn't like that at all. But maybe once we got to Chicago and got jobs and found an apartment, we would learn how to lead our lives. It certainly wasn't going to happen in Bath or, for Alma, in some home in Detroit. We had to go out there and find the way.

So I kept the letter to Ma and Pa, picked up my valise, which had a strap as well as wooden handles. I slung the strap over my shoulder and began walking. It was dusk. The night sounds of peepers and frogs were coming up in the marshy places along South Creek. I felt so bad I sometimes had to stop and take a deep breath. And I'd shift the valise strap to my other shoulder. If Alma were with me, I might have turned around and gone home. But the truth was we'd already begun, we'd already left.

▪ ▪ ▪

Jed reached Kehoe's woods at dusk, that time of the evening when there was still light but no color. He'd been here so often lately that he felt he knew every trunk as he walked directly toward the stump. After he stepped over the last felled tree, he crossed the clearing, which he and Mr. Kehoe had made by removing several stumps. The ground was still uneven where their roots had been torn out of the ground.

He'd set everything up earlier that afternoon. The dynamite and blasting caps were buried under the stump, one stick on the east side, the other on the west. Mr. Kehoe had always been particular about positioning the dynamite and pyrotol so that it would be what he called "even"—he once joked that if you don't space things out right, you end up stumped, with a half stump. It was inefficient, and you'd have to do it all over again. You'd have to use more dynamite, which would mean less to be planted under the school. Jed had set the detonator on the ground next to the stump. Its wire ran under an exposed root, and then it came back up out of the loose dirt, circled around the base of the stump and again disappeared into the ground, where it was connected to the other sticks of dynamite.

He had seen this many times, stumps blown to bits. The explosion was so big, so swift, so definite he knew that there wouldn't be time to feel anything. You just go. You leave your body. Or your body leaves you. Standing next to the stump with the detonator, there was no chance of failure, of doing things halfway. There would be some justice if the explosion was so thorough that they really couldn't find anything of him. Because one thing he'd come to believe was that the real problem with death was the body. With what you leave behind. They joke about how you can't take it with you. Meaning money and possessions. But your body is what's left behind and it's the problem. It's a nuisance. It has to be dealt with before it begins to turn all rotten and bug-laden and smelly. He'd seen it in the fields. Dead animals, cows, horses, deer. After a few days, they began to break down, seeming determined to return to the earth. The smell taints the air and flies swarm. When he'd gotten up close, he could see maggots frantically devouring the remains. That's what the body became: remains. It didn't stay with you. The dead went elsewhere. They didn't need the body any longer. And the living were left with the chore of burying the body. This was not right, digging a hole and putting the corpse in the ground to rot. He'd attended all those funerals, some of them for boys and girls who sat in class with him. He watched the caskets as they were lowered into the ground and he knew it wasn't right. This wasn't what they'd want, if they were here. They wouldn't want to leave their bodies behind so their parents and families and friends would have to stand around a hole in the ground crying. They would want nothing to be left behind, nothing to remain. It was better to simply disappear, as though you'd never been here. Your family and friends then wouldn't have to stand in a cemetery in the heat and rain, or the cold and snow. They'd just have their memories.

That's all that should be left of you. Memories were all right. That's what you should leave behind because that's what you couldn't take with you. Where you were going you didn't need memories. You would have no recollection of this place. You wouldn't know you'd been alive. You certainly wouldn't remember you'd lived in Bath, Michigan. You'd just be you. It would just be you out there, part of the universe. There would be no pain, no sorrow. There would be just a nothingness forever and you won't mind at all.

Jed buttoned his suitcoat. All three buttons. He leaned over and pulled the plunger up, out of the detonator. He liked the sound of the gears turning in the box—there was something definite about gears, sprockets, spark plugs, which had a clear purpose, like numbers—and he liked the feel of the scarred wooden handle. Mr. Kehoe said it was World War I surplus and probably saw action somewhere in Europe. He seemed proud of the fact that this piece of equipment had been overseas. It was in good working order, like his tractor and his machine. *We should all be more like machines,* he once said. *With the proper maintenance, they do what they're supposed to do. Human beings aren't as efficient.*

All it took was one good downward shove.

One time, Mr. Kehoe had let Jed do it.

There was nothing like it, shoving that plunger into the detonator box.

▪ ▪ ▪

When I got to the bend in the tracks, Alma wasn't there. I looked east toward the village and then I looked west. It was getting dark, and I couldn't be sure but I thought I could see someone walking on the narrow dirt road that divided the fields. She—if it was Alma—didn't seem to be carrying her suitcase. I put my valise under a bush and walked quickly down the road—I still couldn't run due to my broken leg.

After I'd gone perhaps a hundred yards, I could see that there were two people on the road, and the one farther ahead was Alma—smaller, wearing a skirt. Nearest to me was a man. It was too dark to see him clearly, other than that he wore what appeared to be a crumpled fedora. I knew who it was, the hobo at the caboose, the man who carried me into the village the night I broke my leg.

I didn't even know his name. I didn't know what to make of him. He had shown me a kindness. I had given him some beans and a can of peaches, and he seemed grateful. Alma had told me he watched us, that he looked out for us. I've thought about this all these years. If she was right, he was like our guardian angel. Not some heavenly being who descends from the sky with a flowing robe and wings, but a true angel who minded how two country girls fared. But after all these years, I still don't know who or what he really was—I know now that I'll never know. What were his intentions? The way he was following Alma, I just didn't know. She said she'd seen him, talked to him, too. She'd also given him something to eat, bread and cheese. Was he following her because he wanted to protect her, or he wanted something from her? At that moment, there in the last light of day, I felt so frightened and uncertain, while at the same time there was something in me that was alive because we were about to go out on our own, to find our way in the world. I just didn't expect him, there, on the darkening road, behind my sister.

I tried to run but it only caused pain in my leg, so I continued to walk as fast as I could—and I was gaining on him. Then I came upon a dress, Alma's yellow dress, lying in the road. After that there was a trail of clothing, until I came to her suitcase, which lay on the ground. The latch had sprung open (it tended to do that and I should have thought to have her tie the suitcase with twine). Ahead, I could see Alma stop at the edge of Kehoe woods. She appeared to look back down the road, and when she saw that he was following her, she quickly disappeared into the woods.

I started to run. It hurt so. I couldn't go very fast but I kept running.

▪ ▪ ▪

Jed heard a twig snap, and then another.

He took his hands off the plunger and straightened up. The woods were dark but he could hear someone breaking through the underbrush, and then Alma ran into the clearing. She stopped when she saw him. She looked confused and scared, although she often did these days.

"Warren?" Her voice trembled as though she were pleading. She glanced back at the woods and then cried, "He's coming after me."

"Who is?"

Jed heard it, too. Someone else was behind her in the woods. Alma ran across the clearing. Unlike Bea, she wasn't light on her feet and stumbled once on the uneven ground. When she reached the stump, she appeared shocked, her hands gripping his arms. And surprised. "*Jed?*"

"What are you doing here?" he said.

"We're leaving."

"We?"

"I was waiting for Bea when—" She glanced over her shoulder. "He follows me. I don't know what he wants, but he watches me. And Bea." She gripped his forearms, her face close to Jed's, her hair wild about her face. "Please, we must get away, we have to go—"

"*Don't!* Don't go!" A man emerged from the woods. Jed recognized him. The hobo, the egg thief. Tall, bearded, heavy coat despite the heat. He had picked Bea up the night she fell in the field. He had carried her to the town hall steps. "Listen to me," he said, "you're not going anywhere." He sounded angry? No. Concerned? Jed wasn't sure. "You're not going anywhere," he said again, lumbering across the clearing. "It's not safe out there." He paused a moment. "You don't understand, you *can't* understand." He sounded as though he were pleading, with himself as much as with them.

Alma tried to pull Jed away from the stump but he resisted. When the man continued toward them, Jed let Alma lead him away from the stump toward the other end of the clearing. At first they walked quickly, but when the man yelled something primitive, something incomprehensible, they ran into the woods. Jed could barely see the tree trunks in the dark woods, but he could hear Alma breathing as she ran ahead of him, pulling him by the hand. Branches whipped his face and bushes snagged on his suitcoat and trousers. The man shouted again just as Alma tripped and sprawled on the ground. Jed fell next to her, his shoulder striking something hard. He sat up next to Alma. Back through the trees he could see the man, who was nearly halfway across the clearing. When he reached the stump he stumbled—maybe on the uneven ground, maybe tripping on the wire—and he lurched forward, his arms outspread as he tried to regain his balance, or as if he might be able to fly. Jed heard the gears in the detonator and he rolled over onto Alma, pushing her head into the moist earth.

The explosion sent a jolt through the ground. They held each other as wood and debris came down, until she shoved him away and sat up in the smoke. Her hands pulled at her hair. Her mouth was open.

She must have been screaming.

■ ■ ■

The blast flushed birds from the trees. Hundreds of them, or so it appeared, swarming high into the evening sky, cawing and squawking. I had fallen to my knees and had to push myself up off the ground. My palms were covered with dirt. I was confused. The fact that it was a bomb didn't surprise me—as though I'd been waiting all these weeks for the next explosion. But a bomb, here in the woods?

I yelled, "*Alma!*" I ran into the woods. I think I was still calling her name, I'm not sure. When I reached the clearing I heard something, a voice, and stopped running. Between my heart pounding and my gasping for breath, it was difficult to hear anything. But then I heard it. Crying. Alma, crying. It could only be her.

The ground was littered with jagged pieces of wood, roots, and clods of dirt. Walking was difficult. I worked my way across the clearing and past the hole in the ground where the explosion had occurred. It was just a hole, dark as the night. The smoke reminded me of that day in the village when everything changed.

They came out of the woods. I knew it was Alma, but it took me a moment to see who she was with. He was wearing a suit. I thought, *Warren?* But then I knew, *Jed.* I was surprised at how tall he looked. I had not noticed over the summer how much he had grown. It wasn't just his suit—he was wearing his Sunday suit out here in the woods. He held Alma by the arm, a courtly gesture, as they walked slowly into the clearing.

Alma paused to lean over and seemed to be doing something to her leg. She straightened up, a handkerchief in her hand. It was stained. I looked down and saw it, blood running down the inside of her leg.

Jed looked at me, confused. "Is she hurt?" He spoke loudly, almost shouting.

"No, she's not hurt," I said.

He didn't understand me. Or couldn't hear me.

"You've started," I said to Alma.

"Yes. Is it too late? The train to Chicago, is it too late?"

"No." I thought about this a moment. "But we're not going anywhere."

Alma gazed past me. "That's what he said."

I turned and looked at the hole in the center of the clearing. The man—the hobo, our hobo—who had been following her, he had caused the explosion? I didn't understand, but I realized that he was gone, disappeared. It was profoundly simple: one moment we're here on this earth, and the next we're gone.

And I knew that something terrible had happened here, yet I felt we had all been saved.

I took my sister by the other arm, and with Jed, we walked her across the clearing, keeping wide of the hole in the ground. "We're not going to Chicago," I said. "There's no point now."

"Where are we going then?" she asked.

"We're staying here. In Bath, Alma. We're going home."

22.

At first, no one in Bath seemed certain what they heard. Was it an explosion? Was it a farmer taking out a tree stump or a boulder? The banging of freight train couplings could carry for miles, sounding not unlike an explosion.

But then a hole in the ground was discovered in Kehoe's woods. Word went around, it was kids. A kids' prank. We knew what they thought—something strange about those Turcott girls. Not to mention that Browne boy. Always riding around on that old swaybacked horse. Hard to tell if they were the way they were because of the school bombing or if they were just made that way. Just goes to show you, you don't know who your neighbors are.

But months later, the Skyler's dog found a bone that didn't look like it belonged to an animal. Which led to the suspicion that Kehoe really did have accomplices. Perhaps there was a hobo involved.

No one knew for certain. It was a strange time in Bath. Conversation seemed framed by remorse, suspicion, and fear. Even Aunt Ginny couldn't keep track of all the rumors and gossip. As I recall, she went silent as her health declined with a swiftness that reminded me of the sugar cubes dissolving in her tea.

■ ■ ■

School began the following week. It was not like going to Bath Consolidated. It didn't seem real, but just a place to send children during the day. It was clear that the new teachers—there were a number of them—didn't know how to deal with us. There were students on crutches. Some still wore bandages. They at least seemed pleased to be out of the house and attempting to do something that seemed normal. The others, the ones who died, weren't coming back to school. I'd never be able to talk with Miss Weatherby again.

Alma stayed home. She helped Ma around the house and did chores with Pa. They didn't know about her period being late, but they came to the realization that they couldn't send her away to Detroit. She was ours, and we had to take care of her—that's what Ma said and that's what we did.

Jed was nearly deaf. A specialist in Lansing said it was psychosomatic—or some such thing—a delayed reaction to the trauma of the school bombing. His hearing might return or it might not. Jed attended school, and he did well, despite being nearly deaf. I spoke slowly so he could read my lips. He learned to modulate his voice so he wasn't shouting all the time. I established a signal with him—rolling my eyes up—which told him he was speaking too loudly.

The night of the Dempsey-Tunney fight in Chicago, I went to Jed's house and we sat in front of the radio in the parlor. I told him what was happening during each round. Soon we were both standing, pretending to exchange punches. When Tunney was knocked to the canvas during the seventh round, I fell to the floor.

"*What?*" Jed shouted. "*What happened?*"

I was confused; the broadcaster was confused. I didn't know what to tell Jed, and then I said, "He's *up.* There was a long count because Dempsey didn't go to his corner right away." I got up off the floor. "And now Tunney's on his feet. He's fighting again."

"What?"

"*He's. Fighting. Again!*"

▪ ▪ ▪

Time. How we are ruled by it. Someone's always keeping the count. Still, as time pulled away from the bombings and the events that immediately followed, I could never really leave them. They were ever present. Decades later, they are still.

Our bodies changed. It was harrowing becoming a woman, as though a different species residing inside me slowly emerged. Childhood is merely the chrysalis, which gives way to pain, confusion, and sorrow the color of blood.

In his teens, Jed eventually regained some hearing. He became a handsome young man with wide shoulders and a straight back. But we tended to avoid each other. He ran with a different crowd. Some said it was the wrong crowd. There were stories about drinking and fighting, always the fighting. There were stories about girls he went with. Then he disappeared. His parents didn't know where he was or they weren't saying. There were rumors. He was seen in Detroit. He was seen in Chicago. He wore a good suit, fedora, and spats. Speculation had it that he'd fallen in with bootleggers. Or he fought for prize money. He'd been seen on trains to Cleveland, Akron, and as far west as St. Louis.

Then there were stories about a woman. A married woman, by some accounts. Sometimes she was described as a blonde, sometimes a redhead. He was seen with her on a sidewalk in Chicago's Loop, in the dining car of an eastbound Michigan Central train. He was good with figures, and some said that he helped keep the books for Capone's organization. Others said it was those Jews in Detroit, the Purple Gang. All these stories came back to me, whispered usually, as though I could verify them. I grew tired of hearing them. (After Aunt Ginny died, gossip had lost its sweet luster.)

I did not see Jed for years. During the Depression, people lost their farms. They lost their jobs at the plants down in Lansing. People I'd known all my life continued to disappear. Eventually, I too left Bath. After getting a teacher's certificate at Michigan State College, I managed to find work, spending several years in towns up north. Indian River, just south of the Mackinac Straits, and then in the Upper Peninsula. Places where the winters were long and spring, if it came at all, came much later than in Bath. In 1936, Pa died of a heart attack while working in the barn. When he didn't come in for supper, I found him lying in the hay, pitchfork in hand. Ma's cousin George moved in and helped keep the farm running. She would have sold the place, but there were no buyers.

Four years after Pa died, Ma had a stroke. I was nearly twenty-nine years old. It was August and I was about to begin a new school year, but I wrote to the principal up in Calumet—I had been teaching English at the high school there the past two years—and resigned so I could stay home and take care of my mother and sister. Throughout that winter, Ma could not get out of bed and she died in June.

When the United States entered the war, our cousin George moved to Ypsilanti, where he found work in the Willow Run factory manufacturing B-24

Liberator bombers. I heard that Jed had enlisted, and there was a story about how he deceived the army doctors into thinking his hearing was adequate. Later I learned that he was a captain with an anti-aircraft corps in the South Pacific. Alma and I remained on the farm. A few men came around, but they were intimidated by my height—I was six-foot-one—but more often by my vocabulary. I once used the word vicissitudes in a restaurant, and the man who was buying me dinner said he'd never had them—did I prefer them fried or baked? That became my litmus test, words such as ineffable and venery. Few men called on me again after venery.

When Alma died, she weighed nearly two hundred pounds. She was in her mid-thirties and her heart just gave out. The night she died, she told me she was going to see Warren. In a sense I envied her. I remained in the farmhouse and taught English at the new public school in Bath. At night I would drink scotch and smoke Chesterfields while grading essays and exams.

▪ ▪ ▪

It must have been nearly a year after the war had ended when Jed showed up on the front porch. He was in uniform. I got each of us a beer and settled on the glider. He sat on the railing, shoulder against a post.

"Long time, Jedidiah Solomon Browne. Captain Browne."

"Town's changed some," he said.

"Has it? We've changed, I suppose. But if you don't leave, Bath seems pretty much the same."

Jed nodded as he stared at my mouth.

"That dog," I said.

"Dog?"

"The one that's barking across the way."

He took a sip from his beer bottle and looked west toward the next farm. "Oh, that."

When he turned back to me, I said, "There is no dog barking, Jed."

He smiled. "Your jokes haven't improved much."

"Nor have your fibs. Your hearing, how bad is it?"

"Gone. Ninety-millimeter cannon took care of that."

"Completely?"

He shrugged. "Other fellas lost more. Everything."

We drank our beers. The silence between us, it had always seemed full, but I wasn't sure now. I spoke slowly. "You've changed? The war, all that?"

"One is never sure," he said, a bit too softly. "You think so, but still there's something that remains the same."

"You're no longer twelve."

He tilted his head, a query. But then he said, "Nor are you fourteen. Consider it a compliment."

I could feel the heat rush to my cheeks.

We didn't speak for a good while. It was late June, muggy with the threat of rain. Beyond him, the trees rustled beneath a fine mist.

Looking right at me, he said, "Guess what I have in my pocket."

"Is it edible? Like jelly beans?"

"Nope."

"What color is it?"

"Silver."

"And?"

"You want a hint?"

"Sure. I haven't played this game in a long time. I need a hint."

"And it has a hole in it."

"How many questions do I have left?"

"How many do you need?"

"You're changing the rules of the game. Why?"

"Why not?"

"I know what it is," I said.

"Do you?"

"Yes."

"Tell me, then."

"No."

"Then how do you know?"

"I just do."

He smiled.

"Where did you get it?"

"I don't know if that's a fair question."

"All questions are fair. Did you steal it?"

"No."

"Was it a gift?"

"Well, not exactly."

"Not a gift," I said, "but an inheritance."

He hesitated, and then he nodded. "It was my mother's."

"Good."

■ ■ ■

We married a few weeks later. I had one stipulation, unusual for the time; I wanted to keep my last name. Jed said he'd never imagined me as Bea Browne. I would always be the taller of the Turcott sisters, Bea.

Our first child was born not a year later. Eventually, we had four children, and Jed found work as an engineer in Boston, where we lived until he died of cancer four or five years ago—I can't be sure anymore.

Years after we married, Jed and I talked about the day the stump blew up in Kehoe's woods. I asked him if he believed suicide was the answer. For the longest time, he said nothing. (It wasn't that he didn't understand me due to his hearing loss. All those years, we faced each other when I spoke, and he read my lips without difficulty, except when I said something that he didn't like, and then he'd usually pretend he didn't understand me.) It was after dinner, the children were upstairs, preparing for bed. It was one of those brief moments during those years when the calamity of daily life fell away and it was just the two of us with plates and glasses on the table. Cod, we had had cod that night—living in a town on Boston's North Shore we'd come to love seafood.

"I was twelve," he said. "I thought suicide might be an answer. It was the stumps. For weeks I had helped him blow them up. I had dug the holes and fitted sticks of dynamite down below the roots as he instructed. I helped run the cable back to the box, where he attached it to the terminals. I'll tell you, it was the plunger. He told me that that box had been used by soldiers in World War I. The box was scarred and worn, the wood chipped. I couldn't imagine how many men it had killed. I would look at that wooden handle and watch as he shoved down on it, the gears in the box clattering the moment before the spark shot down the wire. And I would watch the stump, looking so hard, as though I might keep it from exploding. But then it would go up. The impact strikes you here, in the rib cage. There would be smoke and debris in the air, and when it cleared, the stump would be gone. Just gone. I couldn't understand it—how it happened, how it worked—and I knew I'd never understand it. But I decided I wanted to feel it. I thought I could join them. I thought I could be one of them." My husband got up from the table and began collecting the dinner plates. "But we aren't, and we can't ever be, one of them."

▪ ▪ ▪

Sometimes the enormity of it is a presence in the room, in my mind, in that place we call our spirit or our soul. It's the atmosphere that contains me, and it's a mere kernel, a seed that will grow and flourish, that will blossom and spread. Or. It's a tumor, a growth that resides within unseen organs, spreading and colonizing until the prognosis is dire. It has metastasized; it is inoperable. Or. An ivy, a ground cover that eliminates all else, its roots driving deep in the soil, creating an infinitesimally tangled network of vines and shoots that lend strength to the dirt. Michigan soil. There are no words, there is no language that can approach it. No definition is possible. All attempts at description render you mute. (*Render,* forever a word that reminds me of Kehoe, the man Jed accosted on the sidewalk one spring afternoon.)

Years later during a trip to Oslo, Norway, I stood before a wall of paintings in a museum, my feet nailed to the hardwood floor by unspeakable fear. I was staring at a wall of paintings by Edvard Munch. There are glimpses of the horror in those large figures, women, men, sickly bedridden children, drawn with a simplicity that was cartoonish and tentative and yet menacingly bold. Their eyes are enormous, round with trepidation, alarm, and dread. The eyes of witnesses. Witnesses of the horror, of the incomprehensible threat that lurks about them. In some of the paintings, there are dark forms, not shadows, but a black presence that attaches itself to a figure or floats across the sky, threatening to consume the entire painting, to plunge the canvas into a black void that is as inescapable as death. I stood there, a witness.

Which is worse? To be dead or to know you will die. To know not just that your life will end, but that you will not know when and how it will end. To know that the end will come unannounced, no distant thunder, no angels' trumpets. A death that will be so sudden that it will not be experienced. So swift that the pain will not have time to register. Mercifully, perhaps. Bodies torn asunder. Organs hurled skyward, to be dug out of backyard gardens or draped over newly erected power lines. Intestines to hang from the steering wheel of a smoldering Ford truck which had been packed with dynamite and bolts and nails and shell casings, shrapnel designed to do the greatest damage, a crude but effective predecessor of the splitting of the atom, molecular and monstrous.

You cannot give voice to such an enormity. You cannot embrace it; dare not pretend to understand it. Particularly that, for the moment you presume to understand, it will disappear, evaporate, morph into something entirely other. So you stay with what you know, what you can see. You stay with the color of the sky, the smell of the fields after the night rain, the heat rising off the coat of an old mare. You think it was a man, and you give that man a name, his chosen, Christian name. And you sort through his life, what you know of his life; what you don't know, you invent. You speculate, you presume. But even if you think you know this man you cannot get any closer to what he did. It's what happened. It happened. It was. It always will be. It is now as much as it was then. And it will happen again, and again. We know this now. It will always be. Even when it's all but forgotten, it will still be there, the black void that lurks, that hovers about all of us.

▪ ▪ ▪

I don't know exactly where I am now. Sometimes I think Boston, sometimes I feel like I'm back in Michigan. I'm in what the others call a home. It's not a home; it's the last place I'll be on this earth. A place where some people die without knowing who they are, or who they were. At least I haven't lost my memory, though I've pretty much lost my appetite. But I still love apples, so one of our granddaughters who lives nearby visits with her children, and they bring me McIntosh or Granny Smiths. My eyes are poor, but I can still read if I hold the print close to my face. All I have left are words, and these words are mine.

I lie here and wait. I seldom sleep at night but doze on and off all day. Often I have the dream. It's the cemetery, the same one I dreamt of years ago. Same rows of old headstones, same misty fog, but now something happens, something that never happened when I was younger. The earth opens up and bodies emerge from the ground. I recognize them, the children and the teachers as they were on that spring morning in Bath, Michigan. But they look like wisps of smoke, not exactly ghostly but not substantial in a flesh and blood sort of way, either. They rise out of their graves and drift into the sky, disappearing into the clouds. There is none of that business about heaven and hell. The truth is, this life is all that we can know. The rest will take care of itself. The older I get, the more I think this world is beyond belief, but I do believe in this dream, in a resurrection of the spirit, the kind that frees each of us and promises that we will join together once again. And it will be forever.

ways, rather have talked with him than with me.

Finally, two Jerome-free publications that have informed these discussions. First is John Gribbin's *In Search of Schrödinger's Cat*. This is quite simply a wonderful, measured, intelligent introduction to quantum theory. I'm not sure it has been surpassed, despite having been published way back in 1984. Second is *Astrology Decoded: a step by step guide to learning astrology* by Sue Merlyn Farebrother. Do I need to say that I don't believe it? Well, that doesn't actually matter. I liked its ambition. I think Jerome would approve, too.

That's enough of the written word. I must mention a few people who have assisted me along the way. The staff of the British Library were unfailingly helpful. I have had equally helpful conversations with Ian Maclean, John Henry, Dario Tessicini, Alec Ryrie, Tom McLeish, Giles Gasper, Chris French, and Artur Ekert, among others. The generosity of the Fetzer Franklin Fund enabled me to travel to a gathering of quantum desperadoes in Vienna. I am grateful to Philip Voke, who entrusted Wykes' papers to Reading Library, and generously pointed me towards them. I would also like to thank my friend Helen Bagnall for her encouragement to press on and finish what frequently looked like a doomed project.

Now to those whose sharp minds assisted the production of this book. Here, Artur Ekert merits another mention for his comments on an early draft. My agent, Patrick Walsh, his assistant, John Ash, and Scribe's irrepressible Philip Gwyn Jones have all made invaluable suggestions concerning the manuscript. Molly Slight proved an invaluable copy editor, picking up all kinds of errors and omissions.

Jerome, who still inhabits my dreams on occasion, remains in splendid superposition as my chief critic and supporter. On his first reading of the manuscript, PGJ suggested I might be a little in love with Jerome. Perhaps. I do miss having him all to myself now, I must say.

—Michael Brooks, March 2017

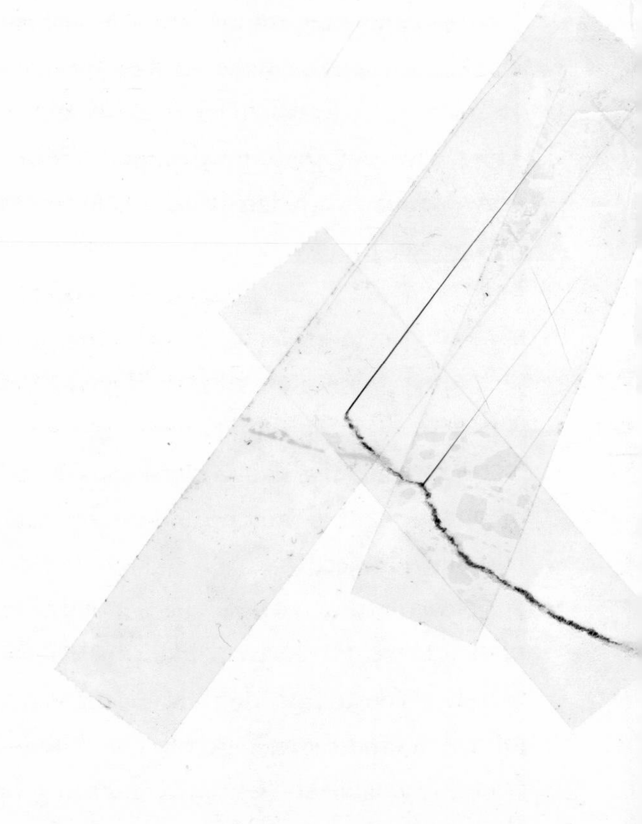